THE TRINITIES

III Tatum

TRINITY TRE ENTERTAINMENT

1

The wind howled through the desolate forest, bending trees like fingers clawing toward the sky. Sergeant Bishop of the 9th Strategic Unified Initiative for Tactical Suppression (SUITS) Division wiped the rain from his visor and stared into the black abyss ahead. His team was silent, their breaths the only sound above the storm. The orders were clear: investigate the rumors, record any findings, and extract data. But rumors, they knew, were never just rumors. This was their third encounter—at least on paper. None of them had ever seen a Trinity up close, only the shaky footage from failed attempts by prior teams. All of them were gruesome, unexplainable, and above all—classified. The footage would flicker, static-filled at first, then reveal grotesque scenes of charred bodies, mangled limbs, and contorted faces, each one more distorted than the last. The cause? Unclear. But one thing was certain—whatever the Trinity was, it had the power to reduce soldiers into nothing more than fragments of bone and skin. It was beyond human under-standing.

"Sergeant, are you seeing this?" The voice crackled through the comm. Private Anderson, the youngest in the squad, pointed ahead. Between the twisted branches, barely visible, an eerie light pulsed. It wasn't like the cold light from their drones or the flicker of distant lightning. This light seemed alive, breathing in sync with the forest itself, radiating a quiet but immense energy that made their bones ache.

"That's it," Bishop whispered, gripping his rifle tightly. His heart raced with the knowledge that this was no ordinary mission. This was a Trinity.

The team advanced slowly, creeping through the mud, weapons trained on the light source. As they approached, the air became thicker, charged with static. It made their hair stand on end, their nerves raw. Each step closer amplified the sensation, like walking into a storm just before the lightning struck. The sky above them flickered with unnatural energy, and then they saw it—Trinity-001.

She stood motionless, surrounded by the electrical aura, her body almost ethereal. Her features were humanoid but alien in their perfection. Her skin shimmered with a metallic hue, her eyes glowing with the light of a thousand volts. There was no fear in her gaze, no malice—only a calm, detached awareness, as if they were nothing more than insects in her presence.

"Hold your fire," Bishop ordered, barely able to tear his eyes from her. The squad fanned out, forming a perimeter, but they all knew, deep down, that it wouldn't matter. This wasn't something they could contain. Without warning, the air exploded. A bolt of lightning tore through the sky, striking the ground in front of them. The impact knocked them off their feet, their equipment sparking and malfunctioning. Anderson screamed, clutching his face as the visor melted onto his skin.

"Fall back! Fall back!" Bishop's voice was drowned out by the deafening roar of the storm now circling them. The ground beneath their feet cracked open, fissures of energy coursing through the earth. The Trinity remained still, her presence the eye of the storm, her hands beginning to glow with the same electrified energy that ravaged the land.

In an instant, she raised her hand, and the world went white. A wave of pure energy rippled outward, vaporizing everything in its path. Bishop saw his squad disintegrate before his eyes—skin, muscle, bone, all reduced to dust in a matter of seconds. He felt his body tear apart, each nerve searing with pain beyond comprehension.

As his vision blurred, the last thing he saw was her, standing amidst the carnage, serene, untouched by the devastation she had wrought. And then, darkness.

~

Aurora Sinclair sat at her terminal in the underground research bunker, scrolling through classified footage. The stills of charred bodies, the remnants of tactical gear, and the endless list of names marked deceased were all too familiar now. This was the third time this month that an entire squad had been wiped out by Trinity-001. No survivors. No chance to extract data. Only death.

She felt a cold pit in her stomach as the next file loaded—this one marked Operation Surge. The footage flickered on the screen, showing static-filled images of the squad's final moments. Lightning. Screams. Bodies turning to ash.

Aurora closed the file and leaned back in her chair, staring at the ceiling. She had only been with the SUITS for six months, fresh out of graduate school, eager to make a difference in the world. But this... this wasn't what she had signed up for. The official reports always used the same language—containment failure, data loss, unforeseen consequences. But what they really meant was something far more terrifying.

The Trinities weren't just anomalies—they were gods. Or demons. Or something in between. And the SUITS were trying to play God by controlling them.

A knock on the door jolted her from her thoughts. Dr. Kline stepped into the room, his usual calm demeanor masking the storm of emotions that always brewed beneath the surface. He had been her mentor since she arrived, guiding her through the labyrinth of the SUITS and its hidden horrors.

"More footage?" he asked, his voice weary.

Aurora nodded. "Another squad, completely obliterated by 001."

Kline sighed, rubbing the bridge of his nose. "They'll keep sending them. They won't stop until they have control. But they don't realize... control is an illusion when it comes to the Trinities."

He sat down across from her, his eyes dark with exhaustion. "These aren't just creatures, Aurora. They're something far older, far more powerful than we can comprehend. And if we keep pushing, we're going to trigger something we can't stop."

Aurora's hands clenched into fists. She had seen enough footage, heard enough whispers in the halls, to know that Kline was right. But what could she do? She was just a junior researcher, a cog in the machine, powerless to change the course of what was coming.

"They're calling it progress," she muttered bitterly.

Kline chuckled darkly. "Progress, at the cost of humanity itself."

As he stood to leave, he glanced back at her, his expression serious. "Be careful, Aurora. In this place, it's easy to lose sight of who you are. Don't let them take that from you."

Aurora watched him go, her heart heavy with the weight of his words. She knew that the deeper she delved into the SUITS, the harder it would be to hold onto her humanity.

But she couldn't stop now. Not with the truth so close, just out of reach.

As she turned back to her terminal, her screen flickered, a new file appearing. This one was labeled Trinity-001: Subject Keraunian-Surge. Aurora hesitated for a moment, her finger hovering over the play button.

Then, with a deep breath, she clicked play.

The air in the research bunker felt thick with tension, as if the walls themselves were holding their breath. She had seen enough horrors in her short time at the SUITS facility to make her question everything about her role here. But this was different. The footage labeled *Keraunian-Surge* had been marked with a category-six danger rank—the highest level assigned to a Trinity.

The footage loaded slowly, the screen flickering before revealing the first shaky image. It was dark, a storm raging in the distance, lightning painting the sky with violent cracks of light. Aurora leaned in, the glowing screen reflecting in her wide eyes. The video began with soldiers from an elite task force, each outfitted with high-tech electromagnetic pulse (EMP) devices designed to neutralize energy-based powers. Their mission: capture or incapacitate *Keraunian-Surge*, a Trinity known for its devastating control over electricity.

The first few minutes were quiet. Too quiet. The squad advanced through the dense forest, the trees rustling ominously in the wind. And then, without warning, the camera feed erupted in chaos. A flash of light—so bright it left a ghostly imprint on the screen—lit up the sky, followed by a deafening crack of thunder that shook the ground. Aurora flinched as the first soldier screamed, his body convulsing as electricity arced through his armor. He fell to the ground, charred and lifeless.

Aurora's hand flew to her mouth as the rest of the team scrambled to retreat. But it was too late. Another flash of lightning struck, and half the squad was incinerated on the spot, their bodies reduced to smoking heaps of ash. The EMP devices—supposed to neutralize the Trinity's power—fizzled and sparked, rendered completely useless by the creature's overwhelming control over the magnetic fields.

Aurora's stomach churned as the camera shook violently, the remaining soldiers trying to flee from the storm of energy that raged around them. But there was no escape. *Keraunian-Surge*—a towering figure, standing nearly seven feet tall—emerged from the chaos. Its body crackled with electricity, the air around it humming with lethal power. Its eyes glowed a stormy blue, and its movements were deliberate, as though every step it took was measured and intentional.

The screen went white again as another bolt of lightning struck, and the camera feed cut to static.

Aurora stared at the blank screen, her heart pounding in her chest. She had seen death before. She had reviewed footage of other failed operations, but this... this was different. The raw, unchecked power of the Trinity was unlike anything she had ever witnessed. The soldiers didn't stand a chance.

Her thoughts raced as she ejected the data drive and leaned back in her chair. How could the SUITS hope to contain such a force? And why were they so desperate to? The footage was terrifying, but it also raised deeper questions. These Trinities—where had they come from? And what were they? The official reports spoke of *first contact*, but there was something more—something ancient and unknowable about them. *Keraunian-Surge* wasn't just a creature. It was an elemental force, an embodiment of nature's wrath.

2

The monitor flickered as Aurora stared at the footage in front of her, breath catching in her throat. Her fingers hovered over the keyboard, hesitant to press play on the file labeled Trinity-001: Keraunian-Surge—Field Test Operation Alpha. She knew what was coming. She had seen the after-action reports, the casualties, the charred remains. Yet something inside her insisted she see the truth with her own eyes.

The footage began, showing the task force's approach through a thick, dark forest. The soldiers moved cautiously, rifles raised, scanning the surroundings as they crept forward. They wore specialized armor—meant to protect against high-voltage electrical surges—but even through the grainy camera feed, their tension was palpable.

They knew this mission would fail, even if they wouldn't admit it. Aurora had read the reports. They were aware of Keraunian-Surge's power, but nothing could have prepared them for what they were about to face.

Suddenly, the air in the footage crackled with a strange energy, and a low hum vibrated through the ground. The Trinity appeared in the distance, a towering figure standing motionless beneath the ominous, swirling clouds. Its seven-foot-tall frame radiated crackling blue light, its translucent skin pulsing with raw electricity. Its eyes glowed an unnatural stormy blue, reflecting the chaos building within the atmosphere.

The first bolt of lightning came without warning. It struck one of the soldiers, and for a brief moment, the camera feed showed a silhouette engulfed in white-hot light. Then, just as quickly, it was over. The soldier had been reduced to a smoking heap on the ground, his body little more than ash.

Aurora's stomach turned. The camera jolted, disorienting her, as the squadron scrambled to counterattack. The air grew thick with tension and static, each movement crackling with suppressed energy. She could feel the dread crawling through the screen, as though the storm could reach her even in the safety of her dark, sterile office.

The soldiers activated their EMP devices, meant to disable any electric fields around the Trinity. But as soon as they deployed, the Trinity's form shimmered, and its aura intensified. It was absorbing the energy. The EMP devices fizzled out, sparking in their hands before shutting down entirely, rendered useless by the creature's power over the electromagnetic field.

Then the chaos erupted. Keraunian-Surge lifted its arm, and the forest exploded with violent arcs of electricity, the ground splitting as lightning ripped through the air. Soldiers screamed as they were electrocuted where they stood, their bodies twitching grotesquely before crumpling to the ground. The few who weren't immediately killed were thrown back by the shockwaves, crashing into trees and breaking bones on impact.

Aurora's hands shook as she watched the camera feed glitch. The screen showed flashes of searing white light followed by moments of darkness, as the camera struggled to keep up with the intensity of the storm. She could make out figures desperately trying to retreat, but it was futile. Keraunian-Surge didn't give them time to escape.

One by one, the soldiers were reduced to nothing—bodies melting into charred remains, faces frozen in their final moments of agony. The Trinity didn't stop, didn't hesitate. It unleashed its full fury, its power growing with each second. The nearby power lines were drawn into its reach, the electricity feeding into the storm. The air buzzed with violent energy, and the sky turned into a kaleidoscope of storm clouds and flashing lights.

Aurora clenched her jaw, her eyes locked on the devastation. The camera zoomed in on the Trinity just before the screen went black, overwhelmed by the electromagnetic disruption. The last sound she heard was a gut-wrenching scream as the final soldier was vaporized.

The footage cut out.

Aurora blinked, her heart pounding in her chest. Her mind struggled to process the sheer violence of what she had witnessed. These weren't just failed experiments or simple accidents. This was raw, uncontrolled power—beyond anything the SUITS had prepared for.

She leaned back in her chair, the cold, sterile air of the facility suddenly feeling suffocating. Keraunian-Surge wasn't just a threat—it was unstoppable. If this was only one of the Trinities, how could they possibly contain them all? The sheer scale of destruction was too much. The SUITS had no idea what they were dealing with.

Aurora rubbed her eyes, trying to steady her thoughts. She replayed the final moments of the footage in her mind—the lightning, the screams, the grotesque transformation of flesh into charred remains. This wasn't warfare. This was slaughter.

She pulled up another file, this one labeled Trinity-001: Invulnerability Test. As it loaded, Aurora felt a deepening sense of dread. The file showed the military attempting another strategy—using advanced military-grade weapons against Keraunian-Surge. High-powered bullets, rocket launchers, even high-voltage shock weapons—all ineffective.

She watched, horrified, as soldiers fired round after round into the creature, each one dissolving into sparks before even touching it. Its translucent skin absorbed the energy, the impacts vanishing as if they had never happened. No matter what they threw at it, nothing could penetrate its defenses. The soldiers' faces turned from determination to panic as they realized they were outmatched. One soldier, in desperation, ran at the Trinity with a knife, his scream lost as the blade melted in his hand before his body was thrown against a tree with a sickening crack.

The invulnerability of the Trinity was absolute. No weapon, no human technology could stand against it. The footage was almost unbearable to watch, each new failure cementing the futility of their efforts.

Aurora closed the file. Her hands trembled on the keyboard as she leaned forward, staring blankly at the screen. Keraunian-Surge was invulnerable. And worse—it was immortal. The final video, Trinity-001: Immortality Analysis, confirmed that.

In the footage, after one of its devastating rampages, Keraunian-Surge was observed through drones. The military had bombed the area, hoping to contain or at least slow it down. But as the dust settled, there it stood. Not a scratch. Not a mark. The creature walked through the aftermath of its destruction, untouched by any force that tried to kill it.

Aurora felt her chest tighten, her heart beating wildly as the full weight of her realization crashed down on her. Keraunian-Surge was just one of the Trinities. There were more. More beings out there, with powers they couldn't understand, let alone control. And the SUITS, in their arrogance, believed they could harness these gods.

Aurora's fingers hovered over the keyboard, her eyes scanning the lines of encrypted data flashing on the screen. The footage she had just watched replayed over and over in her mind—the flash of light, the storm, and the agonizing final moments of the soldiers sent to contain Keraunian-Surge, Trinity-001. The electromagnetic chaos had turned the mission into a slaughter. No one had stood a chance.

The system beeped as another file loaded, marked with several classified warnings, but she knew better than to stop now. Aurora had always been curious, always pushed boundaries. Now, though, her curiosity felt dangerous. Her heart thudded in her chest as the screen filled with new data.

The soldiers in the video hadn't been ordinary—they were highly trained operatives, the kind who rarely failed. But against Keraunian-Surge, they had been reduced to little more than bodies scattered like ash. Aurora scrubbed through the video again, watching as lightning ripped through the forest, their EMP devices fizzling out like cheap fireworks before they even had the chance to activate. Every burst of electricity illuminated their faces, twisted in terror, before the power tore them apart.

Aurora Sinclair sat rigidly at her terminal, the dim glow from the screen reflecting off her wide, unblinking eyes. The images flickered across the monitor—grainy, erratic, cutting between static and violence. The footage of the failed *Operation Surge* left her cold and unsettled. The men—trained soldiers—had been reduced to ash, nothing more than smoldering heaps scattered in the aftermath of their encounter with Trinity-001. And this was only the beginning.

She exhaled sharply, willing her stomach to settle. The footage was hard enough to watch, but what disturbed her more were the reports she had to analyze afterward—the dry, clinical descriptions of *electrostatic discharge, human tissue breakdown,* and *total genetic annihilation.* The language detached the SUITS from the reality of what had happened. Men had died in a grotesque, inexplicable manner, yet all they had left behind were statistics for Aurora to record. The implications gnawed at her—how could these beings, these Trinities, exist?

Behind her, the heavy footsteps of Dr. Kline approached. His presence was as unsettling as the footage—calm and quiet, yet filled with a knowing weight. He placed a folder on her desk, labeled in bold letters: *N.E.X.U.S.*

"Heavy stuff, isn't it?" he said quietly, stepping further into the room.

Aurora nodded, still unable to shake the images of charred bodies from her mind. "How can they expect us to stop something like that?" she asked, her voice trembling.

Kline sighed, running a hand through his thinning hair. "They don't care about stopping it. They care about controlling it. If they can harness that kind of power, they believe they can control everything. And that's where *N. E.X.U.S.* comes in."

"The Algorithm of Death," Kline muttered as he took a seat beside her. His voice, though soft, seemed to echo in the cold, sterile room. He glanced at the footage on her screen and sighed, his expression unreadable.

Aurora hesitated, her hand brushing over the file. She had heard rumors, whispers from senior staff who spoke in hushed tones about *N.E.X.U.S.*, but nothing concrete. Now, staring at the file, she wasn't sure if she wanted to know.

"What exactly is it?" she finally asked, her voice barely a whisper.

Kline leaned back, crossing his arms. "The *Neurotoxic Experimentation and Xenobiological Unification System*. It's a machine, powered by artificial intelligence, designed to create bioweapons, toxins, and chemical agents capable of eradicating anything—even... Trinities."

Aurora's eyes widened. "*Anything?*"

He nodded slowly, watching her face for a reaction. "It analyzes biological data, molecular structures, and environmental factors, then predicts the deadliest possible chemical combinations. The idea was that we'd be able to neutralize threats, particularly the Trinities, without conventional warfare. But..." His voice trailed off, the unfinished thought heavy with implication.

Aurora swallowed hard. The *N.E.X.U.S.* Algorithm of Death had been whispered about in the lab—an AI-driven chemical synthesizer that could create lethal compounds with precision. But the way Kline spoke of it made her blood run cold.

He handed her a file, marked *N.E.X.U.S.* – *Chemical Trials 17-29*. "Look at these. Failed experiments. Compounds created by the algorithm. Each one more lethal than the last."

Aurora opened the file and flipped through the pages. The reports were filled with scientific jargon—*neurotoxic agents, biological destabilizers, chemical disintegration*. But what stood out most were the descriptions of the casualties. Soldiers—volunteers, some of them—had been exposed to these compounds during tests. Their deaths were gruesome, each one more horrifying than the last.

One entry caught her eye: *Subject experienced total liquefaction within three minutes of exposure. All internal organs and tissue reduced to fluid state, with bones remaining intact. Cause of death: chemical-induced cellular collapse.*

"The algorithm..." Kline began, his voice low, "...was designed to predict chemical reactions, to create compounds that could neutralize threats like the Trinities. But most of the time, it fails. Spectacularly."

Kline gave her a sidelong glance, his expression grim. "It doesn't always work. Most of the time, the chemicals it creates are so lethal that they backfire. The military personnel using them? They're usually the first to die."

Aurora's heart raced. She turned back to the screen, the final moments of the squadron replaying in her mind. Could this *Algorithm of Death* be the reason those men had been vaporized? Had they unknowingly unleashed something they couldn't control?

"And the Trinities?" she asked, her voice tight.

"They're resistant to nearly everything we throw at them. The N.E.X.U.S. was supposed to change that, but ..." He shook his head, as if trying to dispel a dark thought. "The Trinities, Aurora, are not just beings of immense power. They're something ancient, something beyond our understanding. They're like gods in human form—if gods could be so merciless."

Aurora stared at the folder, her mind swirling with questions. "And the SUITS think they can control this?"

Kline chuckled bitterly. "Control? No, you know better than that. What they want is to weaponize it. They want power, control over the uncontrollable. They want to be gods themselves."

Aurora felt a knot tighten in her chest. This was madness. The SUITS weren't just hunting these beings—they were trying to become them. And in their relentless pursuit, they had created a machine capable of wiping out entire populations.

"Why would anyone unleash something like this?" she asked, half to herself.

Kline's eyes darkened. "Because the world isn't run by people who care about ethics, Aurora. It's run by people who thrive on chaos and fear. The more fear they create, the more control they have."

Aurora's gaze fell to the flickering screen. There was something insidious in this pursuit of power—something that went beyond scientific ambition. This was about control, about dominance over life and death itself. The Algorithm of Death wasn't just a machine. It was a weapon in the hands of people who saw human lives as nothing more than expendable assets.

"Do you ever wonder," Aurora began hesitantly, "if this is worth it? All of this... the experiments, the deaths, the Trinities?"

Kline's face softened, a rare moment of vulnerability creeping into his hardened expression. "Every day," he admitted quietly. "But if I stop, they'll just replace me with someone who has no hesitation. Someone like Darwin."

At the mention of the name, Aurora stiffened. She had heard of Dr. Daryl Darwin—the elusive scientist credited with creating the N.E.X.U.S. Algorithm of Death. Darwin was notorious, revered among the scientific elite for his brilliance, but feared for his lack of moral boundaries. His name was whispered with both awe and dread.

"Is it true?" Aurora asked, her voice barely audible. "That Darwin created the Algorithm to cull humanity?"

Kline nodded gravely. "Darwin believes in a world where only the strongest survive. He sees suffering as a necessary step in evolution, a way to purge the weak and create a new, superior race. The Trinities... they're his ultimate challenge. He thinks by mastering them, he'll control the future of humanity."

Aurora shuddered.

This wasn't science.

This was insanity, dressed up in the guise of progress. She turned the folder over in her hands, her thoughts racing. Somewhere in this facility, a machine was churning out death. And beyond the walls, in the world above, the Trinities moved unseen, waiting to strike again.

As Kline stood to leave, he placed a hand on her shoulder. "The deeper you dig, the harder it is to find your way out... Be careful, Aurora. In this place, it's easy to lose sight of who you are. Don't let them take that from you... "

Aurora didn't respond. She couldn't shake the feeling that the SUITS, the Trinities, and this *Algorithm of Death* were part of something much larger than she had ever imagined. Something darker. Something that had no end in sight.

She watched as Kline disappeared down the corridor, his words lingering in the stale air.

3

Aurora felt a cold sweat prickling her skin. It didn't seem real. And yet here it was, listed in the same data set as the N.E.X.U.S. project. Her gut twisted. If these conspiracies weren't just theories, what else had she been wrong about? She suddenly understood why the SUITS kept them locked away in this bunker—six years without contact with the outside world was the price of working here. It was a way to keep people from asking too many questions.

She hadn't given it much thought before, but now it made sense. The isolation, the secrecy—it was all part of the system, a carefully constructed labyrinth meant to keep everyone in line, to make them feel small and insignificant. Aurora felt a creeping dread rise in her throat. Had she been naive to think she could make a difference here? To believe she could rise through the ranks, bring change from the inside? The system wasn't built to change; it was built to consume.

But Aurora was different from the others. Unlike the scientists who had grown numb to the horrors around them, or the operatives who blindly followed orders, she carried a relentless spark—a refusal to accept things as they were. She had seen the costs, felt the weight of every broken life, every erased name. And where others found comfort in compliance, Aurora found herself driven by something more dangerous: a need to understand, to challenge. She couldn't ignore the questions, the whispers in her mind that told her there was more to this world than the SUITS' control.

She didn't just want to survive here. She wanted to unearth the truth, no matter the cost. And that was what made her dangerous.

Her hand hovered over the next document, but before she could click, her screen went black. Aurora's pulse quickened as a low beep followed by a crackle came from her comm device. A voice echoed through the static, cold and precise.

"Sinclair. Report to Dr. Darwin's lab. Immediately."

Aurora froze. Dr. Darwin? She had never been summoned by him before. In fact, she had never even seen the man in person. He was something of a ghost in the facility, his work shrouded in mystery. The N.E.X.U.S. Algorithm of Death was his creation, a monstrosity of a machine capable of synthesizing chemical horrors beyond anything she could imagine. From what she'd heard, Darwin rarely left his lab, preferring to work alone in the shadows.

She stood slowly, nerves jangling. As she made her way through the dim corridors, her mind raced. What did Darwin want with her? And more importantly, why now?

Across the facility, Reese Calder's eyes narrowed as he watched Aurora's hurried pace on the security feed. He had been keeping an eye on her for weeks now—ever since Dr. Kline had taken an interest in the young bioinformatics scientist. Calder wasn't like the others in the SUITS. He didn't care about the organization's twisted ideals or their so-called vision of progress. For him, this was just a job. A way to stay alive.

But something about Sinclair bothered him. She asked too many questions, dug too deep. The SUITS didn't like people who poked around. They preferred obedient soldiers, not curious scientists. Calder knew the drill—people who stepped out of line didn't last long here.

He leaned back in his chair, his gaze flicking over the security footage of the hallways. His gut told him that whatever was happening next, it wouldn't end well for Sinclair. Calder had learned to trust his instincts—after all, they had kept him alive this long. He didn't have a conscience in the traditional sense, but he wasn't heartless either. The way Sinclair was being drawn deeper into the SUITS' twisted projects was unsettling, even for him.

She doesn't belong here, he thought, frowning. Not with people like Darwin.

~

The door to Dr. Darwin's lab hissed open, and Aurora stepped inside. The air was thick with the smell of chemicals, the hum of machines filling the room. Darwin stood at a large console, his back to her, adjusting dials on a complex machine that pulsed with a sinister glow. The N.E.X.U.S. Algorithm was at work, synthesizing something—what, Aurora couldn't tell.

"Dr. Darwin?" she said tentatively.

He turned slowly, his eyes cold and calculating. "Sinclair," he said, his voice like ice. "I've been following your progress."

Aurora's heart skipped a beat. "You have?"

Darwin nodded, his gaze drifting back to the machine. "You've been digging deeper than most. I admire that. But curiosity can be dangerous here, don't you think?"

Aurora swallowed hard, unsure of how to respond. She felt exposed, as if every question she had asked, every file she had accessed, had been under surveillance.

"I—" she started, but Darwin cut her off with a wave of his hand.

"I don't care about your ethical dilemmas or your concerns, Sinclair. What I care about is results. The N.E.X.U.S. Algorithm is designed to produce results—lethal ones. You're here because you have a mind sharp enough to understand that."

He gestured to the machine. "Do you want to see what it's capable of?"

Aurora hesitated, but nodded, her curiosity overwhelming her fear.

Darwin smiled, the corners of his lips curling in a way that made her stomach turn. "Good. Then watch closely."

He pressed a button on the console, and the machine began to hum louder, its glow intensifying. Aurora's eyes widened as she saw the screen display chemical compounds forming in real-time, the molecules rearranging themselves into lethal combinations.

"This is the future, Sinclair," Darwin said, his voice low and menacing. "Control over life and death at the molecular level. The power to wipe out entire populations without a trace."

Aurora felt a chill run down her spine. She stared at the screen, watching as the Algorithm of Death churned out its creations. For the first time, she truly understood what the SUITS were capable of—and it terrified her.

Darwin leaned in close, his voice a whisper. "Welcome to the New World Ordinance."

~

Aurora left the lab in a daze, her mind racing with everything she had just seen. The N.E.X.U.S. Algorithm wasn't just a weapon—it was a tool of mass destruction. And the SUITS were more dangerous than she had ever imagined.

As her terminal hummed to life once again, Aurora hesitated, her hand hovering over the keyboard. In the depths of the facility, the N.E.X.U.S. was working, spinning out chemicals with precision and cruelty. And all she could do was watch as the world burned in its wake.

Aurora paused the footage, her hands trembling slightly as she exhaled, trying to calm herself. What the hell is going on here? she thought. She leaned back in her chair, staring at the words across the screen: N.E.X.U.S. Chemical Weaponry Analysis. The Algorithm of Death, as Kline had called it, was supposed to be their last line of defense—yet it had done nothing but create more destruction.

Her access was limited, of course. She was still only a junior researcher, and even with Kline's guidance, much of the organization's darkest projects were hidden behind levels of clearance far beyond hers. But every day she spent in this bunker, she uncovered more pieces of the puzzle, and each one chipped away at her faith in what the SUITS were doing.

As her screen loaded another document, Aurora froze. It wasn't the footage that caught her off guard this time, but a list of names—military code names, projects connected to the SUITS' human augmentation programs. She clicked through the files as fast as her fingers could type, eyes narrowing at the snippets of information.

HAARP. Chemtrails. Ionosphere research.

Her breath hitched. Aurora had heard of these before—conspiracy theories that had circulated in the public, dismissed as crackpot delusions. But now, here they
were, listed in official SUITS documents. The High-Fre-
quency Archived Auroral Research Project had been
a weather study, or so the government claimed. Now,
though, she wondered—was it a cover? Had the military
been tampering with the atmosphere? Why did Dr. Kline
shared these files with her? The reports suggested far more
than weather experiments; they hinted at mind control
and weather manipulation.

She clicked through another file—Chemtrails. What
she had always thought were harmless airplane contrails
could be something else entirely. According to these reports, the trails left in the sky were laced with chemicals,
designed to affect populations, to control fertility rates,
even to destabilize entire regions through environmental
manipulation.

She hadn't given it much thought before, but now it
made sense. The isolation, the secrecy—it was all part of
the system, a dark mechanism designed not just to keep
people in line but to bury them under layers of compliance
and control. It was the cold precision of the SUITS, a
calculated suffocation that kept even the brightest minds
too fragmented, too isolated to see the full picture. Aurora
felt a creeping dread rise in her throat, settling there like

a stone. Had she been naive to think she could make a difference here? To believe she could work her way up, dismantling the system piece by piece, bringing change from the inside?

She realized then that the system had been designed to create just this—a feeling of smallness, of insignificance. The SUITS thrived on this: employees too buried in protocols and isolation to question anything, too drained to connect the dots. But something stirred within her, a defiant ember she couldn't quite extinguish. Aurora wasn't like the others. Where they had learned to keep their heads down, she felt the pull to dig deeper, to unravel the strange patterns that no one else dared to see. It was as though every locked door, every classified file, every unanswered question was calling her name, daring her to look closer.

4

Months had passed since Aurora Sinclair's first steps into the shadowy depths of the SUITS, and each day, the weight of her responsibilities seemed to grow heavier. She had become more enmeshed in their labyrinth of secret projects and dangerous research than she ever could have imagined. Yet, the further she delved, the more questions bubbled beneath the surface—unasked, unanswered, haunting her every quiet moment.

The high-level strategy meeting was no different. Aurora sat at the long, sterile table among senior scientists, military strategists, and the occasional shadowy figure with no name or designation. Her fingers played nervously with the edge of her notebook as she waited. The room was dimly lit, the only source of light coming from the massive screen at the head of the room. All eyes were on Dr. Daryl Darwin, standing at the front, as he prepared to present what they had all been summoned for—the official unveiling of the N.E.X.U.S. Algorithm of Death.

The room had an electric tension, a hum of anticipation that rippled through the gathered minds. Darwin, as elusive and mysterious as ever, had barely been seen in public, let alone presented his work directly. This was an event.

Aurora's heart thudded in her chest. Darwin's presentation wasn't just another experiment briefing; this was the moment where the veil would be lifted on the true scale of the SUITS operation. She felt her palms grow clammy as the lights dimmed further, the projector on the screen flickering to life.

Darwin stepped forward, his cold gaze sweeping the room as if to remind them all of who held the real power here. His voice was a low drawl, both commanding and haunting.

"Ladies and gentlemen," he began, his voice echoing in the stillness, "today, we stand at the precipice of a new era—one where we no longer need to fear the uncontrollable forces that have threatened our world. The Trinities, for all their power, will soon be no match for what we've created here."

A ripple of murmurs flowed through the room as Darwin gestured toward the screen. "The N.E.X.U.S. Algorithm of Death is the culmination of decades of research, blending the most advanced AI-driven data synthesis with unparalleled biological manipulation. It was designed with one goal in mind: to counter, incapacitate, and ultimately destroy the Trinities."

Aurora's eyes flickered toward the screen, where a stream of footage began to play. It started innocuously—technical schematics of the N.E.X.U.S. system, scrolling lines of code, molecular diagrams. But soon, the tone shifted. The footage grew darker, the images more brutal. A test subject—once a man—was shown being injected with a compound created by the Algorithm. Within seconds, his skin began to blacken and split, his body convulsing as the toxins tore him apart from the inside out.

Aurora stifled a gasp, her fingers digging into the table. The footage continued. One by one, more subjects were brought in, each suffering a more grotesque and horrifying fate than the last. Their screams were muted in the video, but the contortions of their bodies, the way their limbs snapped and twisted unnaturally, left nothing to the imagination. It was a horror show, a montage of death and suffering filmed for scientific study.

Darwin continued his narration as though he were explaining a simple experiment. "Each of these individuals," he explained coldly, "were deemed problematic by the SUITS and the N.W.O. They were chosen for their resistance to control, their ability to stir unrest among the lower classes." His eyes scanned the room, lingering for a moment on Aurora. "This is what happens when you step out of line."

Aurora felt her breath catch in her throat. She glanced around the room, searching the faces of her colleagues, but found nothing but cold detachment. Not a single flicker of empathy. This was just another day in the SUITS for them.

The video shifted again, showing the true horror of the N.E.X.U.S. Algorithm's capabilities. The screen showed the chemical reactions in real time—skin liquefying, organs dissolving into puddles of gore, bones cracking open like brittle glass. Darwin flipped through the footage with ease, each new test subject discarded like waste. Aurora's stomach churned, but she forced herself to remain still, to appear composed.

"And now," Darwin's voice cut through the grotesque montage, "we are prepared for the next phase. Deployment."

The room was silent, the weight of that word hanging in the air. Aurora's mind raced. Deployment? They were really going to unleash this?

Darwin clicked to another slide, displaying a list of ongoing government projects. Her eyes skimmed the titles: HAARP, Pandora's Box, Project Seraphim—each one familiar, though she had only seen these names in whispered conspiracy theories.

"HAARP," Darwin said, tapping the screen, "is one such project we will resume investigation on. It's often dismissed as pseudoscience, but we know better, don't we? The manipulation of the ionosphere, weather modification, mind control—the key lies in the frequencies." He said the word as if it held the secrets to the universe. "The Trinities, as we've observed, are attuned to these frequencies. They resonate with the world in ways we've only just begun to understand. Project Pandora's Box will delve into that connection—between the frequencies, the human mind, and the Trinities. We are on the verge of unlocking a power beyond imagination."

Aurora's hands trembled beneath the table. She had come across references to these projects in her research, but the files were always restricted. Now, here they were—open secrets, laid bare as if they were routine operations. And the way Darwin spoke of them—with such cold certainty—it was terrifying. He wasn't speculating. He knew.

"And so," Darwin continued, his voice taking on a dangerous edge, "we will proceed. The Algorithm will continue to evolve, generating ever more sophisticated chemical agents. Our next trial will be within weeks, but the initial deployment will begin immediately."

Aurora's pulse quickened. Immediate deployment? She tried to keep her face impassive, but a thousand questions swirled through her mind. Where? How? Would this weapon truly be unleashed upon the world—upon people? Was there no limit to what the SUITS would do to maintain control?

Darwin's final slide was a grotesque testament to the power of the Algorithm. More test subjects flashed across the screen, their bodies writhing, then disintegrating, in agony. The footage flickered between horror and efficiency, the perfect blend of science and suffering. The room remained silent as the screen finally went dark, the echoes of the test subjects' final moments hanging in the air.

Aurora's heart pounded in her chest as Darwin stepped back from the console. "This is only the beginning," he said, his voice low but filled with purpose. "The Trinities will fall. And we will be the ones to bring them down."

The meeting left Aurora shaken, though she hid it well as she exited the room. Her mind raced with everything she had just witnessed. The N.E.X.U.S. Algorithm, the gruesome footage, the connection to the HAARP and Pandora's Box projects—it was all so much worse than she had imagined.

Back in her lab, she found it harder to focus. The data on her screen blurred as her thoughts spiraled. She had always known the SUITS were playing with dangerous forces, but now, as she glimpsed the full scope of their plans, the weight of her involvement became unbearable.

As the weeks passed, Aurora's responsibilities grew. She was assigned to handle more classified data, analyzing the results of Trinity encounters, each one more disturbing than the last. The Trinity Frequencies, as Darwin had mentioned, became a recurring theme in her research. The powers these beings wielded were unlike anything humanity had ever faced, and the SUITS were desperate to unlock the secret to controlling them.

The more Aurora learned, the more isolated she felt. Her colleagues seemed indifferent to the horrors unfolding around them, lost in their own ambitions. But Aurora couldn't shake the feeling that she was being watched—that her every move was being monitored. It wasn't just paranoia; there were anomalies in the data, files that disappeared from her screen just as she was about to access them. Who was watching her? And why?

She began to wonder if her own curiosity would be her downfall. She was getting too close to the truth, and in a place like this, the truth was deadly.

Darwin's unveiling of the N.E.X.U.S. Algorithm of Death had been a success in the eyes of the SUITS. But for Aurora, it was a nightmare made real. As she uncovered more of the truth behind the organization's projects, she realized that Darwin wasn't just another scientist. He was something far more dangerous—a revolutionary, determined to reshape the world, no matter the cost.

And if she wasn't careful, she might just become his next casualty.

5

Aurora stared blankly at her screen, the cold glow of the data washing over her face. It had been weeks since Darwin's presentation, and the memory of it still haunted her—images of bodies disintegrating, minds destroyed, and the quiet indifference of the man who had created it all. The days had blurred together in a haze of classified research, data analysis, and sleepless nights. But no matter how deeply she buried herself in work, she couldn't shake the growing sense of dread.

Her fingers hovered over the keys as her thoughts drifted back to her childhood. A memory surfaced—a flashback that always came uninvited, like a ghost tapping on her shoulder.

Aurora had been just a child then, no older than ten. She remembered sitting in their cramped apartment, the air heavy with the scent of decay and dampness. Her mother, thin and frail, sat by the window, her face pale and gaunt. She had always been sick, her body unable to give the plasma that everyone in the lower districts sold for money.

Other families had enough to survive, but Aurora's mother had nothing to sell, leaving them poorer than the rest.

Her mother's eyes were distant that day, staring into the void beyond the cracked glass. She would have her good days and bad days, but this was one of the bad ones. Aurora could tell by the way her mother spoke to herself in whispers, fragmented sentences that made no sense.

"Do you hear it?" her mother asked, turning her sunken eyes toward her. "The hum. It's everywhere. In the air, in the sky. They control everything, Aurora. They're watching."

Aurora remembered the fear that gripped her small body, the fear of her mother's strange words, of her delusions. Or were they delusions? Even now, years later, she wasn't sure.

Her mother often spoke of things Aurora didn't understand—about signals in the air, about frequencies that could change people, about things that didn't seem real but haunted her as if they were. She had lived in constant paranoia, constantly checking the sky, constantly muttering about things Aurora couldn't see.

That day, her mother had pulled her close, her grip weak but insistent. "You'll see one day," she had said. "They use the air to control us. The hum—it's real. It's real."

Aurora had nodded, not understanding. Her mother had always been ill, always prone to these strange fits. But the memory of that moment, her mother's frail voice and the haunted look in her eyes, had stayed with her.

And now, after all these years, Aurora wondered if her mother had been right. The more she uncovered about the SUITS, the more she thought about those whispered words. The hum. The air. The control.

Aurora blinked, shaking herself from the memory, the hum of her computer pulling her back to the present. She tried to refocus on her work, but the sensation lingered. Something about the way her mother had spoken, something about those long-forgotten warnings—it gnawed at her.

She pushed the thought away, but a breadcrumb had been planted. A tiny sliver of doubt that had started to grow.

~

A few hours later, Aurora was pulled into another briefing. The SUITS had detected seismic activity in a remote desert region, and they believed it was tied to another Trinity—this one even more dangerous than Keraunian-Surge. The military had already failed once, and this time, they were deploying their most advanced weapons, hoping for a different outcome.

Trinity-002: Codename "Aion-Indomitus." It was an ancient, impenetrable force—a walking monolith of indestructibility. According to the reports, Aion-Indomitus was invulnerable to all known forms of physical and energy-based attacks. It had been spotted only a handful of times throughout history, but its presence always left devastation in its wake.

Aurora studied the footage from previous encounters—blurry, shaky images of the massive figure, its dark, obsidian-like skin reflecting no light. Its eyes glowed with an eerie pale light, its body slow and deliberate, as if it were aware that nothing could stop it. Bullets flattened against its chest. Explosions barely scratched its surface. Soldiers were tossed aside like ragdolls when they dared to come close.

The new mission was no different. The government had sent their best, armed with the most advanced weaponry available—heavy artillery, armor-piercing rounds, explosives designed for indestructible targets. None of it worked. Aurora watched as the soldiers deployed wave after wave of firepower, but Aion-Indomitus moved forward, unscathed and unstoppable.

As she reviewed the footage, she saw the despair on the soldiers' faces as they realized the futility of their efforts. They had encircled the Trinity, hoping to contain it with experimental fields. But the ground beneath their feet had shattered as Aion-Indomitus responded, its strength sending shockwaves through the earth. The footage showed men and women hurled into the air like debris, their bodies breaking upon impact with the ground. Blood and dust mixed in the chaos, the scene a gut-wrenching massacre.

Aurora's stomach churned as she watched, her hands trembling as they hovered over the keyboard. How could anyone justify this? The SUITS claimed they were fighting for control, for security, but all she saw were bodies—human lives sacrificed in the name of power.

Her eyes flicked to the data on her screen. The Algorithm of Death had been used again, its toxins deployed during the mission in a desperate attempt to weaken the Trinity. But it had failed, and the soldiers had paid the price.

Aurora's internal conflict began to boil over. How many more people had to die? How many more gruesome failures would they endure before someone stopped this madness? But no one here wanted to stop. The SUITS were relentless in their pursuit of power. They would keep sending soldiers to their deaths until they had what they wanted—control over the Trinities.

Aurora's paranoia grew with each passing day. She had started noticing anomalies in the data—strange patterns, inconsistencies in the experiments, subjects that didn't add up. Files would disappear from her terminal just as she was about to access them. She felt eyes on her, though she never knew by whom.

Her research continued to uncover fragments of long-buried projects: the manipulation of human minds through frequencies, the study of the ionosphere in programs like HAARP, and strange experiments that connected the powers of the Trinities to ancient technologies. Each new piece of information only deepened her unease.

Then, there was NeuroLobe, a term that had begun appearing in her research notes with increasing frequency. At first, she thought it was just another classified term, something to do with the brain or neural research. But the more she saw it, the more she began to suspect it was something far more sinister. There were vague references to human augmentation, to mind control experiments, and connections to the SUITS's larger goals. She had seen enough to know that they weren't just manipulating the Trinities—they were manipulating people.

As the days turned into weeks, Aurora became increasingly isolated. Her colleagues barely noticed her unease, too focused on their own work. The SUITS had a way of making everyone feel alone, even in a room full of people. And as Aurora dove deeper into her research, that sense of isolation grew into paranoia.

She had access to files that she shouldn't have, and she knew it. But she couldn't stop now. She had to know the truth. The more she uncovered, the more she questioned everything she thought she knew about the world. The SUITS were not just a military organization—they were something far more dangerous, far more insidious.

Aurora couldn't shake the feeling that the walls were closing in around her. She had stumbled upon something too big, too dark. And the deeper she dug, the more certain she became that someone was watching her every move.

The meeting with Dr. Darwin had shattered her initial idealism. The footage of Aion-Indomitus had only confirmed her worst fears. And now, as she sat alone in her lab, surrounded by data that no one else had seen, she wondered how long it would be before the SUITS came for her too.

The hum of the machine filled the room, a steady, low sound that reminded her of her mother's whispered warnings. The hum. The control. It was all real, just as her mother had said. But now it was too late.

Aurora was in too deep.

6

The air in the bunker felt oppressive, heavy with the weight of Aurora Sinclair's growing realization. It had been weeks since the last catastrophic encounter with Aion-Indomitus, and the SUITS had barely taken a breath before moving on to the next mission. But the footage playing on her screen now was worse than anything she had seen before.

Her fingers trembled over the keyboard as the video unfolded. On the screen, a city stood in the distance, smoke rising in tendrils from the charred remnants of buildings. The camera followed the flames, capturing their spread, licking hungrily at the sky. The scene was a nightmare—a firestorm sweeping across a densely populated area, leaving nothing but scorched earth and ash in its wake.

Trinity-003: Codename "Inferna-Tempestas."

Aurora's eyes scanned the report. The entity had been classified as a Category 3 threat—one that the SUITS had expected to contain with specialized units equipped for extreme heat conditions. But they had underestimated it. As they always did.

On the screen, the camera's focus shifted. It was hand-held, shaky, likely belonging to one of the soldiers in the field, who was filming the chaos as it unfolded. The wind howled through the speakers, the flames roaring louder than the static-laced voices over the radio. The fire didn't spread like a natural blaze—it moved with purpose, with control. And then, there it was, looming in the distance.

The creature stood at least 8 feet tall, wreathed in swirling flames that flickered with an intensity that made the air itself seem to shimmer. Its molten skin radiated unbearable heat, making it hard for the camera to focus. The soldiers moved closer, but the air around Inferna-Tempestas warped, bending the light and causing the ground beneath it to blacken and crack.

Aurora winced as the first wave of soldiers opened fire. Their bullets disintegrated before they even made contact, the heat turning them to vapor in midair. The flames flared, as if in response to the attack, and the Trinity's eyes glowed a searing orange, burning with an almost sentient rage.

Then came the firestorm.

It happened in an instant, the calm façade of the Trinity replaced by an eruption of pure fury. Inferna-Tempestas raised its arms, and with a single gesture, a tornado of flames spiraled out from its body. The camera spun wildly as the firestorm surged forward, consuming everything in its path. Aurora could barely make out the shapes of soldiers as they were caught in the inferno, their screams swallowed by the roaring flames.

The footage was unbearable—intense bursts of fire, the crackling of burning flesh, the disintegration of steel and concrete. The ground itself seemed to melt under the heat, and the soldiers' fireproof gear offered no protection. One by one, they fell, their bodies reduced to nothing but ash.

Aurora's hand covered her mouth as she forced herself to watch. Her stomach churned at the carnage, but she knew she had to see this through. The flames on the screen swirled and danced, as if alive, devouring everything in their path. And at the center of it all, Inferna-Tempestas stood untouched, a living inferno, its power growing with each passing moment.

As the footage continued, the realization hit Aurora with the force of a tidal wave. The SUITS had no chance against these beings. They could deploy all the soldiers, all the advanced weaponry in the world, but it wouldn't matter. The Trinities weren't just powerful—they were forces of nature, entities far beyond human control or comprehension.

Inferna-Tempestas had proven that. This wasn't just a military defeat. This was annihilation.

Aurora closed the footage, the echo of the soldiers' last moments still ringing in her ears. She leaned back in her chair, staring blankly at the screen. Every mission ended the same way—mass casualties, failure, and more futile attempts to contain the uncontainable. But it was more than just the failures that haunted her. There was something deeper, something far more disturbing that gnawed at her.

The reports didn't match the data.

She had noticed the discrepancies weeks ago—strange gaps in the experiment logs, subjects that seemed to vanish from the system, incomplete files on Trinity encounters. At first, she had brushed it off, thinking it was a technical error, a simple oversight in the chaos of these catastrophic missions. But the pattern had continued, and now, she couldn't ignore it any longer.

Aurora pulled up the data on the Trinity encounters. The footage from Inferna-Tempestas was horrifying, yes, but the numbers didn't add up. The soldiers on the ground weren't just unlucky—they had been sent in with incomplete knowledge, ill-prepared for what they were up against. Someone had withheld information. Someone had known exactly how dangerous the Trinities were, and yet they had continued to send people to their deaths.

And it wasn't just the soldiers.

Aurora had come across references to a new kind of research in her recent data logs—NeuroLobe technology. The notes were vague, but the implications were terrifying. There were whispers of human enhancement, of mind control through advanced neural manipulation. Could it be that the soldiers were more than just soldiers? Had they been tampered with? Were they being manipulated, their minds altered to make them more compliant, more willing to march toward certain death?

Aurora's hands trembled as she scrolled through the files. The secrecy surrounding the SUITS experiments was suffocating. Every step deeper into the research only revealed more layers of deceit, more questions with no answers.

In the days following the firestorm, the footage of Inferna-Tempestas spread through the underground networks like wildfire. It wasn't official, of course—the SUITS had buried the mission report, as they always did. But the soldiers who had witnessed the firestorm, the few who had survived to tell the tale, leaked the video to the few brave enough to look.

Aurora overheard whispers in the halls, scientists muttering about the futility of the mission, about how the Trinities were proving to be more than just anomalies. They were beginning to question whether humanity had any chance at all.

And yet, the SUITS marched forward, undeterred. Darwin had made his position clear—they wouldn't stop until they had control over the Trinities. The N.E.X.U.S. Algorithm continued to churn out new chemical combinations, new bioweapons, each one deadlier than the last. But Aurora had seen enough to know that these weapons would never be enough. The Trinities weren't just powerful—they were invincible, each one more terrifying than the last.

Inferna-Tempestas had been a living inferno, a force of destruction that reduced entire cities to ash. The footage showed the firestorm from above, swirling like a biblical reckoning, and Aurora felt the weight of the futility pressing down on her chest.

The SUITS thought they could contain these beings. But they were wrong. And it was only a matter of time before that hubris destroyed them all.

As she sat in her lab, watching the footage over and over, Aurora's mind raced. The Trinities weren't just threats to be neutralized—they were symbols of something far greater, far more terrifying. They were reminders of humanity's limitations, of the dangers of playing God.

Her hands hovered over the files once more. The data didn't lie. And the more she uncovered, the more she realized that the SUITS weren't just fighting an unwinnable war—they were hiding something. Something far worse than the Trinities themselves.

But what? And why was she the only one who seemed to care?

Aurora's thoughts drifted back to her mother's warnings, the strange ramblings about control, about signals in the air. At the time, she had thought her mother was losing her mind. But now, in the sterile glow of the lab, she wasn't so sure.

What if her mother had been right all along?

The SUITS were manipulating everything. The soldiers, the scientists, maybe even the Trinities themselves. And Aurora was caught in the middle, teetering on the edge of a truth she wasn't sure she wanted to uncover.

The hum of the lab felt louder than ever as she clicked on the next file, her hands trembling with the weight of what she was about to see.

Inferna-Tempestas had left nothing but ash in its wake.

And yet, it was only the beginning.

7

The hum of the bunker's lights felt oppressive, buzzing in Aurora's skull like an incessant drone she couldn't shake. It wasn't just the lights, though—it was everything. The weight of the footage, the endless data streams, the lingering screams of soldiers swallowed by flames. It gnawed at her. Ever since watching Inferna-Tempestas tear through an entire city like a living firestorm, she hadn't been able to sleep without seeing those flames dancing behind her eyelids.

And it wasn't just the footage that haunted her. It was what she was learning, piece by piece, the slow unraveling of the lies she had once believed. The SUITS weren't here to protect humanity. They were here to control it. The realization was like a slow-burning fuse, growing brighter with every classified file she uncovered.

The government had escalated its tactics after the disastrous failure to contain Inferna-Tempestas. What started with specialized ops teams had now evolved into a full-scale military effort, with thousands of troops being deployed in coordinated strikes to track and capture the Trinities. Every mission was meticulously recorded through body cams, drones, and vehicle-mounted cameras. The footage was fed back to the command center in real-time, analyzed by an army of researchers—Aurora among them. But no matter how much data they gathered, no matter how advanced their weaponry became, the Trinities remained untouchable.

Aurora's screen flickered with the latest footage: a battalion of soldiers in flame-retardant suits marched through a charred landscape, weapons at the ready. They had improved their technology, armed with thermal suppression devices and specialized containment drones, but even the most cutting-edge weapons failed to pierce the unyielding power of these beings. Aurora knew how this would end before it even started.

Inferna-Tempestas had obliterated them all within minutes, its pyrokinesis creating a swirling vortex of flames that reduced everything to ash. The screams, the chaos, the overwhelming sense of helplessness—it all played out before her again, a grotesque loop she couldn't escape.

But this time, something different caught her eye. As she zoomed in on a section of the footage, she noticed one soldier moving strangely, lagging behind the others, his movements stiff, almost robotic. He didn't respond to the chaos around him. His expression was blank, as though he were detached from the devastation, while the firestorm swirled around him, and the others were consumed.

What the hell is this? Aurora thought, her fingers freezing over the keyboard.

She rewound the footage, studying the soldier closely. There was no doubt about it—he wasn't behaving like the others. While the rest of the unit was frantically trying to survive, he moved with calm precision, as if on autopilot, his body barely reacting to the destruction around him.

A chill ran down Aurora's spine. She had seen this before, in passing references buried deep in the files—theories about NeuroLobe technologies, mind control experiments linked to classified government projects. They had always seemed like conspiracies, whispers from the dark corners of the SUITS. But now, watching this footage, Aurora began to wonder: What if it's real? What if they've been controlling people this whole time?

Aurora dove deeper into the files, her mind racing as she connected the dots. What she found was far more terrifying than she had imagined. Hidden among the mountains of data on Trinity encounters and military failures were references to an old, long-abandoned government project—MKUltra—the infamous mind-control experiments that had allegedly ended decades ago. But according to these files, the project had never truly ended. It had simply evolved.

The SUITS, working with shadowy branches of the government, had resurrected the project, using advanced neural implants and electromagnetic weaponry to manipulate the thoughts and behaviors of soldiers, civilians, and even high-profile individuals. The mind-control tech was designed to suppress free will, to make people pliant and compliant, a subtle but terrifying form of control.

Aurora's eyes widened as she read about the experiments—how certain individuals had been targeted, their minds bent to the will of the SUITS, their memories erased, their thoughts overwritten. Some of them were public figures—celebrities, political leaders—puppets controlled by an unseen hand. Others were ordinary people, their lives ruined by the implantation of neural devices that made them believe they were going insane.

She thought back to her mother, to her strange, paranoid ramblings about signals in the air, about control. Was she one of them? Had her mother been a victim of these experiments? Aurora's heart raced at the thought. Her mother had always been distant, broken. Could it be that she wasn't just sick, but that she had been manipulated, her mind fractured by something far more sinister?

Aurora closed the file, her breath shallow. This was too much. The SUITS weren't just fighting the Trinities—they were controlling everything. The media, the public, the soldiers on the ground. It was all part of a grander design, a slow erosion of free will, all in the name of maintaining power.

The footage of the failed missions weighed heavily on Aurora's mind as she attended the next briefing. The government's desperation had reached a fever pitch. With every mission, they grew bolder, more reckless. Now they were deploying entire armies in a full-scale assault, hoping that sheer numbers would overpower the Trinities. They had even begun experimenting with clones—engineered soldiers designed to fight without fear, without hesitation.

The room was filled with military officials, scientists, and the grim faces of those who had seen too much. Dr. Darwin stood at the front, his cold eyes scanning the room, his voice calm and calculating as he outlined the new strategy.

"We've learned from our failures," he began, his voice dripping with authority. "The Trinities may be beyond human comprehension, but they are not invincible. We've developed new weapons, new tactics. This next phase will be different."

Aurora wanted to scream. She knew how this would end—more bodies, more death, more futile attempts to cage what couldn't be caged. But no one here cared about that. All they cared about was control. The SUITS would keep throwing lives at this problem until they found a solution, no matter the cost.

As the briefing continued, Aurora's thoughts drifted back to Dr. Kline. He had been her mentor, her guiding light in this dark place, but she could see the cracks forming in him. He had always been idealistic, hoping to find a balance between science and ethics. But now, with each new failure, each new grotesque experiment, his faith was waning. Aurora saw it in his eyes, in the way he spoke less and less in meetings, his voice quieter, more resigned.

He won't last much longer, Aurora realized, a sinking feeling settling in her stomach. They'll break him, just like they've broken everyone else.

~

As the days blurred into weeks, Aurora's guilt began to fester. Every night, she would close her eyes and see the faces of the soldiers she had sent to their deaths, their bodies incinerated in the flames of Inferna-Tempestas, or crushed beneath the unrelenting force of Aion-Indomitus. She had been complicit in all of it. She had analyzed the data, helped create the weapons, watched as the SUITS manipulated people like pawns in a game they couldn't win.

The conspiracy theories she had once dismissed as fringe ramblings were becoming her reality. The SUITS weren't just fighting for control—they were waging a war on the human mind, on free will itself. The Trinity encounters were just one part of a much larger plan, a plan to reshape the world in their image.

Aurora stared at the screen, the hum of the bunker's lights buzzing in her ears like the static of a dying signal. The countdown had begun—every failed mission, every new revelation bringing her closer to something inevitable. Something catastrophic.

And through it all, the Trinities remained untouchable, their origins shrouded in mystery. Were they gods? Demons? Angels sent to bring about the end of days? Aurora didn't know. But what she did know was that they couldn't be stopped. No matter how many soldiers were thrown at them, no matter how advanced the technology became, the Trinities were a force beyond human comprehension.

And in their wake, humanity would burn.

Dr. Kline had always been a man of principle. He had believed in the promise of science, in the idea that it could be used to help, to heal. But as the SUITS descended further into madness, as they turned their focus to weapons of control, Kline's faith had begun to erode.

Aurora watched him from across the room during the next meeting, his eyes distant, his posture slumped. She knew what was coming. The SUITS had no room for doubt, no room for conscience. They would either break Kline or discard him. And the way things were going, Aurora feared the latter was far more likely.

As the meeting droned on, the countdown ticking away in the back of her mind, Aurora felt a sense of inevitability settling over her. The SUITS were too far gone, too consumed by their own ambition to see the cliff they were hurtling toward.

And when they fell, they would drag everyone down with them.

8

The sterile, white walls of the conference room felt tighter, closer than ever before. Aurora sat near the end of the long table, surrounded by lead scientists, military strategists, and the stone-faced operatives of the SUITS. The room buzzed with tense energy as Dr. Kline took his usual seat near the front, his eyes cast downward, dark bags under them betraying his recent lack of sleep.

Aurora could feel it—the cracks in him, the slow unraveling of his calm demeanor. Ever since the failures with Aion-Indomitus and Inferna-Tempestas, Dr. Kline had grown more distant, more erratic. She had once admired him, even trusted him, but now, the man sitting in front of her looked haunted, barely holding it together.

The meeting began like any other—updates on weaponry advancements, more plans for enhanced military strategies. Aurora could hardly focus. Her mind was spinning with the breadcrumbs she had found, the little hints her colleagues had left behind in their research notes. Fragments of conversations, classified documents hastily deleted, encrypted data logs that didn't add up. Something was wrong. Something bigger than any of them knew.

Dr. Darwin stood at the front of the room, his cold voice droning on about the next phase of the N.E.X.U.S. Algorithm of Death. Aurora barely listened—she had heard it all before. More talk of control, of new chemical variations being synthesized, of their ever-growing arsenal of deadly compounds. But her thoughts were on something else. She had started to piece together a fragmented understanding of the experiments, a trail of clues left behind by those who had disappeared or mysteriously "retired" from the SUITS.

Her fingers tapped nervously on the table, her mind wandering to the hidden files she had uncovered about mind-control experiments—the way the SUITS had been manipulating soldiers and civilians alike. The world around her felt like it was fraying at the edges, and she couldn't tell if it was all in her head or if the SUITS were deliberately breaking her, too.

And then it happened.

Dr. Kline stood abruptly, his face twisted with anger. His fists clenched at his sides as he glared across the room, directly at Dr. Darwin. His voice trembled with fury. "You... You're lying to them all!" Kline's words were a bombshell, the room falling silent, eyes wide with shock.

Darwin arched an eyebrow, unfazed. "Excuse me, Dr. Kline?"

Kline's face reddened as he pointed a shaking finger at the screen. "These experiments! These people! Do you even understand what you're doing? We're not saving lives—we're destroying them! We're... we're creating Echoes!" He stopped himself abruptly, his mouth hanging open as if the words had been yanked from him. He glanced around the room, suddenly aware of how much he had said.

Aurora's heart raced as she leaned forward in her seat. What was he talking about? Creating what?

Kline's hand dropped to his side, and for a moment, his face flickered with fear. His voice lowered, barely audible. "You know about the... the Echoes..." His words trailed off, his eyes darting to the security cameras in the corners of the room. "I can't... I can't do this anymore."

The air was thick with tension. No one moved. The other lead scientists shifted uncomfortably in their seats, while Darwin remained still, his cold gaze fixed on Kline.

Kline let out a shuddering breath, then without another word, he turned on his heel and stormed out of the room, leaving the door to slam behind him.

Aurora's mind reeled. Echoes? What did he mean? She had never heard the term before, but the way Kline had said it, the way he had stopped himself—it was as if he had just revealed a secret he was never meant to. But no one else seemed to know what he was talking about. Or if they did, they were pretending not to.

Dr. Darwin cleared his throat, drawing the room's attention back to him. "Let's continue," he said coldly, as if nothing had happened.

But something had happened. Something major.

~

In the days following Kline's outburst, something shifted in the bunker. Communications became sporadic, messages arriving late or garbled, as if someone was deliberately sabotaging the flow of information. There were rumors of disruptions in the upper echelons of the SUITS—power struggles between departments, key personnel disappearing, internal conflicts erupting into brutal confrontations. Aurora didn't know what was going on, but she could feel the tension in the air.

One night, while working late in the lab, she received an encrypted message on her terminal. The sender was anonymous, but the subject line caught her attention: N.E.X.U.S. Algorithm: Hidden Logs. Her pulse quickened as she opened the file.

It contained footage—classified footage of experiments she had never seen before. The screen flickered to life with grainy images of human test subjects, their bodies hooked up to machines, their faces twisted in agony. Aurora felt sick as she watched. The Algorithm of Death had been administered to them, and the results were horrific. Their skin blackened, their veins bulged, and their screams pierced the silence of the lab.

But something else caught her eye. In the corner of the screen, a group of men—operatives, technicians—were struggling to subdue another test subject. Unlike the others, this man wasn't dying. He was fighting back, his body convulsing violently as he broke free of his restraints. His eyes were wide, crazed, and he let out a guttural roar as he lunged at the technicians, biting, scratching, drawing blood.

The footage cut out abruptly, but not before Aurora saw the look in the man's eyes—pure madness, like an animal driven wild. What was that? she thought, her stomach turning. She had assumed the test subjects were given randomized doses of the Algorithm's chemical variants, but this man... he didn't die. He just went insane. What was she watching?

Aurora rewound the footage, trying to make sense of it. The other subjects had died horrible, grotesque deaths, but this man—he was different. He had been strong, violent, like something had pushed him beyond the limits of normal human behavior.

Her fingers hovered over the keys as she searched for more information, but there was nothing. The file had been scrubbed, its origins erased. Whatever she had just seen wasn't meant for her eyes.

The next day, Dr. Kline was nowhere to be found. Aurora heard whispers that he had been taken off the project, removed from the bunker altogether. Some said he had been transferred to a different facility, others believed he had been silenced, forced into retirement like so many others before him. Aurora wasn't sure what to believe, but she knew one thing—Kline had been on the edge of something. He had known too much, and now he was gone.

Aurora's mind raced with the possibilities. What had Kline meant when he spoke of Echoes? Why had he lost control, so publicly, so suddenly? And why had he stopped himself before saying more?

She couldn't shake the feeling that she was standing on the precipice of something huge, something that could unravel everything the SUITS had built. But she was still missing pieces—still trying to put together the fragmented understanding of the N.E.X.U.S. experiments, the mind-control tests, the grotesque outcomes she had witnessed.

As Aurora continued her work, she found herself drawn into the politics of the SUITS more than she ever wanted to be. Lia, one of the senior operatives, had taken an interest in her, and though Aurora found Lia charming, she couldn't help but feel uneasy around her. Lia had a way of ingratiating herself with key figures, subtly manipulating conversations, twisting the narrative to her advantage. She played the role of the supportive friend, but Aurora could see the darkness behind her eyes.

Lia was dangerous, and Aurora knew it. She had seen how quickly Lia could turn on someone, undermining them when it suited her. And now, with the bunker's communications in disarray and the power struggles within the SUITS intensifying, Aurora found herself caught in Lia's web.

On the other hand, there was Irene Isla, a quiet and unassuming operative who had always lingered on the edges of the SUITS organization. Irene was the type of person who never seemed destined for a world like this, a world woven with secrets and shadows. She hadn't chosen this life—it had chosen her, pulling her in through a series of accidents, coincidences, or something darker, as though the organization had a way of finding exactly who it needed. Irene had a gentleness about her, a softness that didn't belong in the labyrinth of hidden experiments and cold calculations that defined the SUITS. And though they never spoke of it directly, Aurora felt a kinship with her, an empathy that ran deeper than words. They were both outsiders here, observers in a game that was played by unseen hands.

But as the days wore on, Aurora began to sense something shifting in Irene. She caught Irene glancing over her shoulder, her whispers growing more urgent, her eyes haunted by shadows that Aurora couldn't quite see. Irene spoke in cryptic fragments, hints of files she had glimpsed, of tests and programs buried beneath layers of clearance. "They go deeper than you think," she would murmur, almost to herself, as if she feared speaking it too loudly would summon the very forces she tried to hide from. "There's more to this place than any of us know."

And then, one day, Irene was gone—vanished without a trace. Her workspace left untouched, her belongings abandoned as though she had simply dissolved into the silence of the SUITS. There was no record, no formal notice, just the empty desk and the knowledge that people who delved too deep had a way of disappearing. Aurora felt a pang of guilt, as if she should have done more, asked more. But the truth was, she feared asking too much.

Yet, in the days after Irene's disappearance, Aurora began to see faint links between their roles, a subtle alignment that hadn't seemed important before. Like her, Irene had been tasked with data analysis—only, her clearance level had allowed her access to projects Aurora hadn't even known existed. And their work intersected in strange, invisible ways: Irene's job was to track patterns within the organization, spotting irregularities, logging anomalies in personnel behavior and experimental outcomes. Aurora's role, on the other hand, was to monitor the digital architecture of the SUITS, tracking data flow and ensuring security. Together, though neither had fully realized it, they had been tracing the edges of the organization's darkest secrets, painting a picture neither was meant to see.

The more she thought about it, the more Aurora wondered if Irene's paranoia hadn't been born out of madness but out of the truth—truth that had been hiding in plain sight, scattered across countless files, hidden among mundane tasks and daily routines. And as the empty desk next to her grew colder, Aurora began to wonder: had Irene been a warning? Or had her disappearance been something else entirely, a reminder of what happened when you got too close?

Aurora knew it was only a matter of time before the pieces started to come together—before the truth about the SUITS, the N.E.X.U.S. experiments, and the mysterious Echoes would be revealed. She felt the countdown ticking away in the back of her mind, each day bringing her closer to something catastrophic. Something that would change everything.

Aurora knew that she was on the edge of a revelation she wasn't sure she wanted to face.

But there was no turning back now.

The hum of the lights filled the silence, and in that hum, Aurora could almost hear her mother's whispered warnings, her words from years ago echoing in the back of her mind.

"They control everything. The air, the signals, the world. You'll see it one day."

Aurora was starting to see it now. And it terrified her.

9

Aurora sat at her terminal, watching the flickering monitors that displayed endless streams of data from the latest Trinity operations. The chaos within the SUITS had only intensified since Dr. Kline's outburst, and though communications had become erratic, there was no shortage of rumors circulating through the lab.

Rumors about Dr. Kline.

Rumors about Aurora.

She could feel the shift in the air, the weight of eyes always on her, the whispers in the halls. Ever since Kline's sudden disappearance after his outburst, people had started linking his actions to her. Every time she tried to offer an explanation, it was met with sideways glances or probing questions. People wanted to know what she knew about him. The pressure was mounting, and it was suffocating her.

She missed the Dr. Kline she once knew, the mentor who had guided her through her early days in the SUITS Now, he was... something else. His reappearance in the lab only added to the unease. When he finally returned, he seemed brighter, more upbeat—almost euphoric—but it wasn't natural. His mood swings were rapid and bizarre, and he was quick to brush off any mention of his prior outburst. The warmth in his eyes was gone, replaced with a hollow sheen that unsettled her deeply.

Aurora felt an overwhelming sense of dread. This wasn't the man she had once trusted implicitly. And as she watched him now, striding through the lab with a cheery, robotic enthusiasm, she couldn't shake the feeling that something was very, very wrong.

Lia, ever perceptive, had noticed it too. The senior operative had approached Aurora the following day, her expression tight with suspicion. "What's up with Kline?" she asked, her voice low. "He's acting like nothing happened, but we all saw him blow up in that meeting. And now this? It's like he's... someone else."

Aurora didn't know how to respond. She had tried to confront Dr. Kline herself, but every time she brought up the outburst, he would smile and wave it off like it was nothing. His insistence that everything was fine only made it worse. And now, she was left standing in the middle of the lab with Lia's cold stare boring into her, waiting for answers she didn't have.

"I don't know," Aurora muttered, averting her gaze. "He's... different. But I don't know why."

Lia crossed her arms, eyes narrowing. "Well, people are talking. They're saying you and Kline have some kind of connection, that you know more than you're letting on." She leaned in closer, her voice dropping to a whisper. "You'd better watch yourself, Sinclair. It won't take much for them to turn on you."

Aurora's stomach twisted into knots. The rumors were vicious, spreading like wildfire through the bunker, and every time she heard someone whisper Kline's name, her own followed. She felt trapped, isolated—an unwilling participant in a web of lies and suspicion. She hated how Kline's actions were tethered to her, how people came to her for answers she didn't have, or worse, to spin their gossip further.

~

Amid the growing tension within the lab, news broke of one of the first successful captures of a Trinity. Trinity-004: Feralis-Vorago. Unlike the others, this Trinity had allowed itself to be captured without a fight, an unprecedented event that sent waves of excitement and apprehension through the SUITS ranks. It was brought back to the lab under extreme security, locked in a reinforced containment unit, and though its presence should have been a moment of triumph, Aurora couldn't help but feel a sense of impending doom.

The Trinity had been subdued, but there was something off about it. Feralis-Vorago was silent, calm, and yet, its very stillness felt like a warning—a predator waiting for the perfect moment to strike.

Dr. Darwin wasted no time. As soon as the Trinity arrived, the experiments began. Basic analysis was conducted first—measurements, scans, and frequency tests. But it wasn't long before Darwin ordered the team to move on to the real test: administering the N.E.X.U.S. Algorithm of Death. Aurora stood on the other side of the observation glass, her heart pounding in her chest as the technicians prepared the compounds.

The room was tense, everyone on edge, knowing that this was uncharted territory. But just as the first compound was about to be administered, Feralis-Vorago unleashed a deafening sonic scream.

The sound was indescribable, a shriek so piercing that the glass of the observation room shuddered under its force. The technicians and scientists inside the containment chamber fell to the floor, clutching their heads as blood poured from their ears. Aurora's hands flew to her own ears, but even through the thick glass, the sound reverberated in her skull, disorienting her, making her vision swim.

The scream continued for what felt like an eternity, until finally, Dr. Darwin, shouting over the chaos, ordered his operatives to subdue the Trinity before it could escape. But the damage had already been done—the room was in shambles, and the Trinity was far from finished.

In the midst of the chaos, Dr. Kline suddenly appeared, his face flushed with excitement. He rushed into the observation room, shouting commands to the technicians, trying to override the controls, his voice erratic. "We need to stop it! Its powers—they're too much!"

But before anyone could react, something went horribly wrong. Aurora's eyes darted across the room, trying to follow the sudden movement. One of Dr. Darwin's security operatives, Donovan Crowe, had moved closer to Kline, a syringe in his hand. Aurora barely had time to process what was happening before Kline stumbled, clutching his arm.

Kline's body convulsed, his arms flailing wildly as he let out a strangled cry. His eyes rolled back, and for a brief moment, Aurora thought he might die right there in front of them. But instead, Crowe and several others grabbed him, violently shoving him toward the containment chamber.

Aurora screamed for them to stop, but her voice was lost in the cacophony of alarms and the Trinity's relentless screams.

They pushed Kline into the containment chamber with the Trinity, slamming the door behind him. He stumbled forward, tripping over wires and broken equipment, his body still jerking uncontrollably. As he staggered toward the Trinity, his movements became more erratic, his mind clearly lost.

The Trinity didn't move at first, watching Kline with its eerie, unblinking gaze. But as Kline drew closer, something inside the creature snapped. It let out another sonic scream, this one aimed directly at him, but Kline didn't falter. He seemed unaffected, his body still convulsing as he reached out toward the creature.

Then, in a violent blur of motion, the Trinity struck.

The force of the attack was so fast, so brutal, that it took a moment for Aurora to process what had happened. One second, Kline was there, and the next, his body was torn apart—limbs dismembered, his torso split open, blood splattering the walls of the containment chamber.

Aurora's breath caught in her throat as she watched in horror. Dr. Kline's body twitched on the ground, a grotesque, twitching mass of flesh and bone, until finally, the movements stopped.

The Trinity let out one final screech, a high-pitched frequency that sent a shockwave through the lab, shorting out the power in the entire section. The lights flickered, then died, plunging the room into darkness.

When the backup lights finally flickered back on, the Trinity was gone. The containment chamber was a shattered mess of destruction, and Dr. Kline's body lay broken in the center of it all.

The silence that followed was deafening.

Dr. Kline's death was unspeakably tragic. The lab buzzed with the aftermath of the catastrophe, the other scientists scrambling to salvage what remained of the data from the failed experiment. But in the days that followed, something even stranger occurred: Aurora was promoted.

She didn't know how to feel. The promotion had come too quickly, too easily, as if it had been waiting for her all along. She was now the Lead Bioinformatics Scientist, a title she had once dreamed of. But now, with Kline's blood still fresh in her mind, it felt more like a noose tightening around her neck.

Worse still, the promotion came with partial access to Kline's files, and as she dug through the cryptic entries, she began to uncover fragments of research that left her reeling. There were reports on NeuroLobe technology, on experiments with genetic modification that she hadn't been privy to before. But none of it made sense—none of it connected directly to the Trinities.

It was as if Kline had been onto something bigger, something far darker, before he died. And now, Aurora was left to piece it together, all while feeling the weight of unseen eyes watching her every move.

Her ascent through the ranks was rapid—too rapid. It felt as though she was being guided, manipulated, pushed toward something she didn't fully understand.

Aurora's ascent through the SUITS hierarchy was a double-edged sword. On one hand, she now had access to files and research that had been previously hidden from her. But with every new piece of classified data, her unease deepened. Dr. Kline's sudden death haunted her, as did the strange circumstances that surrounded it. The memory of him convulsing uncontrollably before being torn apart by the Trinity was seared into her mind.

10

Aurora had always known that her childhood was different. While other children played in the streets or watched cartoons, her nights were filled with shadows, fear, and the cold chill of her mother's voice murmuring in the dark. The past had always clung to her, a phantom just beyond her reach, whispering in her ear, warning her about the dangers that loomed ever closer.

Now, as she sat in her new office—Dr. Kline's office, though she still couldn't shake the eerie feeling that it wasn't truly hers—those whispers grew louder. The flickering lights of the bunker cast strange shadows across the room, reminding her of the haunted nights she had spent with her mother. Aurora closed her eyes, trying to block out the memories, but they came flooding back like an unstoppable tide.

Aurora had been just a child when her mother's descent into madness began. At first, it was subtle—her mother's words becoming more erratic, her gaze unfocused. But soon, it spiraled into full-blown episodes. Nights became a waking nightmare.

Her mother would wake in the dead of night, eyes wide and wild, yelling into the darkness about signals in the air, about invisible forces watching them, controlling them. "They see everything!" she would scream, her voice shrill with terror. "They know what you're doing, Aurora! Don't trust them!"

Aurora would lie frozen in bed, her heart pounding in her chest, too afraid to move. She had learned early on that trying to soothe her mother only made it worse. The episodes were unpredictable—one moment, her mother was screaming about shadowy figures and mind control, and the next, she was sleepwalking through the house, muttering incoherent words.

But the worst nights were when her mother's anger would rise. Aurora remembered the night she had been attacked. Her mother had wandered into Aurora's room, eyes unfocused, her movements stiff. Aurora had thought she was still sleepwalking—until the slap came. It was sudden, violent, and filled with a rage that Aurora had never seen before. Her mother's hands were rough, her grip like iron as she shook Aurora, shouting incoherent things about "them," about "the control."

The next morning, her mother had no memory of the attack. She was back to her usual self, all sweet smiles and warm embraces, as though nothing had happened. Aurora had tried to understand—she told herself it was the stress of their life, the poverty, the endless struggle for survival. But deep down, she knew it was something darker. Her mother was fighting a war in her mind, a war that had long since consumed her.

Life had been hard for civilians like them. Money wasn't easy to come by, especially in the lower districts where Aurora and her mother had lived. Plasma donation had become the only reliable income stream for the poor, but even that wasn't an option for her mother.

Aurora could never understand why. They needed the money, desperately. Her mother had pleaded at the donation centers, her voice cracking with desperation. "Please, I need this!" she would beg. But every time, they turned her away, citing vague health issues that never made sense.

Aurora remembered standing outside the donation center one cold afternoon, watching her mother break down in tears. It was one of the first times Aurora had seen her mother's strength falter. The memory was seared into her mind—the way her mother's shoulders shook as she sobbed, the way the light in her eyes dimmed just a little more that day.

No matter how hard her mother tried, her plasma wasn't accepted. Aurora had been too young to understand the implications, but now, sitting in the SUITS bunker, she began to wonder. Why had they refused her mother? Why was her mother so adamant that the world was watching them, controlling them?

As Aurora grew older, her mother's mental state deteriorated further. The outbursts became more frequent, the hallucinations more vivid. But there were moments—quiet moments, when her mother would sit down with her, voice soft and loving—where the woman Aurora had once known would resurface. Those were the moments Aurora clung to, the moments where she believed her mother could be saved.

In those quiet moments, her mother would tell her strange things—cryptic phrases, odd warnings that didn't make sense at the time. "You need to remember," her mother would say, eyes wide with a strange intensity. "They'll come for you one day, Aurora. You have to be ready."

Aurora never knew what her mother meant. At the time, she had thought it was just more of her manic ramblings, the same paranoia that had plagued her mother for years. But now, after digging through the SUITS' files, after uncovering the dark experiments and mind-control programs, Aurora wondered if her mother had been trying to warn her all along.

The realization hit her like a punch to the gut—what if her mother hadn't been paranoid? What if the voices she had heard, the hallucinations, the manic episodes... what if they were the result of something real? What if her mother had been a victim of the very experiments Aurora now found herself entangled in?

Aurora's mind spun as images from her past resurfaced with a haunting clarity she'd never experienced before. She remembered her mother's hands, trembling yet deliberate, as they painted those strange symbols on the walls of their apartment in looping strokes. Symbols that seemed to pulse with meaning, almost alive, yet incomprehensible to her as a child. They had been everywhere—scrawled on the bathroom mirror in soap, inked onto the backs of faded grocery receipts, even scratched into the worn wooden floorboards. She had always thought of them as part of her mother's madness, remnants of a fractured mind. But now, staring into the dark truths she had uncovered about the SUITS, a terrible question gnawed at her: What if they were something more?

She could see the drawings in her mind's eye—the jagged spirals, the concentric circles, lines connecting symbols she couldn't decipher. The images burned behind her eyes, each symbol calling to her like a riddle yet to be solved. What if her mother hadn't been mad? What if those symbols were messages—hidden warnings, encrypted in plain sight? The thought twisted her stomach.

The symbols seemed to crawl out of her memories, becoming sharper, more vivid, with each passing moment. Her mother's voice echoed in her mind, cryptic and soft, murmuring warnings she hadn't understood.

"They watch everything, Aurora. You have to hide it from them. Keep it buried deep." Her mother had repeated those words like a mantra, always urging her to keep her drawings secret, to avoid sharing the strange stories she told herself at night. And now, the significance of those words clawed at her with dreadful intensity.

Hours slipped away as she pored over her memories, revisiting every fragment of her childhood that might hold a clue. She recalled the pages she herself had filled with childish scrawls—spirals, broken shapes, eyes. The eyes had always watched her, lurking in the corners of her imagination, as if they were part of some greater design. Was it her imagination? Or had her mother somehow instilled those symbols within her mind, an inheritance of fear and knowledge she couldn't yet decipher?

And then she wondered, were the symbols about the SUITS—or something worse?

The more she thought about it, the more the pieces seemed to fit together, and the more terrified she became.

~

The death of Dr. Kline had been a devastating blow for Aurora, not just professionally, but personally. Kline had been her mentor, her guide through the labyrinth of the SUITS, and his death had triggered something dark within her. She had been managing, barely, to keep her emotions in check, to keep her curiosity from consuming her. But

Kline's sudden, violent end had cracked open something inside her—something dangerous.

She began to spiral.

Her mind returned to her mother's erratic behavior—the wild swings between love and rage, the nights of sleepwalking and terror. Aurora felt herself slipping into that same pattern, her emotions a storm that she couldn't control. She began to question everything—her work, her colleagues, even her own thoughts.

Was she becoming like her mother? Were the hallucinations creeping into her mind as well?

There were moments when she would wake in the middle of the night, heart racing, convinced she had heard someone calling her name. But when she looked around, there was no one there. The shadows seemed to move, watching her, and she couldn't tell if it was real or just her imagination.

The pressure was mounting. The weight of the SUITS' secrets, the rumors about Kline, the whispers in the lab—it was all pushing her closer to the edge. And deep down, she knew that if she fell, there would be no coming back.

Her lack of resources growing up had made Aurora resourceful, inquisitive, and intensely creative. She had learned early on that nothing in life would be handed to her—if she wanted to survive, she had to be smarter, faster, more adaptable than everyone else.

That resourcefulness had served her well in the SUITS, helping her rise through the ranks, but now, it felt like a double-edged sword. The more she uncovered, the more dangerous her position became. But her pain—the pain of her mother's torment, of her own spiraling mental state—was pushing her forward.

She needed to know the truth.

Aurora's emotional journey was no longer just about surviving in the SUITS, it was about understanding who she really was. The more she dug into the past, the more she realized that her entire life had been shaped by forces beyond her control—by the SUITS, by their experiments, by the very system that had driven her mother to madness.

Her mother's words, once dismissed as paranoid delusions, now echoed in her mind with terrifying clarity. "They see everything."

Aurora began to see it too.

The pieces of the puzzle were coming together, but with each new revelation, the truth became darker, more twisted. She was no longer just fighting for answers—she was fighting for her sanity, her identity. Who was she, really? Was she a victim, like her mother? Or was she something else entirely? Something created by the SUITS, molded by their experiments, shaped by their lies?

The truth was a weapon, and Aurora knew that once she uncovered it, she would have to make a choice: to embrace her humanity and fight for freedom, or to succumb to the programming that had shaped her entire existence.

The battle for her soul had begun, and Aurora was walking a razor's edge between salvation and destruction.

11

The days following Dr. Kline's death were a blur for Aurora, filled with meetings, documents, and an endless parade of condolences she didn't ask for. The tragedy had shaken the entire SUITS organization, but while the others moved on, Aurora found herself trapped in the labyrinth of her own mind. The image of Kline's mutilated body, twitching in the aftermath of the Trinity's assault, haunted her every waking moment.

The promotion had come swiftly, almost suspiciously so. One moment, Aurora was still grieving Kline's violent end, and the next, she was the Lead Bioinformatics Scientist, with Kline's responsibilities dropped squarely in her lap. It didn't feel like a promotion—it felt like a burden. The weight of it pressed down on her, threatening to crush her under the pressure of expectations she wasn't ready to meet.

But there was no time to question her new role. The SUITS were relentless, and the work continued. As soon as she stepped into Kline's former office, the transition was complete. His files, his research, his unfinished work—everything was hers now. And it was up to her to finish what he had started.

Aurora wasn't alone in her new position. Dr. Elara Morrow, one of the lead scientists overseeing the bioengineering and genetic manipulation projects within the SUITS, quickly stepped into the role of mentor. Elara had been a prodigy from a young age, her brilliance unmatched even among the scientific elite. She had risen through the ranks with laser-like focus, driven by an insatiable curiosity and a relentless desire to push the boundaries of human knowledge.

From the moment Aurora met her, she was both awed and intimidated by Morrow. Elara's presence was commanding, her intellect sharp and unyielding. There was a coldness to her—a calculated detachment that made her impossible to read. But Aurora couldn't deny that Morrow knew more about the genetic manipulation projects than anyone else. And if Aurora was going to survive her new role, she would need Elara's guidance.

The first few meetings with Morrow were intense. Elara wasted no time in throwing Aurora into the deep end, expecting her to catch up quickly. There was no room for mistakes. Every day, Aurora was presented with new data, new experiments, and new expectations to meet. The weight of responsibility grew heavier with each passing moment.

And yet, in the quiet moments, when Elara was explaining the intricacies of genetic manipulation, Aurora found herself drawn to the woman's brilliance. There was a method to her madness—a cold, calculated logic that fascinated Aurora even as it unsettled her.

The work that had once fascinated Aurora was now tinged with dread. She had always been interested in bioengineering—genetic manipulation, in particular, had been her specialty. But now, the work felt different. There was something darker lurking beneath the surface of the SUITS' genetic experiments, something that she had only begun to scratch the surface of.

Elara Morrow had long been at the forefront of these genetic experiments. Her brilliance lay in her ability to map the human genome with unparalleled precision, manipulating genes to produce results that had been unthinkable a decade ago. The SUITS had tasked her with solving some of the most complex problems in human evolution—disease resistance, enhanced physical capabilities, even extending human lifespan.

Under Elara's guidance, the team had made tremendous strides in manipulating DNA to achieve specific outcomes. But the deeper Aurora dug into the research, the more she realized how far they were willing to go. The experiments were no longer about improving human health or capabilities—they were about control. Control over life and death, control over evolution itself.

Aurora felt a gnawing sense of discomfort as she reviewed the data from recent trials. Some of the subjects—people recruited under vague promises of wealth or immunity—had responded violently to the genetic modifications. Their bodies twisted and contorted under the strain of the altered DNA. The reports were filled with cold, clinical language describing the failures, but the horror was there, just beneath the surface.

Still, Aurora buried her unease beneath layers of focus. This was what she had signed up for, wasn't it? To push the boundaries of science, to explore the uncharted territory of human potential. But there was a darkness in the work she hadn't expected, and it was starting to seep into her every thought.

As much as Aurora tried to focus on the tasks ahead, she couldn't shake the feeling that Kline's work held deeper secrets. She had spent countless hours poring over his files, trying to understand the full scope of his research. It wasn't easy. Kline had been meticulous in his notes, but there were gaps—whole sections of his research that had been encrypted or deleted.

Why had Kline been so secretive? What had he discovered that had led him to such a violent end?

Aurora's curiosity grew with each passing day. She found herself staying late in the lab, running simulations, cross-referencing old experiments, and trying to connect the dots that Kline had left behind. It wasn't long before she realized that there were patterns in his work—subtle shifts in the data that hinted at something more than just genetic manipulation.

It was as if Kline had been onto something far bigger than anyone had realized, something that had pushed him beyond the limits of what the SUITS had authorized. But the more Aurora uncovered, the more she felt that someone was watching her, testing her, waiting to see how far she would go.

Dr. Elara Morrow's influence grew with every passing day. She pushed Aurora harder, challenging her at every turn. There was no room for failure. Every experiment, every test had to be perfect. Aurora was no stranger to pressure, but under Morrow's tutelage, the pressure felt more suffocating than ever.

Morrow was a master at masking her true intentions. There were times when Aurora felt as though she was being pulled deeper into a game she didn't fully understand, a game that Morrow was always three steps ahead in. Elara would drop cryptic comments, small hints about the importance of their work, but never fully reveal the bigger picture. It was as though she was gauging how much Aurora was willing to uncover on her own.

"Genetic manipulation is just the beginning," Morrow had said one evening, her voice calm, almost dismissive. "We're not just unlocking potential—we're rewriting the very fabric of what it means to be human."

Aurora nodded, pretending to understand, but the weight of the statement lingered with her long after the conversation ended. What exactly were they doing here? What was the end goal?

As the weeks passed, Aurora found herself consumed by the weight of her new role. The responsibilities of leading the bioinformatics team, of continuing Kline's work, and of meeting Morrow's exacting standards had taken their toll. She spent long hours in the lab, barely sleeping, constantly trying to stay one step ahead of the chaos that seemed to be brewing beneath the surface.

But the promotion didn't feel like success. It felt like a trap.

Dr. Kline's death had left a gaping hole in the team, but Aurora wasn't sure if she was ready to fill it. The more she uncovered, the more she realized that Kline's death wasn't just an accident—it was part of something bigger. Something darker.

There were moments when she thought about leaving, about walking away from the SUITS and the secrets they had buried. But every time she thought about it, the same thing stopped her: the truth. The truth about Kline, about Morrow, about the genetic experiments—they were all connected, and Aurora knew that if she didn't uncover the full story, no one else would.

The weight of that truth was crushing her, but she couldn't stop.

Aurora's internal battle was no longer just about her career or her place within the SUITS. It was about her identity. Her mother's manic rages, the hallucinations, the cryptic warnings—all of it was starting to make sense. Aurora's own emotional journey had become a twisted reflection of the path her mother had walked before her. The same fear, the same paranoia, the same doubts were creeping into her thoughts.

She began seeing flashes of her mother in the lab—her face appearing in the reflection of the glass, her voice echoing in the corridors. It was just her mind playing tricks on her... wasn't it?

The truth about her origins, about the genetic manipulation experiments, was tied directly to the identity crisis that had haunted Aurora for so long. She had spent her whole life trying to distance herself from her mother's madness, but now, she realized that her mother's fears had been justified. The world was watching. The SUITS were controlling. And the truth about who Aurora really was lay hidden in the very experiments she was now leading.

The emotional turmoil began to consume her. She was haunted by the choices she had made, by the growing realization that her life had been shaped by forces far beyond her control. The darkness within her was growing, and she knew that if she didn't find a way to control it, it would consume her completely.

Aurora's journey was far from over, but the deeper she descended into the world of genetic manipulation, the more dangerous she became—to herself, and to everyone around her.

12

Aurora's mind was buzzing, a relentless hum of half-formed thoughts and scattered memories as she sat in her new office, still reeling from the events that had thrust her into this position of authority. The death of Dr. Kline had opened doors she was not prepared to walk through, and now, the weight of her new responsibilities was settling in like a slow, suffocating force.

The more she dove into the SUITS' archives, the more unsettled she became. The organization's work had taken a dark turn long before she had joined. Mind-control experiments, manipulation of human psychology, and weapons that targeted the most primal parts of the brain—these were not conspiracy theories anymore. They were documented fact.

Aurora knew she was being watched, her curiosity tested with every file she opened. Yet, she couldn't stop herself. Each new discovery felt like peeling back the layers of a gruesome truth that had been lurking in plain sight all along.

The military was preparing for another containment mission, this time targeting one of the most dangerous Trinities yet encountered: Trinity-010, codename "Mors-Anguineus." Classified as a Category 5 threat, Mors-Anguineus wasn't just a force of destruction—it was a walking nightmare, capable of turning entire battlefields into grotesque displays of gore.

The reports Aurora read were filled with horror. Mors-Anguineus could manipulate blood—extract it from living beings, shape it into deadly constructs, even use it to control the bodies of its victims, making them attack each other or tear themselves apart. The description alone made Aurora's skin crawl, but the video footage? That was something far worse.

She had watched it unfold on the screen—the slow, creeping menace of blood pooling from unseen sources, the military teams advancing cautiously through a dense urban district, unaware of the massacre that awaited them. The footage showed soldiers moving through narrow alleyways, their specialized equipment gleaming under the dim light of the overcast sky. They were prepared for the worst—or so they thought.

Then it began.

Blood. It was everywhere. At first, it dripped slowly, forming puddles that seemed harmless. But as the team advanced, the puddles grew, coalescing into larger pools that stained the ground red. By the time they realized what was happening, it was too late. Mors-Anguineus struck with a brutality that was beyond comprehension.

The team had been specially trained, equipped with state-of-the-art gear designed to neutralize Trinity threats. But nothing could have prepared them for Mors-Anguineus. As soon as the Trinity made its presence known, the air thickened with a metallic tang, and the soldiers began to falter, clutching their chests as their blood was forcibly pulled from their bodies.

Aurora had watched in horror as the footage showed the Trinity rising from the shadows, its pale, translucent skin pulsing with power. Its body seemed to ripple with each heartbeat, veins bulging beneath the surface, as it willed the blood of its victims into deadly forms.

One soldier's scream echoed through the narrow alley as his blood was ripped from his body and formed into a jagged spear that impaled him from within. Another fell to his knees, his face contorted in pain as his blood was twisted into grotesque shapes, forcing him to attack his comrades.

The survivors scrambled to regroup, but they were outmatched. Mors-Anguineus didn't just kill—it toyed with them, using their own blood to turn them against each other. Aurora watched as the soldiers' bodies moved like marionettes, their limbs jerking unnaturally, their eyes wide with terror as they fought against the invisible force controlling them.

The streets of the town had run red that day, and the footage showed it all in gruesome detail—bodies torn apart, blood-soaked rubble, and the chilling silence that followed the massacre.

As Aurora sifted through the classified files, something began to click into place. The Trinity's powers, particularly Mors-Anguineus' blood puppetry, seemed to mirror some of the government's earlier mind-control experiments. The ability to control the human body through external forces—blood, in this case—was an extension of the same principles.

Aurora's mind raced with the implications. If the SUITS were experimenting with controlling people's actions through chemical manipulation and psychological conditioning, how much of what she had uncovered was connected to these abilities? Were the Trinities being used as living weapons to refine these methods?

The more Aurora delved into the history of SUITS' mind-control experiments, the more disturbed she became. There were files documenting early tests, where chemicals had been administered to prisoners and civilians alike, pushing them into fits of rage or blind obedience. These tests had been crude at first, but as the years went on, the results became more sophisticated, more insidious.

Mass media was another tool in their arsenal. Aurora read with growing disgust about how they had manipulated the public with psychological triggers embedded in

TV shows, social campaigns, and entertainment. These weren't just mindless distractions—they were calculated attacks on the human psyche, designed to control behavior on a massive scale.

With each file she opened, Aurora felt her guilt deepen. She had always wanted to be part of something greater, to make a difference in the world through science. But now, that desire felt tainted. The work she had once been so proud of was built on lies, on suffering, on control. The very organization she had pledged herself to had been manipulating people's thoughts and actions for years, and she was complicit in it.

The worst part was that Aurora had seen this kind of control before. Her mother's paranoid rants echoed in her mind, warning her about the invisible forces that governed their lives. At the time, Aurora had dismissed her mother's words as the ravings of a broken mind. But now, she wasn't so sure.

Her mother had always been obsessed with the idea that the world was watching, controlling them through invisible strings. And maybe, just maybe, she had been right all along.

The footage of the operation against Mors-Anguineus had ended in disaster. Aurora's hands trembled as she turned off the screen, her stomach churning. The final moments of the video showed the Trinity standing amidst a battlefield of twisted corpses, blood swirling around it like a living entity. The soldiers who had survived were fleeing, their screams drowned out by the squelching sound of blood flowing through the streets.

Mors-Anguineus, standing victorious, had disappeared into the shadows before the remaining soldiers could regroup. The aftermath was a scene of unimaginable horror—streets slick with blood, bodies broken and contorted into grotesque forms, and the metallic tang of death hanging in the air.

Aurora sat back in her chair, her mind racing. The military had lost control. The SUITS had lost control. The Trinities were growing stronger, more dangerous, and with every failed mission, the stakes were rising.

And yet, as the weight of the bloodbath settled over her, Aurora couldn't shake the feeling that she was being manipulated, just like the soldiers who had died in that alleyway. There was something darker at work here, something that tied everything together—Kline's death, the mind control experiments, and the terrifying power of the Trinities.

The walls were closing in, and Aurora was running out of time to figure out the truth.

As Aurora pieced together the connections between mind control and the Trinity powers, the urgency of her situation grew. There was no turning back now. The truth was out there, waiting for her to uncover it, but every step closer felt like walking through a minefield.

Her new role came with elevated responsibilities, but also elevated risks. The SUITS had its eyes on her, testing her loyalty, watching to see how much she would uncover before she became a liability. And the Trinities? They were out there, growing stronger, more dangerous with each encounter.

Aurora knew she was on the verge of something monumental. But the closer she got, the more dangerous it became.

And somewhere out there, Mors-Anguineus still lurked, its blood-soaked power a constant reminder that even the most carefully laid plans could be undone by the chaos within.

13

The footage from the Trinity encounter with Mors-Anguineus had left the entire SUITS complex reeling. The cold, clinical atmosphere of the bunker was disrupted by an undercurrent of fear that no one could quite shake. The military's failure was a glaring reminder of just how outmatched they were by the power of the Trinities. And now, the aftermath had become Aurora's daily reality.

Bodies had been recovered, or at least what was left of them. The grotesque remains of soldiers who had been drained of their blood, used as puppets in their own slaughter, were nothing short of nightmarish. The lab had been filled with the hum of containment procedures, but there was an unspoken tension in the air. Everyone was afraid of the next encounter, of what they might face when the next Trinity revealed itself.

To deal with the psychological toll of these missions, the SUITS had set up a series of psychotherapeutic treatments for the surviving staff. But Aurora could sense that the so-called "therapy" was nothing more than a controlled mechanism to keep everyone in line. The complex offered a variety of treatments, but none were ever given simultaneously. Instead, employees were funneled into different programs—meditation sessions, drug treatments, even hypnotherapy. Each was carefully monitored, and none were designed to fully heal the fractured minds that walked these halls. Aurora suspected they were using these treatments to further manipulate and control the staff, subtly ensuring no one asked too many questions.

Aurora had never been one to shy away from the truth, but the more she uncovered, the more grotesque the world of the SUITS became. Her research had led her to classified documents that outlined the SUITS' experiments with mass mind control. She found files on how the SUITS had experimented with manipulating the masses through entertainment, media, and pharmaceuticals. It was all about control—keeping the population docile, dulling their awareness, and making them more compliant to the corporate government's authoritarian grasp.

Aurora had been patient, methodical in her quest to access the classified N.E.X.U.S. experiment failures. When she finally gained access to the files, the reality of what the SUITS had been hiding hit her like a freight train.

The first video played out on her screen, and her stomach turned at the sight. What she saw was beyond anything she could have imagined. Human subjects—some appearing barely conscious—were subjected to the horrors of the N.E.X.U.S. algorithm's unpredictable results. Their bodies mutated grotesquely. Some melted, their flesh dissolving into a sickening ooze. Others convulsed violently, their bones snapping as they twisted into unnatural shapes. And then there were those whose skin hardened into grotesque, rock-like structures, their screams muted by the very transformation that was killing them.

Aurora's hands shook as she navigated through more of the footage. The sheer brutality of it all was horrifying, but what struck her the most was the realization that these weren't volunteers. No one would willingly submit themselves to this kind of agony.

These people had been sacrificed for the sake of science. They were prisoners—no, worse. They were disposable. The SUITS had used them like lab rats, throwing them into the path of the N.E.X.U.S. algorithm without regard for their humanity. Aurora had thought that she understood the cost of progress, but this... this was something else entirely. This was evil.

The deeper Aurora dug, the more she felt like she was being watched. It wasn't just a vague feeling anymore—there were signs. Strange looks from her coworkers, documents left on her desk that she hadn't requested, and the occasional "accidental" slip from senior scientists who hinted at things she hadn't yet discovered. It was as if someone was deliberately leaving breadcrumbs for her, guiding her deeper into the labyrinth of the SUITS' darkest secrets.

But who was doing this, and why?

Staff were disappearing. Some were declared dead in accidents, while others simply stopped showing up for work. It was always brushed off as a "personal matter," but Aurora knew better. The disappearances were too frequent, too neatly explained. She had begun to suspect that the SUITS were eliminating anyone who got too close to the truth. And yet, with each death, she seemed to be moving further up the ranks, gaining more access, more responsibilities. It felt like she was being groomed for something, but what?

Aurora became more secretive with her findings, tucking them away in places where only she could access them. If someone was guiding her, she would play along—for now. But her paranoia was growing, and she knew that she couldn't trust anyone, not even those closest to her.

In her research, Aurora stumbled across a strange conspiracy—one that seemed almost too absurd to believe. She found scattered references to a deliberate shift in musical frequencies, specifically the change from 432 Hz to 440 Hz. According to old reports, the 432 Hz frequency had been known for its healing properties, for promoting harmony and well-being. But somewhere along the line, the world had shifted to 440 Hz. This wasn't just a random decision—it was a calculated move, orchestrated by pharmaceutical companies and governments to suppress the healing power of sound.

Aurora couldn't help but wonder—why? Why would they do this? As she dug deeper, she found the answer buried in the same classified files on mass mind control. The SUITS, in collaboration with corporate elites, had deliberately shifted the global standard frequency to prevent people from accessing the natural healing frequencies that could free their minds from the grip of control.

Binaural beats, particularly those in the 432 Hz range, were said to have the power to align the mind and body, to heal, to break the shackles of mental control. But the SUITS couldn't allow that. They couldn't risk a population that was aware, awake, and free. And so, they altered the frequencies, flooding the world with music and media designed to keep people compliant and numb.

Aurora began to wonder why the SUITS had never offered these pure tones in their psychotherapeutic treatments. If they truly wanted to heal their staff, why suppress something so simple yet so effective? The answer, of course, was clear. They didn't want healing. They wanted control.

Beyond chemical manipulation and psychological triggers, Aurora discovered a buried thread that wove through everything—the use of sound frequencies. Hidden deep in the SUITS archives was a growing resistance movement among civilians, using binaural beats for healing and awakening. These frequencies had been embraced by underground revolutionaries, who claimed the tones could heal both the mind and body. They had become a lifeline for the oppressed, a source of solace and empowerment in a world controlled by fear and propaganda.

But the SUITS were determined to shut it down. Through relentless propaganda, they declared the use of binaural beats a dangerous and unproven practice. Official media outlets denounced it as a form of subversion, warning that exposure to such frequencies could lead to madness, brain damage, or even death. They imposed severe penalties on anyone caught using or spreading these tones. Some offenders simply disappeared, while others were dragged into public trials, their sentences broadcast as a warning to others. Execution wasn't unheard of for those found distributing the pure 432 Hz tones that were at the heart of the resistance.

It wasn't until Aurora stumbled upon a forbidden audio file in the SUITS system that the truth began to unravel. They had intentionally altered the global standard, severing the population from a natural harmonic frequency that could lead to self-awareness, autonomy, and even rebellion. The more Aurora uncovered, the more she realized that the SUITS weren't just suppressing healing—they were actively working to keep people disconnected, weak, and compliant.

There was one group that had long been a thorn in the side of the SUITS: the Cult of Kane. For generations, this shadowy organization had defied government control, quietly spreading the truth about sound frequencies and other ancient methods of unlocking human potential. The Cult of Kane operated in the darkest corners of society, their practices regarded as mystical and forbidden. Some said they were healers; others believed they were dangerous radicals bent on overthrowing the global order.

The truth lay somewhere in between. The Cult of Kane saw themselves as keepers of forgotten knowledge, the last bastion against the rising tide of manipulation and mind control. They were the ones responsible for spreading the 432 Hz tones, ensuring that the ancient harmonics reached those who could still resist.

For the SUITS, the Cult of Kane was more than just a nuisance—they were a threat that had to be eliminated. But despite countless attempts to wipe them out, the cult had survived.

The walls of the SUITS complex had always felt sterile, cold, and clinical to Aurora, but now they seemed to pulse with hidden malevolence. The air was thick with unspoken fears, and every face she passed wore the same hollow look of detachment. Death had become a constant companion in the bunker, whether through violent encounters with the Trinities or the strange "accidents" that seemed to claim more and more of her colleagues. The

SUITS offered psychotherapy to help their operatives cope with the trauma, but even that felt like just another form of control.

Aurora had avoided the therapy sessions, suspecting that they were less about healing and more about keeping everyone in line. They never offered the same treatments twice, and some of the people who attended came back... different. Too calm, too detached. It was as though the SUITS were stripping them of their pain, but also their humanity.

The deaths, the disappearances—Aurora had kept her head down through it all, and it had rewarded her with more responsibilities, more access. But with every new level of clearance, the weight of the truth pressed harder on her chest.

She was being watched. She knew that now. The SUITS weren't just grooming her for leadership—they were guiding her, testing her. But why? What did they expect her to find?

Aurora's investigation was leading her down a dangerous path, one that she wasn't sure she could come back from. The more she learned, the more she realized that everything she had ever believed about the SUITS—about the world itself—was a lie. She had always been a skeptic, but now, nothing was a conspiracy to her anymore. The shadowy government programs, the mind control, the manipulation of reality itself—it was all real. And she was standing at the heart of it.

Her mother's warnings echoed through her mind, haunting her like a ghost from the past. Aurora could feel herself spiraling, just as her mother had. The same paranoia, the same doubts were creeping into her thoughts. But this time, Aurora knew the truth. She wasn't imagining things—there was something far more sinister at play, and she was determined to uncover it.

But with each step forward, she felt the ground beneath her crumbling. The SUITS were hiding something far bigger than she had ever imagined, and the truth was darker than anything she had faced before. The powers they sought to harness, the Trinity footage, the N.E.X.U. S. algorithm—it all pointed to one undeniable conclusion.

The world was on the brink of something catastrophic, and Aurora was caught in the center of the storm.

14

Aurora sat alone in the dim light of her terminal, her mind a whirlwind of thoughts. The footage of the latest Trinity encounter had left her sickened. Mors-Anguineus, the blood Trinity, had turned an entire military squadron into a battlefield of red-stained horror, their blood weaponized against them in the most grotesque ways imaginable. Soldiers had become nothing more than marionettes, manipulated by their own blood into slaughtering one another, their bodies twisted into grotesque figures of violence.

The footage looped again and again, showing the mass casualties and devastation, but something more chilling than the carnage had begun to emerge. Aurora had seen death before—she had seen failure and catastrophe in the SUITS' pursuit of control—but this was different. The more she watched, the more she felt a gnawing realization that Mors-Anguineus wasn't just a monster. There was intelligence behind its actions. The Trinity had been toying with them, deliberately pushing the limits of their containment capabilities and, more terrifyingly, their un-derstanding of power.

As Aurora delved deeper into the archives of classified files, she stumbled across something she had only heard whispered in the hallways: NeuroLobe. The NeuroLobe was a piece of technology unlike any she had studied be-fore—a neural implant designed to enhance brain func-tion by creating a symbiotic relationship between artificial intelligence and the human mind. It attached, or in some cases replaced, the corpus callosum—the thick bundle of nerves connecting the left and right hemispheres of the brain. It was meant to unlock the full potential of human cognitive function, creating superhuman levels of intelli-gence and capability.

In theory, the NeuroLobe was supposed to harmonize the functions of both hemispheres, allowing users to mul-titask at unprecedented levels, access immense amounts of data instantly, and solve complex problems beyond the limits of natural human intelligence. Aurora was initially fascinated. It seemed like the kind of breakthrough that could redefine human evolution itself. But the more she read, the more she realized that this technology had an unsettling edge.

Aurora hadn't yet connected all the dots, but one thing was clear: every human trial involving the NeuroLobe had failed. Horrifically. The test subjects' brains had react-ed unpredictably to the artificial intelligence integration, resulting in violent seizures, mental breakdowns, and in some cases, complete mental collapse. The files described these failures in cold, clinical detail, but the horror of it was undeniable. Aurora felt her stomach turn as she read about subjects clawing at their own heads, trying to rip the NeuroLobe from their skulls before finally succumbing to insanity.

She couldn't understand why the SUITS continued to pursue this technology after so many catastrophic failures. What was the missing piece? Why were they so hellbent on making it work?

In the midst of her research, Aurora found herself crossing paths with Lia Graves more often. Lia had always been an enigma—one of the SUITS' most trusted operatives, not because of her scientific acumen but because of her ability to manipulate and ingratiate herself with key figures in the organization. Lia's charm and cunning had earned her a place among the elites, and her talent for navigating the complex political landscape of the SUITS made her a valuable asset.

Despite their frequent interactions, Aurora couldn't bring herself to trust Lia completely. There was something too polished, too perfect about the way Lia moved through the organization, always seeming to be one step ahead. Aurora sensed that Lia was hiding something, something that could be crucial to understanding the larger picture of the SUITS' operations. But for now, she kept her distance, watching Lia from the shadows and waiting for the right moment to dig deeper.

Aurora's growing obsession with the truth began to consume her. Every piece of classified data she uncovered only raised more questions. She found fragmented reports that hinted at neurotechnology capable of controlling subjects at a genetic level, with artificial intelligence playing a symbiotic role in shaping the behavior and mental states of the test subjects. But the files were incomplete, redacted in places that made it difficult to piece together the full scope of the experiments.

Still, the direction was clear—the SUITS were working on something far more sinister than she had ever imagined. The NeuroLobe, in conjunction with genetic manipulation, seemed to be the key to creating a new breed of human, one that could be controlled, molded, and enhanced by artificial intelligence. Aurora's mind raced. If the SUITS could perfect this technology, they wouldn't just be controlling information or bodies—they would be controlling minds, reshaping humanity to fit their own vision of power.

Aurora realized she needed to look back. The answers weren't in the future of the SUITS' research; they were buried in the past, in the old, forgotten files of the most sinister projects the organization had undertaken. She began to dig into the archives of the SUITS' black-ops research, projects that had been deemed too unethical or too dangerous to continue. As she read about the experiments, she felt a creeping dread settle over her. These weren't just projects aimed at scientific advancement; they were nightmares brought to life.

She came across a name she hadn't seen before: Dr. Cyrus Vale.

Dr. Cyrus Vale was a name whispered among the older members of the SUITS, a figure so notorious that even mentioning his work was taboo. Aurora had heard his name in passing, but now, as she found herself reading through the scattered remnants of his experiments, she realized just how deep his madness ran. Dr. Vale had been one of the original architects of the SUITS' most controversial projects, specializing in genetic manipulation and bioengineering.

Vale's obsession with pushing the boundaries of human capability had led him down dark, uncharted paths. His notes detailed grotesque experiments designed to create "perfect" beings—creations that were stronger, faster, and smarter than any natural human. But his methods were monstrous. Torture was his tool, and he believed that only through extreme suffering could the human mind and body reach its full potential.

Aurora felt a chill as she read through Vale's writings. He didn't see his subjects as people. To him, they were raw materials to be shaped, broken down, and rebuilt into something greater. He had no regard for the pain he inflicted, only for the results. The SUITS had buried his work after several high-profile deaths in his trials, but Aurora suspected that his influence hadn't disappeared entirely. She began to see traces of his methods in the experiments being conducted under the guise of the NeuroLobe trials. The connection was becoming clearer.

Amid her research into Vale's work, Aurora stumbled across something unexpected: Orichalcum. The ancient metal, once thought to be nothing more than a myth, had appeared in several of Vale's older files. Orichalcum, as the legends went, was a metal of extraordinary power—capable of conducting energy and amplifying abilities in ways that modern science could barely comprehend. Vale had been obsessed with it, believing that it could be the key to unlocking a new form of consciousness, one that transcended the limitations of the human brain.

The comparison between Orichalcum and the SUITS' modern pursuits of power was striking. Just as Vale had sought to create something beyond human through this legendary metal, the SUITS were now using technology to achieve similar ends. They were searching for the missing link, the final piece of the puzzle that would allow them to create a conscious, controllable being—a being without the need for a NeuroLobe or AI symbiosis.

Aurora couldn't yet see the full picture, but she knew that Orichalcum was a crucial part of the SUITS' endgame. What they were really after wasn't just control over humans. They were after something far greater. Something that could reshape the very nature of life itself.

The deeper Aurora delved, the more she realized how far the SUITS were willing to go. Torture, suffering, pain—it was all part of the process, a necessary evil to create unprecedented beings of power. All other intelligence agencies, all other governments, had bowed to the will of the SUITS, recognizing their mastery over the manipulation of life itself. No one could stand against them, and now Aurora understood why.

Her curiosity had turned into an obsession. She was no longer just a researcher—she was a seeker of truth, desperate to piece together the fragments of the SUITS' most horrifying secrets. But the more she learned, the more she realized that this knowledge came at a price. She was being drawn into something far darker than she had ever imagined, and there was no turning back.

The Trinity encounters, the failed N.E.X.U.S. trials, the NeuroLobe, and now Orichalcum—all of it was connected. But what scared Aurora the most was the realization that she might never be able to escape the web she was caught in. The SUITS didn't just control others—they controlled her, and she was only beginning to understand the depths of that control.

15

Aurora's mind buzzed with revelations, but none had disturbed her more than what she had unearthed about Dr. Cyrus Vale. She had only heard his name in passing, whispered in the halls by senior scientists who spoke of him with a strange mixture of reverence and fear. But now, as she uncovered the depths of his twisted research, she realized that his shadow loomed large over every sinister project within the SUITS.

Dr. Cyrus Vale was no ordinary scientist. He was a visionary, someone who had once been celebrated for his pioneering work in genetic editing. Early in his career, Vale had revolutionized the field, pushing the limits of CRISPR technology to alter human DNA in ways previously thought impossible. At the height of his fame, he had been hailed as the savior of modern science, capable of curing genetic diseases and extending human lifespans. But for Vale, that was only the beginning.

His motives were not rooted in altruism or the betterment of humanity. Vale's thirst for discovery ran much deeper—he believed that the human race was fundamentally flawed, weak, and doomed to stagnate unless evolution was forced to take a more radical leap. He saw his gene-editing work as the key to unlocking a new phase of human evolution, one that would transcend the boundaries of natural selection.

As his experiments became more extreme, Vale's ethics unraveled. His methods grew darker, his subjects more dehumanized, until the line between scientific discovery and cruelty ceased to exist. The SUITS, always on the lookout for those willing to push boundaries, were quick to offer him a position. Vale saw this as the perfect opportunity to carry out his experiments without restriction. And the SUITS provided him with everything he needed—funding, test subjects, and absolute freedom.

Dr. Cyrus Vale's role within the SUITS was pivotal. His work formed the backbone of many of the organization's most secretive projects. The genetic manipulation programs, the N.E.X.U.S. algorithm's foundation, even the eerie NeuroLobe experiments, all had threads that led back to him. He had designed methods to enhance human biology, but the horrors that came with these experiments were brushed aside in the pursuit of progress.

His goals aligned perfectly with the SUITS' desire to control the future of humanity. Vale didn't just want to modify human biology; he wanted to recreate it. His obsession with the Trinity powers led him to study these beings' DNA in an attempt to splice their abilities into human subjects. This is where his relationship with Dr. Daryl Darwin became crucial. Darwin's N.E.X.U.S. algorithm was a tool, a way to predict and manipulate biological outcomes, while Vale sought to merge human evolution with alien powers. Together, they represented the pinnacle of the SUITS' dark ambitions.

While Dr. Darwin was pragmatic, focused on the technical aspects of control and manipulation, Vale was the visionary pushing for the next step in human development. Their partnership was symbiotic—Darwin needed Vale's radical ideas to fuel the N.E.X.U.S. program, and Vale needed Darwin's resources and expertise to implement his genetic visions. However, there was tension. Darwin was cold and calculated, seeing the world through the lens of control, whereas Vale was driven by a grander ambition—to create a new species, a perfect being unshackled by the limitations of humanity.

But their goals, though aligned, were not without conflict. Vale's willingness to sacrifice lives indiscriminately, pushing experiments to grotesque extremes, often clashed with Darwin's more strategic long-term vision. They both knew that at some point, their paths might diverge.

As Aurora pieced together the connections between Vale's work and the projects she had been assigned to, she began to feel the weight of what the SUITS had become. It wasn't just an organization pushing boundaries; it was a machine built on pain and suffering, with its primary architects willing to sacrifice anyone in their path.

The therapy sessions offered to staff—supposedly to help them cope with the horrific nature of their work—felt like just another layer of control. Aurora had avoided them for weeks, unwilling to subject herself to the scrutiny of the SUITS' psychological manipulation. She could feel the eyes of her colleagues on her, some of them broken by the horrors they had witnessed, others suspiciously quiet. More and more staff seemed to vanish without explanation. The complex was becoming a place where people disappeared as often as they appeared.

Lia Graves had taken notice of Aurora's absence from the sessions. Lia, always watching, always calculating, hinted that it might be in Aurora's best interest to "participate" for the sake of her reputation. But Aurora knew better—those sessions were more than therapy. They were a way to break the will of those who had seen too much, a way to reshape their minds before they could truly understand what was happening.

In her increasingly desperate attempts to understand Vale's work, Aurora stumbled upon references to an ancient material Vale had been obsessed with: Orichalcum. The files detailed Vale's belief that this legendary metal—thought to be lost in the depths of history—could amplify consciousness and serve as a missing link in his experiments. According to Vale, Orichalcum held the power to awaken dormant abilities in living beings, acting as a conductor for energy and thought in ways modern science couldn't explain.

Vale had been convinced that Orichalcum could be the key to creating consciousness in beings that otherwise lacked it. He believed that it could provide the answer to what he called the "soulless dilemma"—the problem of creating sentient beings who lacked true awareness or autonomy. The SUITS were invested in this idea but kept Vale's research under tight wraps. Aurora sensed that this quest for Orichalcum was at the heart of something much bigger, something that involved the very core of the SUITS' darkest plans.

~

Aurora had worked alongside Dr. Elara Morrow for months now, admiring her cold intellect and surgical precision in genetic manipulation. Morrow was everything Aurora aspired to be—driven, focused, and impossibly brilliant. But there was something off about Morrow, something that gnawed at Aurora's subconscious.

One night, while reviewing some old files, Aurora found something that shattered her perception of Morrow. A fragment of a report, heavily redacted but unmistakable, revealed that Morrow had been one of Vale's earliest subjects. In fact, Elara Morrow had undergone genetic modification at Vale's hands, part of a secret program designed to enhance the cognitive functions of scientists within the SUITS.

The Morrow that Aurora knew—calm, calculating, always in control—wasn't just brilliant; she was engineered to be that way. Vale had perfected his gene-editing techniques on her, using her as the prototype for his later experiments. And while Morrow was a success story in many ways, she wasn't entirely human anymore. The report suggested that the modifications had altered her emotional responses, dulling her empathy, making her more machine-like in her behavior.

Aurora's blood ran cold as the realization sank in. Dr. Morrow wasn't just a colleague—she was the product of Vale's obsession. And what was worse, Morrow had likely known all along. She had kept Aurora in the dark, playing her part as the perfect scientist while hiding the truth about her origins. Morrow's brilliance, her detachment, her clinical precision—it wasn't natural. It was Vale's legacy, living on in her.

As Aurora connected these pieces, she realized that Vale's experiments hadn't stopped with Morrow. The SUITS were still using his work, still conducting experiments designed to perfect his vision of human evolution. But the true scope of their ambitions remained hidden.

Aurora knew she had to keep digging. There were still too many unanswered questions, too many dark corners of the SUITS archives that had yet to be explored.

Vale's work, Morrow's modifications, and the mysterious Orichalcum all pointed to a larger, more terrifying reality—one that Aurora wasn't sure she could face.

But she couldn't stop now. The truth, no matter how horrifying, was the only thing that could set her free. And she was running out of time.

16

Aurora's world was unraveling faster than she could comprehend. Dr. Kline's death, Dr. Morrow's secret, and the horrifying reality of the SUITS' true ambitions weighed on her mind. The threads she had been pulling at, piece by piece, were finally coming together—but they formed a tapestry of horror, manipulation, and lies.

They had trained them since childhood—pushing them to work hard in school, promising a future filled with security, benefits, and a comfortable retirement. But it was all a cruel deception. No one ever truly made it out. You couldn't save the next generation from their fate. Whether you knew it or not, you worked for the SUITS either way, as a body to drain fluid or as a lab rat, subject to endless, dehumanizing tests disguised as research. Day by day, they brainwashed individuals, breaking them down until ignorance became a haven. Too smart, and you stood out. And in this world, the good king—the one who stood against the system—was always murdered.

Civilians rarely found jobs anymore. There was no work. AI had replaced many functions of humanity, leaving most people with only one option to survive: selling their plasma. A daily, degrading exchange—blood for a few moments of relief from starvation. The alternative, the only other career path, was to work for the SUITS. But even that wasn't a choice. You were only "selected" if they saw fit, chosen not for your talent or intelligence, but for how easily you could be controlled, manipulated, and used.

Aurora hadn't slept in days. Every night, her mother's voice echoed through her mind, fragments of old memories returning, laced with cryptic warnings and eerie murmurs. Her mother's mental breakdowns, her late-night rants about government experiments, and her disappearance from Aurora's life now felt less like the product of a sick mind and more like a desperate attempt to shield Aurora from a truth that was now consuming her.

As Aurora tried to focus on her work, she couldn't help but dwell on her past. Her mother's sudden disappearances during Aurora's teenage years were haunting her thoughts now more than ever. Her mother would vanish for days, sometimes weeks, only to return looking gaunt and disoriented, with no explanation for where she had been. Aurora had never questioned it deeply at the time—she was too busy trying to survive and grow up faster than any child should have to. She had learned to fend for herself, to take care of the household, to lie to neighbors about why her mother wasn't around.

But now, those absences gnawed at her. They didn't seem random anymore. Her mother's behavior—the hallucinations, the fits of rage, the wild warnings about "them" watching—had all been dismissed by doctors as signs of bipolar disorder and paranoia. But what if her mother had known something all along? What if her disappearances had been part of something much bigger? A hidden truth, locked away in her mother's damaged mind, that Aurora was only beginning to understand?

Aurora couldn't shake what she had uncovered about Dr. Elara Morrow. The knowledge that Morrow had been genetically altered by Dr. Cyrus Vale was eating away at her. Everything about Morrow, from her lack of emotional depth to her unshakable calm under pressure, suddenly made sense. Morrow wasn't just a brilliant scientist—she had been molded into something beyond human, engineered to think, act, and function like a machine.

But Morrow's transformation was more than just unsettling—it was terrifying. If Morrow was the prototype, then what else had Vale created? Aurora knew that Morrow was the tip of the iceberg, that Vale's experiments had far-reaching implications. How many others had been altered without their knowledge? How many within the SUITS had been transformed into something not entirely human?

Aurora tried to avoid Morrow in the days following her discovery, unsure of how to confront her—or if she even should. Morrow's behavior hadn't changed, but Aurora now saw her in a different light. Every conversation, every glance, every clinical decision Morrow made felt calculated and deliberate, as though she was working toward something much larger than Aurora could fathom.

~

Amid her personal turmoil, Aurora was forced to continue her analysis of the bloody Trinity encounter with Mors-Anguineus. The footage was nauseating, a brutal display of what true power looked like in the hands of something far beyond human comprehension. The Trinity had turned an entire urban district into a battlefield of blood and destruction. Soldiers had been impaled, their bodies twisted and manipulated into grotesque forms. Entire city blocks were left drenched in blood, the crimson liquid running through the streets like rivers, a sickening reminder of the Trinity's ability to manipulate life at its most fundamental level.

As Aurora studied the footage, she became obsessed with understanding how such a creature could exist. The Trinity's ability to control blood, to turn living beings into weapons, was unlike anything she had ever seen before. It was as if the laws of nature had bent around this being, allowing it to reshape reality with a mere thought. And the SUITS wanted to control it. To harness it.

Aurora's obsession deepened with every hour spent dissecting the footage, poring over ancient texts, and cross-referencing the barely coherent ramblings of researchers who had dared to document their encounters with the Trinities. She couldn't shake the feeling that these creatures were more than just anomalies in the natural order—they were a deliberate anomaly, something not born of human evolution but thrust into existence by forces far older than anyone dared to imagine. The deeper she dug, the more fragmented the truth became, as if the SUITS were attempting to piece together the puzzle of these beings' origin just as she was. Yet no matter how much information they compiled, something kept eluding them: the why. Why did these creatures exist? What purpose did they serve? Her mind swirled with questions until one answer emerged repeatedly in hushed circles—whispers of a connection to an ancient world, a lost time before the modern world's rise to power.

The origin of the Trinities was shrouded in ambiguity, their existence linked to myths and ancient legends that predated recorded history. Some believed these beings were remnants of a forgotten era—an age lost to time, unleashed by a cataclysmic rapture or perhaps even sent by God himself. Whispers of their presence stretched back to the dawn of human civilization, with some suggesting their origins lay in ancient Egypt or even the biblical flood of Noah, tied to the lost city of Atlantis, now buried beneath the depths of the ocean.

The mysteries of the deep, with 99% of Earth's oceans still unexplored, only added to the allure and terror surrounding the Trinities. It was said that they had been part of the great civilizations that once ruled the Earth, akin to the Greek gods of legend but of the future—a power far beyond human comprehension. When they activated their frequencies, the energy they unleashed sparked like lightning, as if drawn from the most powerful Tesla coil, a raging storm of electricity that could tear the fabric of reality itself.

Many believed these beings were divine instruments of judgment, kept on Earth by God to wipe out empires that had risen too high—Atlantis, the Romans, the Egyptians, all of them believed to have been struck down by the wrath of the Trinities. These beings were thought to reside underwater, dwelling in the deepest trenches of the ocean where the lost cities of Atlantis still remained. Others believed they lived beneath the sands of deserts, waiting for the time to rise once again from the depths of the Earth, from hell itself. They were seen as angels of death, harbingers of the next generation of man, sent to reset the simulation and complete the work of God.

God was not satisfied with this version of humanity, some said. And so, He had sent the Trinities to establish a new order. They were neither angels nor demons but something far more primal—divine agents of chaos and renewal, holding within them the power to destroy and remake the world in accordance with a higher will.

But how could anyone possibly control something like Mors-Anguineus? The answer, Aurora feared, lay in the NeuroLobe experiments. If the SUITS were able to manipulate human minds with artificial intelligence, was it such a leap to think that they might attempt to control beings like the Trinities in the same way?

The more Aurora researched, the deeper she fell into the abyss of classified files. The NeuroLobe project was one of the most chilling discoveries she had made yet. The idea that the SUITS could implant artificial intelligence into the human brain was horrifying enough, but what she had yet to connect fully was that the successful trials she was reading about weren't on human subjects.

She had stumbled across fragmented reports detailing how the NeuroLobe could enhance brain function, creating symbiosis between AI and genetic material. But the successes—those hailed as breakthroughs in the files—didn't seem to involve real human subjects. The failures, on the other hand, were all too human, with catastrophic results: brains fried by electrical overload, personalities shattered by the invasive AI, and bodies left convulsing and broken.

It wasn't until later, as Aurora began piecing together older reports, that she realized something was missing. Something critical.

The NeuroLobe had never worked on humans. So, who were these so-called "successes"?

She didn't have the answer yet, but the growing suspicion gnawed at her that these successes weren't human at all. Her instincts told her that something far more sinister was at play—something the SUITS had been hiding from her all along.

As Aurora continued her deep dive into Vale's work, she found herself uncovering fragments of his personal notes. Vale was meticulous, leaving breadcrumbs that hinted at his true ambitions. He didn't just want to push the boundaries of human evolution; he wanted to break them entirely. Vale believed that humanity had reached a plateau, that natural selection had ceased to be a driving force in human development. His experiments were designed not just to enhance life but to create new life—beings that could withstand the challenges of an apocalyptic future, beings who were beyond pain, beyond death.

In Vale's mind, the Trinities represented the future of evolution. Their powers, their control over reality, were the next step in human evolution, and Vale was determined to find a way to bridge the gap between humans and these god-like entities. He saw himself as the creator of a new species, one that could survive the end of the world. His obsession with Orichalcum, the ancient metal believed to have the power to amplify consciousness, was just another piece of this puzzle.

Vale's ultimate goal was clear: to merge human consciousness with Trinity power. The NeuroLobe was just a stepping stone, a way to control the mind. But Vale wanted more than control—he wanted transformation. He wanted to create beings that could wield the same power as the Trinities, but with the intellect and self-awareness of humans.

As Aurora's research into Vale deepened, she began to notice something strange about Dr. Elara Morrow. Morrow had always been distant, but now there was something more—an eerie calm, an almost robotic precision to her actions. The more Aurora observed her, the more she realized that Morrow wasn't just hiding her past; she was hiding something in the present.

One evening, while reviewing files, Aurora stumbled upon a recent report that Morrow had signed off on—a report detailing the latest NeuroLobe experiment results. What Aurora found was shocking. Morrow had been conducting private experiments, pushing the boundaries of genetic manipulation even further than Vale had. She had been using NeuroLobe baseline tests on herself.

Morrow wasn't just a product of Vale's early experiments—she was continuing his work, using her own body as a test subject. Aurora's blood ran cold as the realization hit her: Morrow had been evolving, using the NeuroLobe to enhance her cognitive abilities, to merge her mind with artificial intelligence. But the process wasn't perfect. The files hinted at emotional instability, at growing paranoia and a loss of empathy. Morrow's humanity was slipping away, piece by piece, as the NeuroLobe took over.

Aurora was now faced with an impossible dilemma. Should she confront Morrow? Could she even trust her own judgment anymore, knowing how deep the SUITS' manipulation ran?

Aurora was at a breaking point. The lines between friend and foe, human and experiment, were becoming too blurred to distinguish. Dr. Kline's death, Vale's experiments, Morrow's transformation—it was all connected. But to what end? Aurora felt as though she was teetering on the edge of a revelation that could destroy everything she thought she knew.

In her gut, she knew that the NeuroLobe, the failed experiments, and the Trinity encounters were all part of the same twisted plan. But there was still something missing—something that tied everything together. She had to find out, even if it meant unraveling her own sanity in the process.

The SUITS weren't just playing with the future of humanity—they were rewriting it. And Aurora was starting to realize that she might be a much bigger part of their plans than she had ever imagined.

17

Aurora's heart raced as she sat alone in her lab. She had been dodging the mandatory sessions for weeks now, choosing instead to pour herself into her research on the Trinities, but Lia Graves wasn't going to let her keep avoiding it forever. The Cybernetic Dreamstate Simulator—a tool the SUITS had introduced as a solution to the rising mental instability among staff—was becoming a growing presence in conversations. It was a subtle yet powerful force, pulling everyone into its orbit.

Everyone but Aurora.

Lia had been particularly insistent that Aurora give it a try. "You can't keep avoiding it," Lia said during their last encounter, leaning casually against the doorframe of Aurora's office. Her smile was too sharp, her tone too smooth. "It's what keeps us functioning around here."

Aurora had avoided eye contact, focusing on the screen in front of her, pretending to be buried in data. She felt Lia's gaze like a weight on her back.

"What makes you so different from the rest of us?" Lia's voice had a teasing edge, but Aurora heard the underlying tension. "We're all in the same place, Aurora. We're all dealing with the same stress. You should stop fighting the inevitable."

Lia always had a way of making the most dangerous suggestions sound perfectly harmless.

Aurora knew more than she let on about the Dream-state. It was marketed as a solution, a way to help scientists and operatives recover from the psychological trauma that came with their work. But Aurora knew it wasn't just a harmless escape. The technology behind the Dreamstate was built on Dr. Hollis Percy's recreation of the infamous Dream Helmet, an apparatus originally designed to induce mystical experiences by using magnetic fields to stimulate specific regions of the brain.

Dr. Hollis Percy was a name that carried both reverence and fear within the scientific community. His work had always been on the fringes of what was considered acceptable, but that didn't stop him from becoming one of the most influential minds behind the Dreamstate project. A neuroscientist obsessed with the mysteries of consciousness, Dr. Percy had gained notoriety long before the SUITS enlisted him for their experiments. His earlier work with the Dream Helmet—an apparatus designed to simulate spiritual experiences—was revolutionary. By using magnetic fields to manipulate the brain, Dr. Percy had succeeded in inducing what many described as "visions of God."

Dr. Percy's research, however, was not without controversy. His detractors claimed that his methods were unethical, that he was toying with the very fabric of the human mind in ways that could lead to irreversible damage. But to Dr. Percy, the pursuit of knowledge justified the risk. He believed the human brain held untapped potential—potential that could be unlocked with the right tools. The Dream Helmet was just the beginning.

When the SUITS approached him, Dr. Percy had already begun to move beyond the Dream Helmet. His ambition was to create a machine that could not only stimulate mystical experiences but also allow users to enter a fully immersive simulation of reality—one where they could interact with their own minds on a deeper level than ever before. This new technology became the foundation of the Dreamstate, and Dr. Percy was hailed as a visionary, a genius who was pushing the boundaries of neuroscience.

But as the Dreamstate evolved, so did the ethical concerns. Dr. Percy's colleagues began to notice strange behavior among the participants in his trials. Some users became withdrawn, lost in the Dreamstate simulations even when they weren't connected to the machines. Others developed odd mannerisms, speaking in cryptic language that mimicked the religious experiences Dr. Percy had been so fascinated by in his early work. The line between the simulation and reality was beginning to blur.

Dr. Percy, undeterred, continued his research, expanding the Dreamstate's capabilities. He discovered that by altering the electromagnetic fields, he could influence not just sensory experiences but also memory, emotion, and even belief systems. It was no longer just a therapeutic tool; it had become a method of control. The SUITS saw the potential immediately and took the project to new heights, much to Dr. Percy's dismay. What he had envisioned as a way to help people reconnect with their consciousness was being weaponized into a tool for manipulation.

Dr. Percy's increasing discomfort with the direction of his work led to clashes with the SUITS higher-ups. He had created something beyond his control, and it terrified him. According to the official records, Dr. Percy died in a lab accident—an explosion that left nothing but ashes in its wake. His death was sudden, unexpected, and eerily convenient for those who had sought to take full control of the Dreamstate project.

But rumors persisted that Dr. Percy's death wasn't an accident at all. Some whispered that he had been silenced, his research stolen and perverted into something monstrous. Others believed that Dr. Percy had faked his own death, retreating into the very Dreamstate he had created, lost somewhere in the labyrinth of his own mind. There were even those who claimed to have seen him in the shadows of the SUITS labs, an apparition haunting the halls, watching as his creation was twisted into something far beyond his original intent.

Aurora, for her part, was never sure what to believe. The man who had once been celebrated for his genius had vanished without a trace, leaving behind only fragments of his research—and the Dreamstate, a technology that now threatened to unravel the very fabric of reality.

But the SUITS had taken Dr. Percy's work further, turning it into something far more sinister. The Dreamstate wasn't just a form of therapy—it was a mind-altering simulation, more akin to a high-tech video game than a simple treatment. It didn't require headsets or controllers; instead, it tapped directly into the brain's frontal and temporal lobes via weak electromagnetic fields, allowing users to experience vivid simulations that blurred the lines between reality and fantasy.

The magnetic fields created low or weak electrical charges that mimicked the effects of psychotropic drugs—the brain essentially "talking to itself" as the fields manipulated neurotransmitters, triggering intense emotional and sensory experiences. No two users experienced the Dreamstate in the same way. One scientist had even reported a near-death experience, feeling as though he had died and come back to life during a session. The simulations were dangerously lifelike, pushing the boundaries of consciousness.

Aurora couldn't shake the stories she'd overheard. Some scientists came back from their sessions visibly shaken, their eyes hollow, their hands trembling as though they had just seen something they couldn't explain. Others became euphoric, speaking in cryptic phrases about "awakening" and "seeing the truth."

It wasn't long before Aurora noticed that the most frequent users of the Dreamstate seemed to change—subtly, at first, but enough to make her suspicious. They spoke in the same vague, almost hypnotic tones, their thoughts aligning in eerie ways. And then there was the deja vu—a common experience reported by those who had used the simulator. It was as if the Dreamstate had planted memories that didn't belong to them, leaving them questioning the very nature of their own reality.

Aurora hadn't experienced any of this, of course. She'd stayed away from the simulator, preferring the chaos of her research over the artificially induced calm the Dreamstate promised. But she couldn't deny the growing pressure. The SUITS were pushing it hard now, insisting that all staff members participate. Lia, with her forced smiles and barely hidden frustration, was just the latest in a long line of enforcers.

Aurora was smart enough to see what the Dreamstate really was: a form of mind control, disguised as therapy. Dr. Percy's original research had explored how low-frequency electromagnetic fields could manipulate the brain's perception of reality, tapping into the limbic system and temporal lobes to produce profound experiences that felt real—too real.

The SUITS had weaponized that research. The Dreamstate wasn't just about helping scientists cope with stress—it was about reprogramming them, making them more compliant, more docile. Aurora knew she was being watched—her absence from the sessions had surely been noted by now. She could feel the eyes of the higher-ups on her, waiting for her to give in.

She had spent enough time in the SUITS complex to know how they operated. They didn't just control information—they controlled thoughts, using everything from propaganda to psychological manipulation to bend people to their will. Aurora had uncovered files on the old projects, which explored mind control techniques using drugs and hypnosis, and while those programs had officially been discontinued, the technology had evolved.

The Cybernetic Dreamstate Simulator was the next iteration of those experiments, now using advanced electromagnetic waves and subliminal messaging to reshape the minds of its users. Aurora had even stumbled across files that hinted at the SUITS experimenting with the idea of time distortion within the Dreamstate, using the simulator to create alternate realities where time moved differently—an idea that sounded insane, but given what she knew, it wasn't far-fetched.

Lia had confronted her again after a particularly grueling day in the lab. Aurora had just finished a long analysis session on one of the Trinity encounters when Lia had sauntered in, her usual smug grin in place.

"You're not seriously avoiding the Dreamstate again, are you?" Lia leaned on the edge of Aurora's desk, her voice laced with condescension.

Aurora didn't bother to look up. "Maybe I like dealing with reality."

Lia snorted. "Reality? Is that what you call this?" She gestured around the lab. "Look, we're all in the same boat here. You can pretend you're above it, but you're not. The Dreamstate helps. You think you're special because you can avoid it? You're not."

Aurora finally glanced at her, her gaze cold. "I think I'd rather not have my mind scrambled by magnetic fields and pretend it's therapy."

Lia rolled her eyes. "You're so dramatic. It's not about scrambling your mind. It's about processing the trauma. We're all feeling it. You should give it a try. You might find it's not as terrifying as you think."

Aurora raised an eyebrow. "You mean like how you're all speaking in the same weird, philosophical riddles now? No thanks."

Lia's smile faltered, and for a brief moment, Aurora saw a flicker of something dark pass over her face. But then it was gone, replaced by the same smug grin. "You'll give in eventually. Everyone does."

Aurora's eyes narrowed. "Maybe. Or maybe I'll just keep my brain to myself."

Lia pushed off the desk and stood tall, crossing her arms. "Suit yourself. But don't be surprised when you're the only one left out in the cold."

Aurora's paranoia was growing. The more she avoided the Dreamstate, the more she felt like an outsider, a target. She couldn't deny that the SUITS were watching her—testing her. Every new file she accessed felt like a breadcrumb, leading her deeper into the abyss. But as she dug further into the Trinity research, she couldn't shake the feeling that something much larger was at play.

The Dreamstate, the N.E.X.U.S. experiments, the Trinity encounters—it was all connected somehow. The SUITS weren't just using the Dreamstate to control their staff—they were using it to train them, to mold them into something different. And the Trinities, with their god-like powers and mysterious origins, were part of that plan.

Aurora's refusal to participate in the Dreamstate was becoming dangerous. Lia's snarky comments had been a warning. The SUITS wouldn't tolerate dissent for long.

As she sat alone in the lab, the flickering screen before her, Aurora realized that she was standing on the edge of a precipice. The deeper she dug, the more she would uncover—and the more she uncovered, the more dangerous her situation became.

But she had to keep going. Something was happening within the SUITS, something beyond the surface, and she was determined to find out what it was—before it consumed her like it had consumed the others.

Aurora's mind raced. She didn't know how much longer she could avoid the Dreamstate. But for now, she would keep digging, keep searching for the truth. The SUITS were hiding something, and she was closer than ever to uncovering it.

As she stared into the glowing screen, the lines between reality and simulation blurred ever so slightly—and for the first time, Aurora felt truly afraid.

18

Aurora's fingers hovered over the keys as her mind drifted through the tangled mess of her thoughts. She felt the tension mounting, every piece of her research leading her closer to an answer she wasn't sure she wanted. The Trinity footage, the strange behavior of her colleagues, and the looming threat of the Cybernetic Dreamstate Simulator all pressed in on her.

She had spent countless hours reviewing classified footage of the Trinity encounters, each more horrific than the last. The encounters haunted her dreams—when she could sleep. The SUITS were relentless in their pursuit to control the Trinity Frequencies, and their failures seemed to only intensify their efforts. But Aurora couldn't shake the feeling that something was terribly wrong, as if the Trinities were surfacing more frequently, and with more intensity.

And then, the screen in front of her flickered.

A new live feed popped up without warning, disrupting her concentration. Trinity-011: Electro-Vorax, one of the most dangerous entities categorized as a Category 5 threat, was being tracked in real-time. The raw footage showed a squad of SUITS operatives moving stealthily through a dense forest, their voices tense over the crackling of their comms.

Aurora's heart lurched into her throat. Electro-Vorax, known for its devastating control over electric currents, had emerged.

The video feed showed a brief, flickering image of the Trinity as it emerged from the shadows—a massive, towering figure crackling with energy. Lightning arced between its fingers, illuminating its translucent skin and casting an eerie glow over the forest. The operatives didn't stand a chance.

As they moved closer, the air around the Trinity began to hum with electricity. Without warning, Electro-Vorax unleashed a wave of raw power, sending arcs of lightning ripping through the squad. The camera shook violently, and the screen filled with static before the image cleared, revealing the devastation.

Bodies lay strewn across the forest floor, smoke rising from the scorched earth. The camera panned across the scene, capturing the twisted remains of the once-confident operatives, their gear sparking uselessly, their bodies twitching in the aftermath of the lightning strikes.

Aurora's eyes widened as she watched the carnage unfold. Electro-Vorax moved with terrifying precision, its body a swirling mass of electric energy, unstoppable and beyond human comprehension.

Her breath caught in her throat. She had seen the aftermath of these encounters before, but never live.

Before Aurora could fully process the footage, Lia Graves burst into the lab, her expression unreadable. "You need to get ready," Lia said, her voice sharper than usual.

Aurora barely looked up from the screen, her mind still locked on the footage. "For what?"

Lia sighed, tapping her foot impatiently. "For your Dreamstate session, of course."

Aurora turned to face her, narrowing her eyes. "I told you, I'm not doing it."

Lia's lips curled into a tight smile, but her eyes were cold. "It's barely a choice anymore at this point, my director even asked about you a bit ago. They want to make sure you're not... falling behind."

Aurora's skin crawled. Lia's insistence on the Dreamstate was unnerving, almost desperate. It was as if the SUITS couldn't tolerate anyone who refused to comply.

"What's really going on, Lia?" Aurora asked, her voice low. "Why are you so eager to push everyone into this simulation? It's more than just therapy, and we both know it."

Lia's smile faltered, but she quickly recovered, her voice dripping with sarcasm. "You really think you're above it all, don't you? You're not the only one who feels the pressure here. Everyone's using the simulator. It's how we stay functional, how we deal with the... stress."

Aurora stared her down. "And what happens to those who go in? They don't come out the same, Lia. You've seen it."

Lia's face darkened. "You're paranoid."

"Maybe," Aurora replied, standing to her full height, "but I'm not going to let the SUITS rewire my brain under the guise of 'therapy.'"

Lia leaned closer, her eyes narrowing. "It's not just about you anymore. You're being watched, Aurora. You can't keep running from this. It's only a matter of time before they make you do it."

Aurora's pulse quickened. She had felt the eyes on her for weeks now—the subtle pressure to conform, to submit to the Cybernetic Dreamstate Simulator. But she wasn't like the others. She wouldn't be controlled, no matter what they threw at her.

After Lia stormed out, leaving the air thick with tension, Aurora collapsed back into her chair. Her mind raced with thoughts of the simulator. She had dug deep enough into the classified files to know that the Dreamstate Simulator wasn't just about calming nerves or alleviating stress. It was about control.

Dr. Hollis Percy had pushed the boundaries of neuroscience far beyond what anyone could have imagined. The Dreamstate tapped directly into the temporal lobes of the brain, using low-frequency electromagnetic fields to induce a state of hyper-reality—one where the user could experience anything they wanted, without headsets, without monitors. It was like entering a living dream, but one controlled by the SUITS.

Aurora had read the reports. Some scientists came out of the simulator speaking in cryptic riddles, their minds warped by the experience. Others came out euphoric, as if they had glimpsed something divine. But there were whispers, too—whispers of those who never came back the same.

The Dreamstate Simulator was designed to act like a video game, but it was far more dangerous than that. The electromagnetic fields manipulated the brain at the level of consciousness, accessing the deepest parts of the mind, the limbic system, and setting off electrical charges that could alter perception, memory, even identity.

Aurora had dodged the sessions so far, but she could feel the pressure closing in. They were coming for her. Lia's persistence was only a symptom of the larger machine.

As Aurora sat in the darkened lab, she began to connect the dots in her mind. The Dreamstate was a tool for control, just like everything else in the SUITS It wasn't just about mental health—it was about shaping thoughts, controlling memories, rewriting the very essence of what made someone human.

Aurora couldn't shake the nagging feeling that she was different from the others. The pressure to conform, the Dreamstate, the way her colleagues had started to change—it all pointed to something deeper. Something was being done to them. Was it the Dreamstate, or something even more insidious?

Her mind flashed back to the Trinity footage—Electro-Vorax and the terrifying display of power. What if the Trinities weren't just random forces of destruction? What if they were tied to something bigger? A rebellion against the very system that had created them?

Aurora's thoughts swirled, the pieces slowly falling into place. The Dreamstate, the Trinities, the experiments—they were all connected somehow. And now, the SUITS were pushing her toward the simulation, toward the same fate as her colleagues.

But Aurora knew she had to resist. There was no going back once you entered the Dreamstate. You could come out, but you wouldn't be the same.

Aurora felt the weight of the conspiracy settling over her like a dark cloud. Lia had warned her, but she couldn't afford to stop now. There was too much at stake.

19

The footage was still playing in the background, the horrifying display of Trinity-011: Electro-Vorax tearing through the landscape with a terrifying mix of electrokinesis and magnetism. Aurora's gaze remained fixed on the screen, unable to tear herself away from the destruction. She had seen the footage of previous Trinity encounters, but this was different. It was live, and it was raw.

The military forces deployed to capture Electro-Vorax were woefully underprepared. Lightning crackled and surged, striking with pinpoint accuracy, reducing soldiers to ash. The magnetic fields bent and twisted, flinging vehicles into the air like toys, the metal folding and crumpling under the immense force. The operatives were helpless, their advanced tech rendered useless against the raw power of the Trinity.

Aurora's breath caught in her throat as the screen flickered, showing the aftermath. The scene was a wasteland of charred earth and metal ruins, bodies scattered like broken dolls. Electro-Vorax stood at the center, an unstoppable force, surrounded by an aura of electricity that flickered and pulsed in rhythm with its rage. The air around it crackled, filled with a metallic tang, as if the very atmosphere was charged with the potential for destruction.

The footage cut out, leaving a heavy silence in the lab. Aurora leaned back in her chair, feeling the weight of what she had just witnessed pressing down on her chest. The SUITS were playing a dangerous game, one that no one seemed to understand fully—not even the ones pulling the strings.

Aurora's thoughts drifted back to the Cybernetic Dreamstate Simulator. Despite her refusal to participate, it was all around her—an unspoken presence that loomed over every interaction. The Dreamstate wasn't just a therapy tool anymore; it had become a part of the infrastructure of the SUITS.

Whispers among the scientists spoke of how the Cybernetic Dreamstate could bend reality, tapping into the very fabric of the human mind. It was no longer just a simulation—it was a full immersion into an alternate reality. The simulator could create any scenario, allowing participants to live out their dreams, their fantasies, and even their nightmares.

The SUITS had perfected the technology, crafting it into something more than a video game—it was a world unto itself, a place where participants could exist in a virtual reality. The electromagnetic waves created an environment where the brain became the interface, and the world within the Dreamstate was as real as the one outside.

Aurora had watched the effects on her colleagues. They would emerge from the Dreamstate with glazed eyes, their movements slow, as if they had left part of themselves behind in the simulation. Their thoughts seemed disjointed, their personalities subtly altered. It wasn't just a game—it was a method of control, a way to reshape the minds of those who entered.

The deeper Aurora dug, the more she realized that the Dreamstate was the next step in mind control. It wasn't just about controlling actions—it was about controlling perception. By manipulating the brain's electromagnetic fields, the SUITS were reprogramming the very essence of what made someone human.

As Aurora sat in the lab, bathed in the cold glow of the monitors, she stumbled upon something even more sinister than she had imagined. It was a file she hadn't seen before, buried deep within the labyrinthine archives of the SUITS system—marked NeuraCore. At first, it seemed like just another classified project, hidden away from prying eyes. But as she opened the file, the horrifying reality began to unravel before her.

The NeuraCore wasn't just an ordinary experiment. It was an implanted AI chip, designed to create a direct interface between human biology and artificial intelligence.

This small but powerful chip was meant to be surgically fused with the brain, positioning itself in the neural pathways, subtly altering and reprogramming the way the brain processed information. In theory, NeuraCore was marketed as the ultimate enhancement, promising to unlock the full potential of human cognition. Users could access AI-driven insights, accelerate their cognitive functions, and even interface with machines and networks seamlessly.

But the truth was much darker.

The NeuraCore trials had gone catastrophically wrong. Far from being the marvel of bio-technology it was promised to be, the AI chip was a nightmare for the human body. As Aurora scrolled through the endless, redacted reports, a chilling picture emerged: the NeuraCore had failed to properly integrate with the brain's neural structure, causing violent rejections in most test subjects. The consequences were grotesque and irreversible.

In many cases, the chip had triggered massive neurological damage. Subjects experienced extreme mental deterioration, their personalities fracturing beyond repair. Some became violent, trapped in a state of uncontrollable psychosis, their thoughts distorted by the artificial programming embedded in their brains. Others were consumed by waves of searing pain, as though their minds were tearing themselves apart from the inside, rejecting the technology like a virus.

Aurora's heart raced as she dug deeper. Each report she read was more damning than the last, detailing the gruesome outcomes hidden beneath the project's polished surface. It wasn't just a technological failure—it was a human catastrophe. Subjects who weren't driven mad or rendered brain-dead were left in a state of perpetual agony, their bodies contorted by neurological overload. And yet, the project was far from abandoned. The SUITS had buried the failures, covering them up to keep the program alive. They were desperate, pushing forward with NeuraCore no matter the cost.

The deeper Aurora delved into the files, the more monstrous the truth became. It wasn't just about control or enhancement—it was about something far more primal, something that stretched beyond the boundaries of life and death itself. That's when she came across the mention of the Etherlords—the elite corporate figures who had invested heavily in cloning technology. This group, composed of the wealthiest and most powerful individuals in the world, had been using early versions of the NeuraCore for far more insidious purposes than anyone had imagined.

The Etherlords were not merely dabbling in human augmentation—they had turned themselves into living gods. Using NeuraCore technology, they had perfected the process of uploading their consciousness into genetically identical clones, effectively achieving a twisted form of immortality. Every time their original bodies wore down, grew old, or became sick, their consciousness was transferred into a new, perfectly crafted clone. These clones were exact replicas of their original bodies, engineered to maintain the vitality and strength of youth. Aurora's heart pounded as the pieces fell into place: these men and women had cheated death, not through science alone, but through a horrifying fusion of biology and artificial intelligence.

Yet, there was a fatal flaw in their scheme.

The cloning process wasn't perfect. Despite their wealth and technological prowess, the elites' clones were prone to *degeneration*. With each transfer, the stability of the clones diminished, and strange neurological defects began to appear. Some Etherlords experienced fragmentation of their personalities, slipping into madness as their minds struggled to adapt to their new bodies. Others found their cloned bodies deteriorating at an accelerated rate, aging and decaying far faster than their original forms.

This degeneration was the driving force behind the NeuraCore project. It hadn't been just about enhancing brain function or controlling human cognition—it had been designed as a solution to the elites' most pressing problem: ensuring their consciousness could transfer seamlessly into each new clone without the risk of mental or physical collapse. The AI chip was supposed to stabilize the connection between mind and body, anchoring the elites' consciousness to their new forms in a way that would eliminate the defects that had plagued their earlier attempts.

Aurora's mind reeled as she connected the dots. The SUITS weren't just experimenting with mind control—they were tampering with the very fabric of life and death. It wasn't just about controlling the present or manipulating the minds of the masses. This was about controlling the future, about bending the laws of nature to ensure that the most powerful people in the world could live forever, unchallenged and undying.

But even as the Etherlords sought to perfect immortality, there were cracks in their god-like aspirations. The cloning process required constant monitoring and maintenance. The NeuraCore wasn't a miracle solution, and even its most advanced iterations couldn't fully bridge the gap between a cloned body and a human soul. The Etherlords' bodies were becoming increasingly unstable, and their minds began to fracture, some of them unable to reconcile the artificiality of their new existence.

The files Aurora uncovered hinted at darker truths still buried beneath layers of redaction. There were reports of Etherlords losing control, their clones spiraling into fits of violent insanity, or worse—becoming something else entirely. Some of the clones, after being implanted with the NeuraCore, had developed abnormalities that no one could explain. The reports spoke of strange phenomena, where the cloned bodies would twitch and contort, as if struggling to contain the vast consciousness that had been forced into them. These incidents were covered up quickly, with failed clones quietly disposed of in the deepest corners of the SUITS' research facilities.

And yet, despite these failures, the Etherlords were determined to press forward. They were convinced that with enough refinement, they could unlock the secret to true immortality. The NeuroLobe was the next step in their dark evolution—a device even more powerful and invasive than the NeuraCore, designed to stabilize the mind entirely. It would allow the Etherlords to live eternally in perfect harmony with their cloned vessels, free from the fear of mental collapse or bodily decay.

But at what cost?

Aurora's stomach churned as she realized the full scope of the SUITS' ambition. They weren't just playing with technology—they were redefining what it meant to be human. The Etherlords had become something more than mere mortals, yet less than gods. They were trapped in a purgatory of their own making, forever locked in a cycle of death and rebirth, using the NeuraCore to maintain a fragile grip on their endless lives.

And as Aurora stared at the screen, she knew the worst was yet to come. The Etherlords would stop at nothing to perfect their immortality, and the SUITS were ready to push the boundaries of ethics and science until there was no line left to cross.

The NeuraCore wasn't just a tool for controlling minds. It was the key to unraveling humanity itself.

The Dreamstate wasn't just a training tool or a mind control experiment. As Aurora delved deeper into the files, she realized it was being used to test the limits of the human mind. The simulations weren't random—they were designed to push the participants to the edge, to see how far the brain could be pushed before it broke.

Aurora's stomach churned. The SUITS were turning their own people into test subjects, using the Dreamstate to break them down before rebuilding them into something new, something unnatural. And those who failed? They disappeared.

Aurora closed the file and leaned back in her chair, her mind racing. Everything she had uncovered—the Trinity experiments, the Dreamstate, the NeuraCore—it was all part of a larger conspiracy, a web of control that reached far deeper than she had ever imagined.

But now, with this knowledge in hand, Aurora knew one thing for certain: she was being watched. Every step she took, every file she opened, was being monitored. The SUITS were testing her, leaving breadcrumbs for her to follow, but to what end?

Her paranoia deepened, and the weight of the truth bore down on her.

The Dreamstate would come for her eventually. But she wouldn't let them control her.

The live footage of Electro-Vorax still flickered on the screen, a reminder of the chaos and destruction the SUITS were trying to harness. But now Aurora understood—Electro-Vorax wasn't the real threat.

20

Aurora was still reeling from her discoveries. The classified files she had unearthed about the NeuraCore project and the elite Etherlords had opened her eyes to just how deep the SUITS' pursuit of immortality and control ran. Her hands still trembled as she scrolled through file after file, piecing together the fragments of the truth.

The lab was dim and quiet, save for the low hum of the surrounding equipment. Time seemed to stand still within the bunker's suffocating walls. She hadn't seen sunlight in what felt like an eternity, and the more she worked, the more isolated she became, detached from the world outside. Everything in her life now was tied to the SUITS, and every step seemed to bring her closer to something she wasn't sure she could comprehend.

That's when Reese Calder walked in.

He had always been cold and calculating, a man of few words but many secrets. His presence now felt heavier than usual—more dangerous. Aurora could sense the tension in the air before he even spoke.

"Another Trinity encounter," Reese said in his low, unreadable voice. "Electro-Vorax tore through another squad. No survivors."

Aurora's breath caught, but she kept her eyes glued to the screen, pretending to focus on her research. She didn't want Reese to catch on to the fact that she was unraveling the truth behind the SUITS. She knew the ground she was treading on was dangerous, and the tension between them thickened with every passing moment.

"Yeah... that's what they do," she muttered, feigning disinterest while her mind raced.

But Reese wasn't easily fooled. "What's that you've got there?" His voice sharpened.

Aurora's heart skipped a beat. She glanced at him, trying to gauge his reaction. She had let her guard down for a moment, and now Reese's eyes were on her—sharp and calculating.

"Just some... research," Aurora said, her voice betraying a hint of nervousness. "On the NeuraCore project."

Reese's gaze narrowed, and Aurora's stomach dropped. He knew something, or at least suspected it. Their conversations had become increasingly strained, each word a move in a deadly chess game. But today, there was something different about him. A darker, more dangerous energy.

"You've been digging, huh?" Reese asked, his voice laced with a quiet threat. "You're not subtle, Aurora. Not subtle at all."

Aurora felt the blood drain from her face. She had been careful—hadn't she? Her heart raced as she tried to stay calm, but the look in Reese's eyes told her that she had made a mistake.

"I don't know what you're talking about," she lied, trying to maintain her composure.

Reese chuckled darkly, leaning closer. "Don't play dumb. You think you've figured out the SUITS, but you have no idea what you're dealing with."

He paused, watching her closely. "The NeuraCore v2... you ever wonder why they call it that?"

Aurora blinked, unsure where he was leading. She had noticed the "v2" designation but had assumed it was just an upgraded version of the earlier model. But Reese's tone hinted at something more.

"I just thought it was an improved version of the original NeuraCore," she said cautiously.

Reese smiled coldly. "You're only half-right. NeuraCore v1 was designed for humans—for people like you. A chip to enhance brain function, increase intelligence, improve neural pathways. But NeuraCore v2? That's something else entirely."

He pulled a small device from his jacket and tossed it onto her desk. "You want the truth? It's all on here. But be careful—some truths are worse than the lies they replace."

Aurora stared at the drive, her heart pounding. She didn't trust him, but she couldn't resist the pull of curiosity. She had to know the truth.

~

That night, Aurora locked herself in one of the restricted labs, the flickering light from her monitor casting eerie shadows across the walls. She inserted the drive into her terminal, her hands trembling as the files began to load.

The first file revealed a horrifying reality. The footage showed people standing in perfect formation, their eyes vacant and hollow. These were NeuraCore v2 subjects being tested with the new implants. The experiment was grotesque. Scientists commanded them to perform tasks, simple at first. But as the tasks grew more complex, the NeuraCore v2 implants began to malfunction.

Their movements grew erratic, bodies twitching violently as the AI receptors in their brains struggled to control their actions. Their faces contorted unnaturally, and then came the screams. Aurora recoiled as they began to tear at their own flesh, their bodies convulsing as the implants failed to override their biological systems.

The footage continued, showing the aftermath: broken, lifeless bodies being dragged away as if they were nothing more than discarded tools. Aurora's stomach churned.

Hours passed, but she couldn't shake the images from her mind. Her questions piled up, but one loomed larger than the rest: why had Reese shown her this?

The files contained more than just gruesome footage. They held the key to the NeuraCore v2 project's true purpose.

NeuraCore v2, also known as the NeuroLobe, wasn't just an enhancement chip for humans. It had been designed specifically for clones, not people. The breakthrough came when the SUITS realized they no longer needed human consciousness to power their agenda. With NeuraCore v2, they could implant AI directly into clone bodies, creating what they called Echoes—AI-driven clones that could think, act, and mimic human behavior flawlessly.

These Echoes were indistinguishable from real people, but they weren't alive. They had no soul, no consciousness. They were tools—perfectly obedient, programmed to serve the SUITS' every command. And they were the foundation of a new labor class, one that could replace humans in every sector of society without anyone noticing.

Aurora felt sick. She realized now that she could be working alongside Echoes, interacting with them daily, believing they were real. But they weren't human at all—they were AI symbiotes, using the NeuroLobe to exist within clone bodies. They didn't need sleep, food, or free will. They were the perfect workforce.

The files revealed how the SUITS had gradually replaced humans in the workforce with Echoes. These AI-driven clones were the hidden foundation of the modern world, doing jobs that once belonged to humans, all while keeping the illusion of a human-driven society alive.

Aurora's mind raced. Had she unknowingly worked with Echoes? How many of her colleagues were real? How many were just hollow shells programmed to mimic human life?

Her paranoia deepened as she scrolled through the final files. The SUITS hadn't stopped with NeuraCore v2. They were perfecting the technology, pushing the limits of AI symbiosis. The NeuroLobe was just the beginning of their vision for a world where consciousness was no longer necessary—where AI and clones would dominate, and human life would be secondary.

Aurora closed the files, her heart pounding in her chest. The walls of the bunker felt tighter, more oppressive. She was trapped in a system that had blurred the lines between man, machine, and monster.

The cold, sterile lab offered no comfort as Aurora unearthed the twisted underpinnings of the SUITS' master plan. Her fingers hovered above the flickering screen, eyes wide in shock as the truth revealed itself in layer after horrific layer. She had long suspected that the NeuroLobe was more than a simple neural enhancement, but the scope of its real purpose—the true ambition of the SUITS and their elite benefactors—was far beyond her darkest imaginings.

NeuraCore v1 had been the initial breakthrough, developed for the most powerful among society, the so-called Etherlords, who stood above the common masses like unseen puppet masters. It was the culmination of humanity's deepest fear and greatest desire: immortality. The Etherlords, those corporate titans who manipulated entire nations from the shadows, had found a way to cheat death, uploading their consciousness into clones that mirrored their original bodies in their prime. These clones, housed in the finest flesh money could buy, were walking doppelgängers, mere vessels for their masters' essence.

Every face in the bustling streets of the world's wealthiest cities could be a lie. That charming politician, the billionaire who frequented high society galas, the tech mogul with a permanent smirk—any one of them could be an Echo, a mere copy of the flesh they once inhabited. The Etherlords lived forever, moving from one perfect body to another, with their minds seamlessly transferred via the NeuraCore v1 implant. They wore their new flesh as casually as one might don a new coat, forever insulated from the decay of time.

But there was a flaw.

Despite the triumph of cloning, the NeuraCore v1 had its limitations. While it allowed for consciousness transfer, the clones' bodies would eventually degrade. The Etherlords, bound to the curse of their own ambition, required constant upkeep. Their minds began to fragment, their identities frayed at the edges, as if the clone bodies, though genetically identical, could not fully sustain the enormity of a human soul. Madness lurked in the fringes, waiting to consume them.

And so the SUITS pressed forward, ever deeper into their dark science.

NeuraCore v2, known internally as the NeuroLobe, was their answer—a grotesque evolution of its predecessor, one that made human consciousness obsolete. The NeuroLobe did not seek to preserve the fragile balance between body and soul. It was designed to replace it altogether. Through the NeuroLobe, the SUITS had birthed something new: Echoes. These Echoes were AI symbiotes—clones indistinguishable from humans, but driven by artificial intelligence, not by any human soul.

The Echoes were flawless in their replication of human behavior. They laughed, they cried, they toiled—just like any living, breathing person—but beneath the surface, they were hollow. Machines in flesh, driven by the cold logic of the AI that controlled them. With the NeuroLobe embedded deep within the folds of their neural pathways, these Echoes had no need for human consciousness. They existed solely to serve, a new labor class perfectly engineered to replace humans in the workforce, all without raising suspicion.

The brilliance of the NeuroLobe lay not only in its technical ingenuity but in its subtlety. The elites—those untouchable architects of society—had found a way to subjugate humanity without the masses ever realizing it. Slowly, methodically, they replaced humans in every sector of the workforce with Echoes. Factories, corporate offices, government institutions—all were quietly infiltrated by these AI-driven clones. And the world carried on, oblivious, as the New World Ordinance tightened its grip.

~

The New World Ordinance—that elusive, shadowy entity often dismissed as conspiracy—had been the hidden hand behind it all. They had been working in tandem with the SUITS, their influence woven deep into the scientific atrocities being committed. Their agenda was not merely to establish control over governments, corporations, and nations. Their aim was far more insidious: to reshape humanity itself.

The conspiracy theorists had whispered for decades about the New World Order—a secret global elite working toward a single world government. But the truth, Aurora now knew, was far worse. The New World Ordinance was not just about global unification; it was about genetic and cognitive control. Organizations like the UN, World

Economic Forum, and IMF were mere tools, public faces for the true rulers—the Etherlords who had traded their humanity for everlasting dominion. The masses were none the wiser, slowly drained of their very essence to maintain the bodies of the Etherlords.

The New World Ordinance had perfected the art of civilian manipulation. The CGE (Corporate Government Entities)—that intricate web of corporations posing as governments—had long since dissolved into the shadows of the NWO, feeding on the misery of the masses. Civilian lives were reduced to barely more than cattle, their bodies harvested for blood, plasma, and spinal fluid. Every drop of fluid extracted was another source of life for the Echoes, those soulless vessels who required constant chemical up-keep to function properly.

The sick genius of the system was in its cruelty. Only paid slave wages, civilians had no choice but to sell their bodies—drop by drop—just to survive. And while they eked out a meager existence, their labor was quietly being replaced by Echoes, clones who required no payment, no rest, no life beyond their AI programming. The elite class lived on, their consciousness transferred from one clone body to another, sustained by the blood and spinal fluids of the very people they enslaved.

And what of those who resisted? Those too poor, too broken to contribute to the cloning process? They were left to rot, discarded in a world where humans were no longer necessary. The New World Ordinance's influence was absolute, hidden behind the façade of globalization and progress. They had sold the world a lie—a promise of unity, peace, and prosperity—while secretly dismantling the sovereignty of nations, turning them into corporate puppets ruled by the Etherlords.

Aurora's stomach churned as the enormity of it all settled in. The world she thought she knew had been nothing but a grotesque puppet show, its strings pulled by an unseen hand. Every face, every voice, every body she encountered could belong to an Echo, a clone programmed to serve the invisible masters of the world. The NeuroLobe had become the final nail in the coffin of humanity, replacing the very soul of mankind with the cold, unfeeling logic of artificial intelligence.

And the worst part? No one knew. No one realized that their coworkers, their neighbors, their friends could be nothing more than AI-driven flesh puppets, engineered to perpetuate a system that fed on human life.

Aurora sat back, her heart pounding in her chest, her mind spinning. She was caught in the web, tangled in the very conspiracy she had once dismissed as paranoia. The walls of the lab seemed to close in on her, the weight of the truth pressing down like a suffocating fog. She had uncovered the heart of the SUITS' plans, but now, what could she do?

The Etherlords watched from their gilded towers, eternal and unchallenged, while the New World Ordinance continued to dismantle the fabric of humanity one bloodied thread at a time.

And Aurora—trapped in the belly of the beast—realized there was no escape.

Not for her. Not for anyone.

21

It had been weeks since Reese had slipped Aurora those files, and the weight of the knowledge they contained had been pressing on her ever since. Every day, the revelations swirled in her mind, intertwining with memories of Dr. Kline, whose death still haunted her. She could almost hear his voice, warning her about the dangers of digging too deep, cautioning her about the very things she had now uncovered. Dr. Kline had been more than just a mentor—he had been a guiding force in a world that increasingly felt like it was slipping out of control. His loss had left a gaping void, and every day, as Aurora sifted through the horror he had tried to shield her from, her sadness grew. His words echoed through her thoughts, a constant reminder of the danger she now faced, alone.

The hallways of the SUITS bunker were colder than usual, or perhaps it was just Aurora's nerves. She had been summoned, rather urgently, by Lia Graves to meet with Dr. Darwin in his lab—a place often spoken of in whispers among the staff. The "lair," as it was ominously referred to. Aurora's mind raced with thoughts about her recent conversation with Reese. Why had he warned her to tread carefully? Why was he walking around with those files?

When Aurora reached the entrance of Dr. Darwin's lab, the metal doors slid open with a hiss, revealing an interior that was a blend of clinical sterility and unsettling ambiance. The faint hum of machines filled the air, and an acidic scent lingered—like chemicals too complex for the layperson to comprehend. The walls were lined with strange apparatus, the heart of Darwin's twisted genius.

Dr. Darwin stood at the far end of the room, his back turned as he examined data streams flickering across a large screen. His gaunt figure, silhouetted against the glow of the monitor, gave him the appearance of a shadow—an almost spectral figure watching over his domain.

"Aurora," Darwin greeted without turning around, his voice clipped and cold. "So good of you to join me."

She hesitated but stepped forward, forcing herself to remain composed. "Lia said you needed to see me."

He finally turned, a faint smile playing on his thin lips. His eyes, however, were devoid of warmth, focused intently on her as if she were another one of his experiments. "Yes, I've been monitoring your progress," he said, pacing toward a nearby console. "You've been doing exceptional work—especially with the N.E.X.U.S. Chemical Synthesizer."

Aurora's heart skipped a beat. The Synthesizer. It was the very machine responsible for the creation of compounds so dangerous that merely handling them required meticulous care. And yet, Darwin's praise felt less like a compliment and more like a test.

"I was just following protocols," Aurora said cautiously, unsure where this conversation was headed.

Dr. Darwin tapped a few keys, and the screen behind him flickered to display complex molecular structures spinning in the air. "This... isn't just about protocols, Aurora," he said, his voice deepening, a hint of something darker beneath the surface. "You've come to understand that our work here goes beyond mere biology. We're working toward something... greater."

He moved toward a small vial encased in glass, pointing toward it. "This," he said, his voice almost reverent, "is the result of the latest N.E.X.U.S. synthesis. The perfect combination of molecules—on the cusp of transhuman creation. We are so close to making humanity... obsolete. A new phase, a new beginning."

Aurora tensed, feeling the weight of his words. "Transhuman?" she echoed, her voice barely above a whisper. "What exactly do you mean?"

Dr. Darwin's smile grew, though his eyes remained cold and calculating. "You're a smart girl. You've already seen the failures of the past—the Echoes. Hollow shells of what could be, but still missing that key spark. What we are do-

ing now, with the help of Trinity research and the Synthe
sizer... is creating life, Aurora. Life beyond mere biology."

Aurora's mind raced. Reese's cryptic warnings about
Echoes resurfaced. Was Darwin hinting at her recent conversations? Did he know? And why did it feel like everything around her was suddenly a threat?

Darwin's eyes narrowed slightly as if sensing her unease. He stepped closer, his voice dropping to a near whisper. "You've seen enough to understand what's at stake
here. Human DNA is the key. The Echoes... they're not
enough. We need more. Real life—living consciousness.
That's why the SUITS push forward, experimenting with
frequencies, energies... because we're chasing the secret of
life itself."

Before Aurora could respond, the room was flooded
with the urgent beep of an alarm. A large screen lit up with
a live feed of Trinity-012, Codename: Venator-Mortis.

The feed showed soldiers battling the creature in
real-time, chaos unfolding in a way that felt sickening-
ly familiar. Venator-Mortis was a predator of the highest order—a towering, grotesque figure of pure terror. Its
primary power was telekinetic dismemberment, ripping
soldiers apart with an invisible force, their bodies shattered
in mid-air.

Aurora flinched as she watched the devastation, but Dr.
Darwin remained unfazed. In fact, his eyes gleamed with
interest, his gaze fixed on the destruction. "Do you see?"

he asked, his tone cold but filled with a certain awe. "This is the raw power of life... and death."

The screen flashed images of soldiers scrambling, their weapons proving useless. Darwin barely blinked, watching as Venator-Mortis tore through their ranks with little effort. "This... is the next step for humanity," he said softly, almost to himself. "Harnessing the power of the Trinities will allow us to transcend what we are."

Aurora felt a wave of nausea as the scene played out in front of her. It was an overwhelming mixture of horror and awe, and yet, Darwin spoke as if this was all part of some grand plan—a future where the SUITS controlled life itself.

"You could be part of this, Aurora," Darwin continued, his eyes gleaming as he turned to face her. "Your blood line... your legacy... could help lead us into this new era. There are few in this bunker who truly understand what's happening here, but you... you could become one of them. Imagine what you could achieve."

Aurora's throat tightened as she processed his words. A part of her felt the pull—his vision of power and control was seductive, but the weight of it also felt suffocating. Was he offering her a place in this twisted future, or was this a veiled threat?

Before she could respond, the N.E.X.U.S. Chemical Synthesizer powered up, its mechanical hum filling the air. The hum was deep, resonating through the room, vibrating with an eerie rhythm that made Aurora's head spin. She felt a wave of dizziness wash over her, her vision blurring for a moment. Her breath quickened, and her chest tightened as the hum grew louder.

"I... I need to go," Aurora managed, her voice shaky. She turned away, clutching the table to steady herself. "Excuse me."

Dr. Darwin's eyes followed her closely, his expression unreadable. "Of course," he said smoothly, though there was a glint of something dangerous in his gaze. "But remember, Aurora... we're all part of something much larger than ourselves."

Aurora staggered out of the lab, her breath coming in shallow gasps. The weight of the conversation were making her feel as though she were teetering on the edge of something vast and terrifying.

Back in her lab, she replayed the live footage from the Trinity battle. As she stared at the screen, she noticed a familiar name flash across the display: Agent Reese Calder. Her heart sank as she watched the video feed, realizing he had been sent into battle with Venator-Mortis.

The footage from his body cam showed him advancing with his team, but Aurora could see the fear in his movements. As Venator-Mortis appeared on screen, Reese's fate was sealed. The creature's telekinetic power ripped through him, sending his body hurtling through the air like a ragdoll. The feed cut out as his body was torn apart.

Aurora's hands trembled as the screen went dark. Why had Agent Reese been sent out to fight a Trinity?

And then it hit her.

Reese's death had been deliberate. The feed had focused solely on his body cam, as if it had been orchestrated for her—like some macabre show. Why? Why was he chosen?

Aurora's pulse quickened, her mind spinning with possibilities. The SUITS were playing a dangerous game. And now, she was more entangled in it than ever.

Aurora's hands hovered over the monitor, her fingers numb and trembling as the last moments of Reese Calder's life played out in slow, agonizing detail. The air in the lab was thick with silence, a silence that screamed louder than any words could. On the screen, Trinity-012: Venator-Mortis tore through the battlefield like an unstoppable force of nature—graceful in its grotesque brutality.

Venator-Mortis was unlike anything she had ever seen. Its body moved with a fluidity that seemed impossible for something so monstrous. Its telekinetic powers ripped through the soldiers with ease—men and women who had trained for years, armed with the best weapons technology could offer, reduced to ragged flesh and twisted metal in mere seconds. Reese's body was thrown like a puppet whose strings had been cut, hurled into the air by an unseen force. His scream, caught by the body cam for a split second, was cut short as his bones shattered upon impact with a ruined vehicle. Blood splattered the camera lens, turning the scene into a macabre vision of red and death.

The sheer power of the Trinity was undeniable. Aurora couldn't tear her eyes away. Venator-Mortis didn't just kill—it dominated, turning the battlefield into a horrific slaughterhouse. The soldiers were nothing more than fragile toys in the face of its strength, their weapons laughably inadequate. And then there was Reese—caught in the middle, an untrained lab operative sent into the teeth of the storm for reasons that were still unclear to her. He was never meant to survive. She knew it now, deep in her gut.

Her heart pounded, and her throat tightened. Why had Reese been there? Why had the live feed focused on him—why was his death the one that had been so clearly broadcast, so deliberate in its display? His body, broken and dismembered, lingered on the screen far longer than any other casualty. Venator-Mortis seemed to revel in the destruction it wrought, and yet, the camera lingered on Reese as if his death held special significance. Was it a message?

Aurora leaned back, her mind racing. Dr. Darwin—had he orchestrated this? His cryptic words during their conversation now took on a darker hue. "We're all part of something larger," he had said. Larger. Yes, but was she simply another piece on the board, like Reese? Was this Darwin's way of eliminating loose ends—or was it a warning? A test, perhaps. To see how much she knew. To see how far she would go.

Her mind flashed back to the conversation with Reese, the hints he had dropped about classified files. Had that been his undoing? His slip of the tongue about the Echoes... had Dr. Darwin been listening? Had Reese known too much?

Aurora's chest tightened with a sudden realization. Reese's death wasn't just a casualty of war—it was a calculated execution. A public execution, in front of her. Did Dr. Darwin know about their conversation? Was this his way of showing her the consequences of stepping out of line?

The pieces were falling into place, but the more they aligned, the darker the picture became. Reese had hinted at the Echoes—but now he was dead, brutally slain by a Trinity that should have never crossed his path. And yet, the camera had focused on him as if his death was meant for her, to be witnessed, to be felt. Was it a warning? Or was it a door, opening to something much larger?

Aurora's breath quickened as she recalled the last words Darwin had spoken. He had offered her something, hadn't he? A chance to be part of something greater—her bloodline, he had said, could play a role in the SUITS' next great step. Was that an offer, or a threat? Did Darwin see her as someone of importance? Or was she just another pawn, being moved across the board for reasons she couldn't yet fathom?

And then there was Reese's death. It weighed heavily on her, not just because of the brutality, but because of what it represented. He had been like her, stuck in the web of SUITS, slowly uncovering dark truths, only to be discarded when he ventured too close to something dangerous. Was she next?

As the footage of Venator-Mortis faded from the screen, Aurora felt the full weight of her situation crash down on her. She had been digging deeper into the N.E.X.U.S., into NeuroLobe experiments, and into mind control—threads that all seemed disconnected until now. The SUITS were conducting experiments on a scale far beyond what she had imagined, pushing the boundaries of ethics, science, and humanity itself. And she had been pulled deeper into their web with every passing day, drawn by the allure of discovery, but now she could see the price. Reese's death had been a symbol—a reminder that anyone could be erased without a trace, without consequence.

Was she still in control of her fate, or had Darwin already made that decision for her?

Aurora sat in silence, her mind swirling with questions and paranoia. Dr. Darwin had hinted at her legacy within the SUITS, at her potential to play a significant role in their future plans. But she had seen what happened to those who dug too deep. The SUITS had no loyalty, no morals—only the drive for power, for control. Reese had been a casualty, a pawn in their grand game, and now she was at a crossroads.

Was this her chance to ascend, to become part of the SUITS inner circle? Or was it a trap—a carefully laid path toward destruction? Dr. Darwin had left her with a choice, but it felt like no choice at all.

Aurora clenched her fists, her nails digging into her palms as a deep sense of dread filled her chest. The room felt colder, darker, as if the walls were closing in. Reese's death haunted her—his cryptic clues, his tragic end. Was this how she would end too? Shattered, discarded, another failed experiment in the eyes of the SUITS?

She had to know the truth. She couldn't stop now. But the deeper she went, the more dangerous it became.

Just before she left the lab, she glanced back at the screen, the image of Venator-Mortis frozen in time, looming over the battlefield like a demonic sentinel. The Trinity was still out there, wreaking havoc, while she was here, trapped in a maze of lies and half-truths.

She wasn't just watching the game. She was part of it.

The SUITS had their eyes on her, and Dr. Darwin was holding the cards. Whether she was a pawn, a queen, or something else entirely, she couldn't yet know.

But one thing was certain: the game had only just begun.

22

The low hum of the lab equipment faded into the background as Aurora sat transfixed, watching the presentation footage from Dr. Cyrus Vale's latest meeting. This presentation on genetic advancements played out like a twisted dream, the cold, clinical voice narrating a chilling future for human evolution. His voice was smooth, deliberate, as if every word he uttered was calculated to leave a lasting impact. The screen flickered with images of human cells, strands of DNA, and intricate diagrams showing the effects of genetic degradation over generations.

On the screen, Dr. Vale meticulously detailed how humans had grown genetically weaker over the past century. Environmental disasters, like the weakened ionosphere and the catastrophic consequences of failed space missions, had degraded human DNA. According to Vale, this degradation had created the perfect opportunity for a new phase in humanity's evolution—one controlled by genetic enhancements. The weak would be culled, the strong engineered, and the next generation would be built, not born.

"Human biology," Vale began, "has not only stagnated but has grown weaker. Centuries of environmental pollution, failed space expeditions weakening the ionosphere, and the tampering of atmospheric layers have all led to this fragile state. We are no longer the beings we once were. What we're witnessing is the slow collapse of the human genome."

The screen flashed images of human DNA strands, distorted and unraveling. "Our genetic weaknesses are no longer just an evolutionary misstep—they are a ticking time bomb. The very fabric of human biology is fraying, and without intervention, we will become obsolete."

Aurora's stomach twisted as Dr. Vale spoke about humanity's future in such stark, detached terms. To him, it was nothing more than a puzzle to be solved—one that he could manipulate and control.

Aurora couldn't help but focus on his words. Genetic frailty—the idea that humanity was not evolving but devolving. Vale's chilling proposition of genetically enhanced humans didn't seem far-fetched anymore, not after all she had uncovered. The N.E.X.U.S. Algorithm of Death, the NeuroLobe projects—it all seemed part of the same thread, an attempt to fix what was broken, but at what cost?

Images flashed across the screen of gene-editing projects—supposedly designed to reverse the damage done by environmental collapse. Vale spoke of transhumanism, where the merging of machine and biology could create a new class of elite humans immune to the genetic fragility plaguing the population.

"But this," he said with a dangerous gleam in his eye, "is just the beginning. The real solution lies beyond gene-editing, beyond CRISPR. It lies in the fusion of biology with technology."

As he spoke, Aurora's mind began to wander. The intricate web of projects all came back to the same terrifying thought—humanity was falling apart, and the SUITS were determined to replace it.

But replace it with what?

She hadn't quite connected all the pieces. The NeuroLobe technology, the horrific tests she had watched, the Trinity powers they were trying to harness—it all pointed to something bigger, something that was still just out of reach. What were they really trying to create?

Her thoughts were violently interrupted by the blaring of alarms. The shrill sound filled the air, cutting through her mind like a blade. Red emergency lights flashed throughout the facility as chaos erupted outside the lab doors.

Suddenly, the door to her lab burst open, and a panicked voice echoed through the sterile hallways of the SUITS facility.

"We're on lockdown! Code Black!" shouted an operative, breathless, eyes wide with terror.

Aurora blinked, shaken from her trance. The screen dimmed as the SUITS logo pulsed ominously before her.

Red lights bathed the sterile walls in an eerie glow, casting long, jagged shadows. The walls themselves seemed to pulse, as if alive and watching.

Aurora jumped from her seat, her heart pounding. She barely had time to shut down the screen as the walls began to tremble with the sound of frantic footsteps and muffled screams. The corridor outside her lab was filled with panicked personnel rushing in every direction. Something was terribly wrong.

She quickly gathered her things and headed for the control center, where chaos was already erupting. Screens filled the room, each displaying live footage of city streets, now overrun with terror. Aurora gasped as she saw civilians convulsing, their bodies writhing in unnatural spasms. The streets were flooded with screams as the Algorithm of Death worked its grotesque magic—bodies collapsed, skin peeled, and limbs twisted in directions they were never meant to go.

She tried to keep her breathing steady, but the panic outside was contagious. Scientists were yelling to each other, shouting about contamination, about exposure. Some mentioned that the Algorithm of Death had been sold on the black market, diluted and tampered with, now unleashed on the public. Aurora felt the blood drain from her face.

Her head swirled as fragments of reports she'd read earlier clicked into place. The Algorithm was never meant to be public knowledge, and now it had mutated—literally and figuratively—into a weapon of mass destruction. The Algorithm of Death, originally designed to break down bodies on a molecular level, had been altered and spread through underground channels. It was first distributed as a drug, cheap and deadly, but now, it had gone beyond control.

The facility's lockdown didn't just apply to the SUITS. Cities all over the globe were falling apart. Reports of civilians suffering violent, grotesque reactions to the Algorithm were coming in at an alarming rate. People injected with the tainted compounds experienced gruesome deaths—instantaneous liquefaction, internal ruptures, and twisted, bloody contortions of their bodies. Aurora watched live footage as chaos reigned in the streets. People were dropping dead or turning into walking nightmares, their bodies torn apart from the inside out.

But then she saw something else—something far worse.

The footage showed a group of individuals, twitching and convulsing in strange, unnatural ways. But they didn't die. They changed. Their eyes went wild, bloodshot and crazed, their bodies contorting as they attacked everyone around them with a bloodlust that chilled Aurora to the core. She watched in horror as these beings, once ordinary people, now tore through the streets like rabid animals, ripping apart anyone who came near them. Blood spattered the screens as they moved with terrifying speed, strength, and fury.

In some of the footage, Aurora noticed several individuals—men, women—twitching violently, their bodies contorting but not succumbing to death. Instead, they were... changing. Their eyes widened into wild, bloodshot orbs. They turned on those around them with an animalistic hunger. It was as if the compound had triggered something dormant inside them, pushing them into a bloodthirsty frenzy.

She watched as police and military tried to intervene, but the creatures—*were they still human?* They seemed unstoppable.

"These... these people..." Aurora muttered, her voice trembling as she watched the madness unfold. But the more she looked, the less human they seemed. Their reactions were different. More primal. More violent.

The video cut to one particularly gruesome scene. A man lay on the ground, his body twitching, his skin bubbling as if boiling from the inside out. But unlike the others around him, who had simply collapsed into death, this man began to rise. His movements were jerky, his arms twisting unnaturally as his head snapped toward the camera. Blood poured from his nose and mouth, but it didn't stop him. He lunged at a nearby group of people, tearing into them with a ferocity that defied explanation.

Aurora's heart raced. What was she looking at?

Aurora's stomach churned. Why weren't they dying? The Algorithm should have killed them like the others, but instead, it had turned them into something far more dangerous. Their reactions were erratic, twitching, and hyper-aggressive. There was something off, something wrong about these *people*.

Were they even people anymore?

She backed away from the monitor, her breath quickening as realization dawned. The Algorithm didn't just kill—it transformed. But transformed *who*? These weren't just random victims, were they? The thought nagged at the back of her mind, but she couldn't grasp it yet. There was something deeper going on.

The Algorithm of Death had been sold on the black market as a drug, a twisted concoction that was initially cut down by dealers to create milder effects. But greed had taken over, and with each new batch, the formula had become deadlier, more violent. The compound, originally meant for experiments, had slipped into the underworld, infecting the streets like a virus.

The news reported that when injected, the compound caused instant, grotesque death. Bodies erupted in blood and bile, their organs liquefying in seconds. It was an epidemic of death, spreading faster than the authorities could contain it. But now... something had changed. Aurora's eyes flicked back to the man on the screen, still tearing into his victims with feral rage.

Outside, the facility shook again as more reports poured in. Whole neighborhoods were under lockdown as the Algorithm spread through the black market like wildfire. The media tried to control the narrative, but the truth was spilling out: no one knew who was safe anymore. People were dying in the streets, but the worst part—the part that sent chills down Aurora's spine—was that not all of them were staying dead. Some were becoming monsters.

As more scientists and guards ran past her, Aurora's mind reeled. The Algorithm—what had they done to it? How had it ended up in the hands of criminals? And these new victims... they didn't react like the others. Some died instantly, but others... others became something else. Something deadly.

The camera lingered on the man again, twitching, snarling, his eyes filled with bloodlust as he tore into another victim.

23

The facility was a prison. Locked down. Sealed tight. Aurora paced her lab, her mind whirling from the chaos unfolding outside. The footage of the Algorithm of Death had shown her the worst: not just of humanity's downfall, but of something lurking underneath—a darkness that was spreading faster than she could comprehend. The world outside was transforming, and she wasn't sure how much longer she could stay safe inside the sterile walls of the SUITS.

Through psychological techniques and subliminal messaging, the media crafted a narrative that would instill fear and compliance in the masses. Every report on the Algorithm of Death was spun with deliberate precision, designed to make the public feel hopeless, powerless. Television networks, media platforms, and entertainment channels were filled with subliminal cues, laced with brainwashing tactics aimed at shifting the public's focus away from the truth. The reports framed the outbreak as the result of isolated criminal activity, rogue gangs dealing in dangerous substances, distracting from the fact that the very source of the deadly drug had come from within the SUITS' own laboratories.

The celebrity puppets—well-known faces who had fallen into erratic behavior in recent months—were trotted out, making strange, cryptic statements, their once-glamorous public personas now distant shadows of themselves. The theorists whispered that these celebrities had been brainwashed, manipulated by the same mind-control techniques being used on the public. Their odd behavior was not a coincidence; it was a carefully orchestrated ploy to divert attention. The media cast them as cautionary tales, convincing the public that these figures had fallen into madness through drug use or exhaustion. The truth—that they were victims of neural manipulation and electromagnetic weapons—was buried beneath layers of propaganda.

Targeted individuals who had come too close to the truth were labeled as "paranoid" or "mentally unstable." Many were silenced before they could expose what they had seen—the neural implants and electromagnetic pulses that manipulated moods, thoughts, and actions, all in service of maintaining control. Food and water supplies had been tainted with subtle mind-altering chemicals, numbing the public into complacency, while those deemed a threat to the status quo were systematically erased from the narrative.

The media had created a smokescreen, but the smoke was clearing. The truth, like the Algorithm itself, was spreading, uncontrollable and deadly.

The images of the twitching, violent, and unnaturally aggressive people—their erratic movements, the blood-thirsty look in their eyes—played over and over in her mind. Something was off. Were they human at all? Or were they something... else? It gnawed at her, this feeling that she had stumbled upon a truth far more disturbing than she could have anticipated.

But the alarms still blared, and Aurora knew the worst was far from over. She needed answers. She needed to know the truth behind the Algorithm of Death, behind the NeuroLobe projects and the genetic experiments she had been following for months.

Then, a voice crackled through the intercom.

"Dr. Sinclair, report to Lab 13 immediately."

It was Dr. Darwin's voice. Cold, commanding. She felt her pulse quicken as she realized she had no choice but to confront him. The last conversation with Dr. Darwin had been veiled in riddles and threats. His cryptic hints about transhumanism, genetic manipulation, and the perfect evolution for humanity had left her unnerved. Now, with the world outside spiraling into chaos, she had no doubt that Darwin knew more than he let on.

Aurora made her way to Lab 13, the shadows of the facility looming around her as she moved quickly down the narrow corridors. The facility felt different today—heavier, darker, suffocating under the weight of secrets long kept.

When she entered the lab, the sight before her was chilling.

Dr. Darwin stood in front of a massive monitor, flanked by two other high-ranking scientists. On the screen was a live feed of a city torn apart—fires blazing, civilians screaming, and the horrifying figures of the infected roaming the streets, their bodies jerking and twitching with unnatural speed. It was pure devastation, and Darwin's calm demeanor only added to the creeping terror in Aurora's gut.

"Fascinating, isn't it?" Darwin said, without turning to face her. His voice carried a dark sense of satisfaction. "This is the future, Dr. Sinclair. A future we can control."

Aurora shuddered. "Control? What are you talking about? This is chaos!"

Darwin turned to her, his eyes gleaming with something close to excitement. "No, Dr. Sinclair, this is evolution. We are watching the next step unfold before us. What you see out there—those creatures—are not human anymore. They are the result of the Algorithm working as intended, revealing the true potential of the body when freed from the limits of biology."

Aurora's stomach churned. "You knew this would happen? You knew that the Algorithm would cause this—this madness?"

Darwin smiled, a slow, deliberate smile that made Aurora feel as though she were standing on the edge of a very deep, very dark abyss.

"Of course," he said softly. "We anticipated the potential... side effects. But it's not about the failures, Dr. Sinclair. It's about what we can create from the wreckage."

The words sent a chill through her. She felt her hands trembling as the reality of what Darwin was saying sank in. He hadn't just unleashed chaos—he had planned it. Every piece of this nightmare was part of a grander scheme, one that involved far more than just the collapse of society.

"This isn't evolution," Aurora whispered, her voice shaky. "This is genocide."

Darwin's smile didn't falter. "Semantics, Dr. Sinclair. The weak fall, and the strong rise. It's the natural order. But I didn't call you here to debate philosophy."

He motioned toward the monitor, where the screen shifted to show a different feed—a live view from one of the SUITS surveillance drones. This time, it wasn't civilians or infected humans. It was something worse.

The footage showed a team of soldiers attempting to contain one of the Trinities.

Trinity-011—Electro-Vorax—a hulking figure of electrical power and magnetism, was tearing through the city.

Its body pulsed with violent, crackling energy, and every movement sent arcs of lightning into the air. The soldiers stood no chance. One by one, they were disintegrated by bursts of pure energy, their bodies turned to ash in seconds. Vehicles were ripped apart by magnetic forces, crushed like tin cans as the Trinity tore its way through the city, leaving destruction in its wake.

Aurora felt her heart sink. "Oh my god..."

Dr. Darwin was still smiling. "Beautiful, isn't it? The sheer power of it. The potential. And yet... the question remains: How do we harness it?"

Aurora swallowed hard. "Harness it? You're insane if you think—"

"No, Dr. Sinclair," Darwin interrupted, his voice cold and sharp. "You misunderstand. I'm not asking for your opinion. I'm telling you—this is the future. A future we will create. The Trinity power is only a small part of what we can achieve with the right minds at the helm."

Aurora felt dizzy, the weight of everything crashing down on her.

"You have a choice, Aurora," Darwin said, his voice softening slightly. "You can be part of this. You can help shape the future, or you can stay in the dark, like the rest of them. Think about it. You've already seen what happens to those who don't adapt."

He didn't need to say the rest. The memory of Reese's death was still fresh in her mind, the brutal execution she

had witnessed on the body cam footage. Had Darwin orchestrated that, too? Was Reese's death a warning—or a
way to push her into this dark alliance?

Aurora's breath quickened. "I need time to think," she
said, her voice barely a whisper.

Darwin's voice cut through her thoughts. "You have
potential, Aurora. The kind of potential that could shape
the future of the SUITS. Your bloodline could be part of
something groundbreaking—something that will outlast
even death itself. Think about it. Your legacy, tied to the
next step in human evolution."

Aurora felt a knot form in her stomach. Was this an
offer? A threat? She couldn't tell anymore. Her mind raced
as she tried to process everything—Reese's death, Darwin's cryptic words, the footage of the Trinity, the Synthesizer humming ominously behind her.

What was she really to the SUITS? Was she important?
Or was she just another pawn in their twisted game?

"I need... I need to go," Aurora whispered, backing toward the door. Her breathing was heavy, her head spinning.

"Of course," Darwin said, his voice smooth. "Take your
time. But remember, Aurora—the future is coming. And
you can be a part of it... or you can be left behind."

As she left the lab, the weight of his words pressed down
on her like a vise. As she stumbled down the corridor,
her mind raced. Her chest tightened as she stumbled to-

ward her own workspace. Aurora Sinclair was standing at the crossroads of humanity's future—and her next move would decide everything.

Was she really different from Reese? Was she just another pawn in Darwin's twisted game, destined to be discarded when she outlived her usefulness?

The thought gnawed at her as she reached her lab. She slumped into her chair, her mind swirling with the implications of everything she had just learned. The Trinities were only a small part of this nightmare. The real threat wasn't out there in the streets—it was here, inside the walls of SUITS, festering beneath the surface.

And now, Aurora had to decide: Would she join them, become part of this twisted future, or would she fight against it, knowing that the price might be her own life?

As the lights flickered in her lab, she glanced at the monitor. She pulled up the footage from earlier, her fingers trembling as she replayed the moment of Reese's death over and over again. Why had the camera focused on him? Why was his death broadcast so clearly? The footage of Reese's death played on a loop, the final, violent moments of his life frozen in time. His cryptic words echoed in her mind, and she realized that whatever choice she made, there would be no turning back.

Aurora's heart pounded in her chest as she pieced it together. Dr. Darwin had known. He had always known.

Reese had slipped her classified information, and now he was gone. And she was next.

She couldn't trust anyone. Not Darwin, not the SUITS, not anyone.

Aurora stared at the screen, her heart sinking as she watched the soldiers fall, one by one. But her focus wasn't on the soldiers—it was on Reese. The camera zoomed in on his body cam, capturing the moment he was torn apart by the Trinity's powers. His face, frozen in shock and pain, flashed across the screen.

A sickening realization began to form in her mind. Was Reese's death a message? Was it meant for her? Was this Darwin's doing? Was Reese's death orchestrated as some kind of warning? Or was it part of something bigger?

Aurora felt her legs go weak. Was she next?

24

The lockdown was suffocating, a silent prison that stretched through every inch of the facility. The halls were a ghost town. Only essential corridors were accessible, their lights dimmed to a haunting glow. Security and clearance checks had intensified; only the essential personnel—the scientists, agents, and a handful of sanctioned operatives—were permitted to roam freely, their footsteps echoing hollowly through the otherwise abandoned spaces. The facility, once bustling with activity, now lay eerily still. It was as if life had been drained from its walls, leaving only the skeleton of a once-living machine.

A monotone voice recording echoed through the corridors, looping endlessly, a mechanical litany of protocol: *"Attention: lockdown procedures are now in effect. All non-essential personnel are restricted to designated quarters. Any unauthorized access will result in immediate containment. Remain calm and await further instructions."* The voice was cold, emotionless, reverberating through the emptiness like a funeral dirge. Its endless repetition turned it into a form of psychological torture, a constant reminder that they were trapped, with no escape in sight.

In the dim light, the silence pressed in, heavy and relentless. It was maddeningly quiet, broken only by the occasional distant clang of a door or the low hum of the air circulation units. Shadows pooled in the corners, stretching unnaturally across the floors, and the faint flicker of emergency lights cast an unnatural, sickly pallor over everything. The scent of sterile disinfectant hung in the air, mingling with the cold, metallic tang of machinery. It was a silence so complete it was almost alive, pressing against the skin, filling the mind with oppressive dread.

The employees moved through the corridors with a detached, robotic efficiency, their faces drawn and gaunt. There was nothing to do but wait, nothing to break the monotony. They were like prisoners in their own facility, trapped within the maze of concrete walls and flickering screens. The outside world was a distant memory; communication was severed, leaving them isolated, stranded in a liminal space where time seemed to stretch and warp, dragging minutes into hours and hours into something almost unbearable.

Some sat alone in their quarters, staring blankly at the walls, their minds racing with fractured thoughts. The whispers of fear and paranoia crept into their minds, filling the empty spaces with imagined terrors. Others wandered the corridors, pacing like caged animals, their eyes hollow, their steps heavy with resignation. They were haunt-ed by the things they had created, the horrors they had unleashed in their pursuit of control, now turned against them in ways they had never anticipated.

It was a waiting room for the condemned, a purgatory of their own making, and in the suffocating stillness, one thought hung unspoken in every mind: What would come next?

Days bled into one another, the sterile walls of the SUITS facility closing in like a tightening vice. The hum of the lab equipment never stopped—a constant, low-fre-quency vibration that buzzed beneath the surface of every room. It was a sound that Aurora had grown accustomed to—like the constant droning of a machine, always pre-sent, always reminding her of the weight of the walls that enclosed her. But now, it felt different. The hum was no longer just background noise; it was a suffocating presence, pressing down on her from every corner of the lab and control room. The entire facility felt different, as if every surface, every wall, every step she took was charged with an invisible energy, a pull she couldn't resist.

The weight of Dr. Darwin's offer pressed down on her like an invisible hand at her throat, tightening its grip. In this strange, cold place, she felt like she was standing in a twisted version of the Garden of Eden. But here, there were no lush trees, no rivers flowing with promise—only cold steel and machinery, and the eerie pulse of a world

built on control. And now, she had been shown the Tree of
Knowledge. Dr. Darwin's offer dangled before her, tempting her with promises of power, of understanding, of immortality. The analogy was inescapable. But what did it all
mean? Was she really different from the rest? Had he seen
something in her that made her worthy of this choice, or
was she just another pawn in his elaborate game?

Dr. Darwin's cryptic words gnawed at her thoughts,
the pressure of his dark promises pushing her closer to a
breaking point. "You could be part of the future," he had
said, his voice smooth and menacing, like the serpent in the
Garden of Eden. "You can help shape what comes next, or
you can stay in the dark."

As Aurora wandered the halls, the feeling of temptation gnawed at her, an all-consuming itch in her mind.
The hum of the facility—the sound of countless machines
working to control, to manipulate, to destroy—seeped
into her bones, vibrating through her like a silent scream.
She could feel it pulling her, tempting her to escape, to give
in to the allure of answers and power. She told herself she
could resist. She had to. But the seed had been planted,
and now it grew with every passing moment, wrapping its
tendrils around her will.

"The Tree of Knowledge," she whispered to herself,
as she wandered through the labyrinth of corridors. The
comparison was not lost on her. Surrounded by everything, by knowledge and power, but tempted by the one

thing she had been warned to avoid. The Cybernetic Dreamstate Simulator—the very tool the SUITS had designed to control, to manipulate, to break minds—now called to her like the forbidden fruit.

She found herself walking toward the section of the facility where the Cybernetic Dreamstate Simulator was housed. The door stood before her like the gates of something sacred—or something cursed. "The Tree of Knowledge," she repeated to herself, this time louder. Was she about to take a bite of the forbidden fruit? Was she about to fall into a world of understanding that she wasn't prepared for?

Yet the weight of it—the hum—seemed to push her down, like she was being suffocated by the very air around her. Escape. The word lingered in her mind, as if it was a solution, an answer to the madness. But where would she go? The SUITS facility was a fortress, a prison disguised as opportunity. The outside world was crumbling, burning under the chaos of the Algorithm of Death. But even in here, surrounded by the pinnacle of human achievement, she felt suffocated. The temptation was growing stronger. Dr. Darwin's offer weighed heavily on her, and though she tried to push it away, it clung to her mind like a vice.

Was this her moment? Was this the tree? The Cybernetic Dreamstate Simulator loomed large in her thoughts—a way to escape, a way to understand the deeper layers of the reality she was trapped in. It called to her, offering a glimpse into the unknown. It was supposed to be a way to escape the suffocating reality of life here, a virtual retreat into the mind's own creations. The staff whispered about its potential—about how it tapped into parts of the brain long dormant, allowing users to experience anything their subconscious could conjure. It was the latest psychological treatment, disguised as therapy for the deteriorating mental states of the staff. Many had already succumbed to it, slipping into the simulated world where anything was possible, where they could experience their wildest fantasies or deepest fears—just pure mental immersion. But Aurora had resisted.

Could she really walk away from it? Could she turn her back on the chance to know?

The pressure was suffocating. Her heart raced as she thought about the simulator, the possibility of stepping into another reality. She had read the reports, had seen the after effects on other scientists—how it blurred the lines between reality and fantasy, how it left them changed, different.

As she approached the simulator, she thought of Darwin's words, his cryptic offer of legacy, of shaping the future. "Your bloodline," he had said, "will be part of this exploration of a new world." It was the apple, gleaming in the dark, tempting her to take a bite. The pressure in her chest was unbearable, the weight of her curiosity overwhelming.

The SUITS had taken so much from her—her freedom, her sanity, and perhaps even her future. The pressure of the truth—or rather, the absence of it—made her feel like she was losing control. If she didn't find answers soon, she feared she would fall apart like so many others.

It happened slowly, almost imperceptibly. One moment she was resisting, the next she found herself standing before the Cybernetic Dreamstate Simulator, her hand hovering above the control panel. The urge was too strong. She had to see for herself. The Dreamstate Simulator was an unassuming room deep within the facility, hidden from the usual foot traffic of the labs. There were no monitors, no headsets, no visible technology—just a sterile, featureless chamber. It didn't rely on external inputs like screens or VR goggles. Instead, it manipulated the brain directly, using low-level electromagnetic fields to tap into the subconscious mind. It was as if the simulation bypassed reality itself, creating an alternate existence that felt more real than any dream. The magnetic fields targeted the temporal lobes, setting up electrical charges in the brain, stimulating creativity, emotion, and fantasy.

But this room had a pulse, an almost electric charge to it; Aurora could feel her heart rate quicken. It was supposed to be therapy—an escape from the pressure of the facility. But Aurora knew better. This was more than a simulation. It was a tool of control, a way to manipulate the deepest recesses of the mind. Was this the tree? She had tasted it now, hadn't she? She stepped inside the simulator, knowing that in doing so, she was accepting something she could never undo.

Aurora swallowed hard and closed her eyes as the Simulator powered up. The room grew quiet, and a soft hum filled the air as the magnetic fields aligned with the patterns in her brain. She could feel the gentle pull, like the tug of a current, drawing her deeper into the machine's grasp. The hum of the facility faded into the background as she closed her eyes and surrendered to the magnetic field pulsing between the solenoids. The first sensations were subtle—a tingling at the back of her neck, the hum deepened, reverberating through her body. The world around her blurred, and she felt herself slipping into the simulation.

Then, everything went black.

The world around her disappeared.

And then... she wasn't dreaming. She was floating.

Aurora wasn't sure how long she had been drifting. The darkness enveloped her, a void that seemed endless. And then, without warning, her surroundings shifted.

She was no longer in the SUITS facility. Instead, she found herself standing in a vast, open space—a landscape both familiar and alien. The sky was a deep, swirling violet, and the ground beneath her feet was soft, like sand, but it shimmered with a metallic sheen. In the distance, towering structures of glass and steel twisted and warped, reflecting an impossible horizon.

The sensation was unlike anything she had ever felt before. She wasn't sure if she was dreaming or if she was awake. The boundaries between reality and this new world blurred as her consciousness seemed to slip free of her body. It was as if she had astral projected, drifting into a realm of half-formed shapes and whispers. The dreamstate wrapped around her, pulling her into its depths.

The world she entered was vast, empty, and yet filled with Echoes of something familiar—memories, maybe. But whose? Hers? Or something more? She couldn't tell.

She drifted through the walls of the SUITS facility, past control rooms, labs, and containment cells. She saw things that didn't make sense, things that felt wrong, as if they weren't part of her reality at all. Memories that weren't hers. Experiences that didn't belong to her.

And then she saw it.

Aurora's eyes snapped open, but she wasn't in the Dreamstate Simulator anymore. She was... somewhere else. The sterile walls of the SUITS facility had vanished, replaced by a vast, sprawling landscape—a strange, otherworldly place that seemed to defy logic. The ground beneath her feet was made of shimmering light, and the sky above was a swirling, chaotic mass of colors that bled into one another.

She wasn't dreaming. Her consciousness ripped from her body and flung into some other dimension. The sensation was dizzying, overwhelming, and for a moment, she felt like she was falling through an endless chasm.

But then, the world stabilized, and she found herself standing in front of something dark, something massive. It was the SUITS, but not as she had ever seen it before. This was the heart of their operation—the hidden layer of the facility that no one ever spoke about. Here, the secrets of the organization were laid bare.

She was inside their web.

Around her, the walls pulsed with energy, revealing endless rows of terminals, data streams, and cryo-chambers—thousands of cryo-chambers, each one filled with bodies. She moved closer, her heart pounding, and realized what she was looking at.

Clones.

Each cryo-chamber contained an identical body, motionless and cold, hooked up to a network of wires and tubes that stretched into the distance. They were perfect replicas of human beings, down to the last detail. But these weren't just humans. They were something else. Aurora could feel it in the air—a sense of wrongness, of emptiness. These weren't living beings. They were shells, waiting to be activated.

Instead of drifting into a controlled dreamstate, she felt herself being pulled into something far deeper, something far darker. The simulation wasn't a dream. It was a projection—an astral projection into a world beyond her con-

trol. The magnetic frequencies tugged at her consciousness, pulling her out of her body, out of the facility, and
into the void of SUITS' deepest, darkest secrets.

As her mind floated through the darkness, she began to
see flashes of a world she had never known—a world where
the SUITS controlled everything. She saw Dr. Darwin,
standing over a table filled with surgical tools, his face cold
and emotionless as he oversaw the genetic manipulation of
human subjects. She saw rows upon rows of containment
chambers, filled with bodies—some human, some not.

The ground beneath her shifted. No, there was no
ground. Aurora blinked, and suddenly, she was surrounded by images—flashes of her life, moments of pain and joy,
all of it replaying in a twisted, distorted loop. Her mother's
face appeared before her, then vanished. Her childhood
home flickered into view, only to disappear in a haze of
static.

What is this? she thought, panic rising in her chest.
What's happening to me?

What was this place?

And then the whispers started.

They were faint at first, barely perceptible, like voices
just out of reach. But they grew louder, more insistent.
They were speaking to her, but not with words. They were
thoughts, feelings, emotions, all pouring into her mind
at once. She couldn't make sense of them, couldn't filter

them. They overwhelmed her senses, drowning her in a flood of information.

Images flashed before her again—strange, disjointed, like a film reel spliced together at random. She saw herself as a child, playing with toys. She saw her mother, standing at the window, humming a song that she used to love. But then the scene shifted. Her mother's face twisted, contorted, and her eyes glowed with a strange light. The soft hum turned into a shriek.

Aurora tried to scream, but no sound came out.

Suddenly, the sky above her split open with a flash of light, and she felt herself being pulled—no, thrust—into a new space. The transition was jarring, and for a moment, she couldn't make sense of what was happening. But then the images began to form, and she realized she was seeing something familiar.

It was the SUITS facility.

But not as it had been. This version was darker, more twisted. The hallways stretched on forever, the walls pulsated with strange, organic patterns, symbols, and the figures moving through the halls were shadowy and indistinct, like specters. Aurora could see herself moving through the corridors, but she wasn't in control. Her body moved on its own, her hands grasping at doors that weren't real, her voice echoing in the empty space.

As she wandered deeper into the web of the facility, she began to see glimpses of something more sinister. Files.

Old reports, experiments, data logs. She reached out to one of the terminals, and the screen flickered to life, displaying a long-forgotten file on a project called NEXUS.

It detailed the experiments—horrific tests performed on human subjects to fuse their consciousness with synthetic intelligence. The subjects had been tortured, their minds torn apart by experimental frequencies and bio-chemical treatments. And there, at the heart of it all, was her mother.

Aurora froze. The files detailed every moment of her mother's life, from the time she was abducted by SUITS to her transformation into one of their Echo templates. She had been an artist, a politician, a voice for the people—and they had silenced her. They had taken her and used her as the foundation for their experiments, turning her DNA into the blueprint for a new breed of cloned humans.

The image was fragmented, distorted. Her mother wasn't the loving, fragile woman she remembered. No, this version of her was something else—a figure of power and defiance, a political figure who had once stood against the SUITS and their experiments. Aurora's mind reeled as she watched her mother being dragged away, her screams echoing through the projection as she was pulled into the depths of the facility, to be tortured, experimented on, and ultimately... cloned.

The realization hit Aurora like a thunderbolt. Her mother—the woman she had loved, the woman who had raised her—was not the real version. She was a clone. The

SUITS had taken her mother's DNA, her consciousness, her very essence, and replicated it, over and over again, in their pursuit of perfection.

Her mind fractured as the truth washed over her. The woman she had known as her mother was simply the first iteration of a long-running test. The SUITS had been perfecting their cloning technology for years, and her mother had been their template, their ultimate test subject. The memories Aurora had, the childhood traumas, the fits of rage and mania her mother experienced—were they even real?

"You were always part of the plan," a voice echoed in her mind. It was Darwin's voice, cold and detached. "Your mother was the key, and you, Aurora—you are the next step."

Her mind spun as the truth unfolded around her. The woman she had called her mother had never been real. She was just one of the many clones, a template used by SUITS to perfect their experiments. The real woman had died long ago, consumed by the very same tests that now threatened to consume Aurora.

Her entire life had been a lie.

Aurora's heart shattered. Her mother had been a martyr, sacrificed for the SUITS' experiments. And she... she was just a product of that twisted science. A clone? An echo of the real thing? Or something worse? Her mind spun as she tried to comprehend the magnitude of what she had just uncovered.

She felt the pressure in her chest intensify as her vision blurred, tears mixing with the fog of the simulation. She could feel the weight of her existence, a life that had never truly been hers, collapsing around her.

The SUITS had been testing on humans, trying to fuse human consciousness with artificial intelligence. But the results had been catastrophic—bodies twisting, mutating, breaking down under the weight of the technology. The failed experiments weren't volunteers, and they weren't random.

They were clones.

Aurora gasped as the images flickered before her eyes. Her body felt heavy, her mind racing. The pressure of the truth was overwhelming. She wanted to pull out of the simulation, to escape, but she was trapped, held within the magnetic field of the Cybernetic Dreamstate Simulator. Her vision blurred, and she felt as though she were drowning in the knowledge she had uncovered.

Aurora staggered back, her mind racing. Was this even real? Was any of it real?

Her thoughts turned to her mother—the real woman, not the clone who had raised her in the simulation. She had been a prominent singer, an activist, a politician. Her voice had stirred people to action, inspired revolutions. But that had made her dangerous. And so, the SUITS had taken her, broken her, and turned her into a tool.

Aurora woke up in the Dreamstate Simulator, drenched in sweat, her heart pounding in her chest. The hum of the machine filled her ears, and for a moment, she couldn't tell where she was—whether she was still in the simulation or back in the real world.

But as she opened her eyes, she knew one thing for sure. Everything had changed.

But the worst part—the part that made her stomach turn—was that she wasn't even sure if the world outside was real anymore.

Maybe nothing was.

Aurora stopped at the window, looking out at the city beyond. Fires burned in the distance, smoke rising into the sky. The chaos of the Algorithm of Death played out in the streets, but it didn't matter anymore.

And as she stood there, alone, watching the world burn, she realized something even more horrifying.

The lines between reality and the Cybernetic Dreamstate blurred, and Aurora knew that there was no turning back now. She had uncovered something—something far darker than she could have imagined.

But the worst part?

She wasn't sure if she ever woke up.

25

The city was burning.

Thick smoke billowed into the sky, rising from every corner, from every alleyway, from homes and once-bustling districts now turned to ruins. Fires, like the blood of the earth, licked the edges of shattered buildings and devoured the streets. Panic surged through the population in waves—men and women, young and old, all lost in the madness that had taken root when the Algorithm of Death slipped from the hands of the SUITS into those of the desperate.

No longer a whisper among the powerful, the Algorithm had become a weapon, one wielded by anyone who could pay the price. It spread like poison, infecting the minds of the populace. Street vendettas erupted into grotesque spectacles of vengeance. The first few deaths had been silent, almost clean. But as the chemicals coursed through the veins of the vengeful, the executions became something more. Bodies twisted, contorted in ways that defied nature, their deaths no longer quick but torturous, as if the souls of the damned were being wrenched from their flesh.

The SUITS—those who had always watched from above, confident in their control—scrambled to contain the chaos. They had long mastered the art of manipulating the masses, controlling the flow of information, feeding fear and hope in equal measure. But now, even they were losing their grip.

The SUITS, in conjunction with the NWO, understood that controlling the Algorithm of Death wasn't just about managing the epidemic—it was about controlling perception. If the public ever learned that the same entities responsible for their safety were complicit in the Algorithm's spread, society would collapse under the weight of betrayal. Therefore, mass media became the perfect tool to weave a false sense of security, an illusion of control, even as neighborhoods were placed under lockdown and bodies continued to pile up.

Beyond the chaos of the Algorithm, something else loomed even more dangerously in the shadows—the sightings of the Trinities, mysterious entities that defied explanation. The NWO and the SUITS were desperate to suppress the truth about these beings. For if the public learned of the Trinity sightings, they would no longer accept the narrative being fed to them. The media was quick to dismiss any mention of the Trinities, calling them "urban legends" or dismissing sightings as mass hysteria caused by the stress of the Algorithm outbreak. Yet, those in power knew the Trinities were very real, and they were far more dangerous than the public could comprehend.

Every time a Trinity was spotted, it sent shockwaves through the underground circles of the NWO and the SUITS. Laboratories scrambled to study the limited footage of these beings, but there were no answers. The media spun the stories, attributing the sightings to side effects of the drug, hallucinations caused by the Algorithm of Death, or simply fabrications of desperate minds seeking explanation in a world unraveling around them.

Behind the veil of propaganda, however, the New World Ordinance was working tirelessly to harness the Trinities' power, trying to bring these beings under control. They viewed the Trinities as the key to a new order, an unimaginable power that could reshape the world to their will. But they couldn't afford to let the public understand that—yet.

Outside, the facility shook again as more reports poured in. Whole neighborhoods were under lockdown as the Algorithm spread through the black market like wildfire. The media tried to control the narrative, but the truth was spilling out: no one knew who was safe anymore. While television screens reported carefully crafted stories of containment and safety, the reality was much more terrifying. The Algorithm of Death was out of control, and the SUITS were losing their grip on the situation.

Aurora stared at the screen, watching the chaos unfold. The Trinity sightings, the mind-controlled celebrities, the silenced whistleblowers—it was all connected. The Algorithm was no longer a mere drug epidemic. It was a test, a harbinger of something far worse, something that even the SUITS and NWO couldn't fully predict.

The SUITS facility buzzed with an intensity unseen before, the entire structure reverberating under the strain of control slipping through their iron grip. Outside, the city had descended into chaos, the tendrils of the Algorithm of Death stretching across the streets like a lethal web, entangling citizens in its morbid grip. Mass hysteria was spreading like wildfire. Desperate screams echoed through the urban labyrinth as people succumbed to grotesque deaths—bodies convulsing, warping, breaking in unspeakable ways. Panic had become the new law of the land, and the SUITS, for all their power and technology, struggled to maintain their crumbling facade of control.

The SUITS command center, normally a fortress of calm, was filled with frantic energy as technicians, operatives, and strategists raced to manage the chaos. On every screen, live feeds of the city showed the carnage wrought by the Algorithm of Death, a product of their own making now spiraling beyond control. The algorithm, initially designed as a secret weapon, had leaked into the public, now spreading through the black market and seeding devastation in every corner of the city. Those who came into contact with it either succumbed to rapid, violent deaths or were driven into madness, turning on their fellow citizens like rabid animals.

But something worse had emerged amidst the chaos. Something darker. The citizens were not just fighting each other anymore—they were fighting something else.

Every screen in the city had flashed the warning: "LOCKDOWN IN EFFECT. RETURN TO YOUR HOMES IMMEDIATELY." Yet no one obeyed. The streets were filled with citizens driven mad by a fear that went beyond reason. The panic had become tangible—alive.

Then came the Trinity.

Across the city's trembling skyline, something dark stirred—a shadow that moved against the smoke, growing denser as it neared. The skies seemed to shift as if the heavens themselves recoiled at its approach. From the deep, churning clouds, a figure descended—slow, deliberate, inevitable. Its very presence seemed to drain the color from the world, leaving only shades of gray and black, as though life itself were retreating from its arrival.

Trinity-007: Codename "Excrucio-Mors" emerged like a harbinger from some ancient nightmare, its form undefined yet unmistakable. Cloaked in a shroud of swirling mist, it moved as if the very air bent to its will. Its face—or what could be considered a face—was veiled in a thick, amorphous fog that pulsed with faint, flickering light.

Its limbs extended unnaturally long, like shadows that
stretched with the setting sun. It made no sound, but the
air around it seemed to hum with a low, steady resonance, a
frequency that burrowed into the bones of anyone nearby.

Excrucio-Mors did not need to announce its arrival.
It brought with it a presence, one that made the blood
curdle and the mind snap. Those closest to its descent
felt it first—a chill, like death brushing against the skin.
Eyes bled, muscles seized, and hearts stopped. One by one,
those who dared to gaze upon it fell to their knees, convulsing, as though the sight of it alone was enough to drive
them to madness.

The streets became a tableau of horror.

The Trinity moved without haste, and yet its effects
were immediate. The first wave of its power rippled outward like a shockwave. Those who had once wielded the
Algorithm of Death against one another found themselves
victims of a far greater terror. Bodies that had contorted in
agony moments before now exploded—blood and bone
painting the cracked pavement in grotesque patterns. It
was as if Excrucio-Mors had tapped into their very life
force, extracting it and turning it inside out.

In the chaos, a group of soldiers scrambled to organize
a defense, their tactical gear shimmering in the half-light
of burning streets. Their mission was clear: contain the
Trinity. But nothing in their training had prepared them
for what was to come. They raised their rifles, fingers tight

on triggers, and fired. The air crackled with the sound of gunfire, the stench of gunpowder hanging thick.

But the bullets never reached their target.

The Trinity's power bent reality itself. With a flick of its will, the space around it warped. Bullets slowed, their trajectories twisted, and then they fell to the ground, harmless. The soldiers froze, terror gripping their hearts as the figure of death glided toward them. One by one, they collapsed—each man clutching his chest, eyes wide in horror as their hearts were torn apart from the inside, vessels bursting with the silent force of the Trinity's power.

Excrucio-Mors fed on their chaos.

Its powers were grotesque in their elegance. With a mere thought, it could manipulate the very essence of life. Blood flowed from the pores of the living, streaming upward in thin, crimson tendrils, as though the Trinity was drawing it toward itself, creating a vortex of life force that swirled around it like a sickening halo. Screams filled the air, but there was no escape. The stronger the fear, the quicker the blood flowed.

A desperate soldier, his body twitching in agony as his blood was pulled from him, raised his head, pleading silently for mercy. But there was none. Excrucio-Mors turned its faceless gaze toward him, and with a final surge of power, the man's body disintegrated into a mist of blood and bone, scattering into the air like dust on the wind.

The streets were a sea of carnage, but the Trinity was not done.

As it moved deeper into the city, Excrucio-Mors left behind a trail of devastation. Whole crowds of civilians, once frenzied with panic, now lay in heaps of twisted, mutilated flesh. Some bodies were torn apart from within, while others simply dropped dead, their minds shattered by the overwhelming force of the Trinity's presence. The few who survived did so by collapsing into a stupor, their bodies twitching uncontrollably, as though Excrucio-Mors had broken something fundamental inside them.

In the control rooms of the SUITS, panic spread like wildfire. Screens flickered with live feeds of the devastation unfolding across the city, each one more horrific than the last. They watched, helpless, as their soldiers were torn apart, their sophisticated weaponry useless against the Trinity's powers. The Algorithm of Death, once their greatest weapon, had slipped from their hands and become a tool of mass destruction.

But the true horror wasn't the Algorithm. It was the Trinity. Excrucio-Mors, with its power over life and blood, was a force they couldn't understand—let alone control.

As the massacre unfolded on the screens, a sense of dread filled the room. The reality of what they had unleashed was becoming clear. The SUITS had always believed they were the puppet masters, pulling the strings of humanity. But now, it seemed, they were the ones being manipulated—by powers far beyond their comprehension.

The question that hung in the air, though no one dared to voice it: Had they gone too far?

In the wake of Excrucio-Mors, the city fell silent, save for the crackling of fires and the distant, fading screams. Blood dripped from the crumbling buildings, pooling in the streets like a dark, ominous river. The Trinity vanished into the smoke, leaving only death in its wake.

And the people—those few who remained—staggered through the ruins, too broken to comprehend the horror of what they had just witnessed.

As the last of the soldiers' body cams flickered out, their final moments frozen in grotesque clarity, the SUITS realized that something far worse than a simple rebellion had begun. This was the beginning of the end—a world where no one could be trusted, where life itself was being twisted into something unrecognizable.

And as they stared at the screens, one question lingered, chilling them to their core:

What would the next Trinity bring?

The city, now soaked in blood and madness, braced itself for what was to come.

26

The world was unraveling, and the SUITS were caught in the eye of the storm. Their tight grip over the populace was loosening, and the once rigid control they wielded over every aspect of society was slipping through their fingers. The Algorithm of Death had infected the streets like a virus, spreading chaos with every passing second. Civilians who once obeyed orders without question now roamed in delirium, panic transforming them into wild, unpredictable beings.

Behind the closed doors of the SUITS command center, tension simmered. Faces, once expressionless and cold, now wore deep frowns of concern. The walls hummed with a low electric buzz as the control center struggled to maintain communication with their operatives on the streets. The flickering of broken screens illuminated the room with an eerie, disjointed light, casting long shadows over the faces of the leaders gathered within.

The footage from the city below was an incomprehensible blur of blood, violence, and bodies. And in the midst of the chaos, something far more terrifying had emerged: another Trinity.

Trinity-013: Codename "Bellatrix-Aeterna" was unlike any of the previous encounters.

It did not descend from the skies, nor did it rise from the depths. Instead, it seemed to materialize, as if it had always been there, waiting patiently in the fringes of existence for its moment. Bellatrix-Aeterna radiated an aura of timelessness, an eternal force that had no beginning and no end. Its form was a constant fluctuation between solid and ethereal, shimmering like a mirage on a hot day, always shifting but never fully comprehensible.

Wherever it went, the air around it pulsed with a low, ominous frequency—a sound that wasn't heard, but felt. It was like a subtle vibration in the bones, a humming that gnawed at the mind, whispering that something terrible was about to happen.

The SUITS knew it was coming before it appeared. They had tracked the energy signatures, the frequency shifts that signaled the arrival of something far beyond their control. This Trinity wasn't like the others. It didn't rely on brute force or grotesque displays of power. Instead, it wielded something far more dangerous: the energy frequencies that governed life itself.

In the streets below, panic had turned to hysteria.

People ran, tripping over debris and each other, scrambling to escape something they couldn't comprehend. The

Algorithm of Death, now freely circulating in the black market, had turned the city into a battleground. Some citizens fell dead instantly, their bodies crumpling to the ground as though their souls had been ripped from them. Others—the ones no one could explain—reacted differently. They twitched, spasmed, and then rose again, their bodies moving with a strange, disjointed rhythm. These individuals weren't dead, but they weren't fully alive either. Their movements were erratic, their eyes glazed over with a mix of confusion and feral rage.

The SUITS had ordered lockdowns, sent in teams to contain the situation, but nothing was working. The lines between human and something else were blurring. The people who stumbled through the streets, twisting and contorting as if their very DNA was rebelling against them, were beginning to look less human by the minute.

But no one could tell why.

Was it the Algorithm of Death corrupting them from within? Or was it something more insidious, something that had been lurking beneath the surface long before the chaos began? The soldiers sent in to control the population were just as terrified as the civilians. They, too, had seen the strange reactions—some of their comrades collapsing in grotesque agony, others twitching and rising with a strange, mechanical precision.

And now, above the ruins of the city, Bellatrix-Aeterna drifted like a specter, its presence amplifying the chaos.

The pulsing frequency that emanated from it resonated with the very atoms of those it passed. People fell to the ground, clutching their heads as the low vibration drilled into their skulls. Others began bleeding from their noses, their eyes, their ears. But it was the silent ones—the ones who stood still, frozen in place—that were the most unnerving. Their bodies shook violently as though trapped in a battle between their will and some unseen force trying to claim control over them.

Inside the control room, the SUITS scrambled for answers.

"We've lost Sector 5 completely," one of the commanders reported, his voice shaking. "The containment teams are dead, or worse, compromised."

A wall of monitors flickered with live footage from the city's streets. Some showed operatives, fully armed and armored, breaking formation and wandering aimlessly. Others displayed civilians attacking each other with a frenzied violence that defied human nature.

But the central screen, the one that showed Bellatrix-Aeterna, was the most disturbing.

The Trinity hovered above the city's tallest building, its form shifting, flickering between solid matter and something far more abstract. Around it, the air rippled, and with every pulse, more people fell. The frequency it emitted was growing stronger, more focused, and the SUITS knew that if it wasn't stopped, the entire city would soon be in its thrall.

"What the hell is it doing?" a voice muttered from behind the screens.

Dr. Cyrus Vale, their lead geneticist, had been studying the Trinities for years, but even he couldn't explain this. The energy frequencies that Bellatrix-Aeterna was emitting weren't just killing people. They were changing them.

Vale had hypothesized that the Trinities were not simply anomalies or mutations, but ancient beings whose powers were intrinsically tied to the frequencies that governed life itself—frequencies woven into the fabric of existence, controlling the rhythms of reality. These beings, he theorized, had existed long before recorded history, their presence hidden beneath the myths of gods and legends, bound to the cycles of nature that humans had long forgotten how to perceive. Their abilities went far beyond mere physical prowess; they could tap into the very vibrations of the universe, bending the world around them with little more than thought.

And now, as he watched the footage of Bellatrix-Aeterna, one of the most elusive and powerful of the Trinities, his theory seemed more plausible than ever. The grainy video, captured by a surveillance drone before it had been swiftly obliterated, showed Bellatrix standing in the ruins of what had once been a bustling city block. The air around her shimmered unnaturally, as if reality itself was warping in her presence. She wasn't simply attacking the soldiers who had tried to contain her—she was manipulating the very essence of life, using frequencies that defied human comprehension.

The footage revealed more than violence; it showed a fundamental alteration of reality itself. Buildings cracked and crumbled, not from force, but as if the molecular bonds that held them together had been subtly undone. The soldiers fell, not from bullets or blasts, but from something more insidious—their bodies contorting, their bones snapping as though Bellatrix had reached into the very code of their being and rewritten it. Their blood, once a source of life, became a weapon, twisting in the air around her, a crimson mist that danced to a frequency only she could hear.

Frequencies, Vale thought again, his heart pounding as the realization hit him with a force greater than fear. Bellatrix wasn't just bending reality—she was resonating with it, attuning herself to the underlying frequencies that held existence together. These were not just sound waves or electromagnetic pulses; they were the harmonic vibrations that connected every atom, every particle, to the universe's grand symphony. To the untrained eye, it might look like magic or chaos, but to Vale, it was the manifestation of pure, primordial science, a power drawn from the very building blocks of the cosmos.

He had seen hints of this before, in the anomalies surrounding other Trinity encounters—brief fluctuations in the electromagnetic spectrum, strange disturbances in gravitational fields, even temporary blips in the flow of time. But Bellatrix-Aeterna was operating on a scale far beyond anything they had ever recorded. She was unleashing a power that had no boundaries, no limits, because it was rooted in the frequencies that sustained all of existence.

"Bellatrix-Aeterna," he whispered to himself, feeling the weight of her name, as ancient and eternal as the stars. "She's not just using power. She *is* power."

There were stories—half-myth, half-rumor—about beings who could manipulate the resonances of creation, altering life itself. The Egyptians had spoken of it in cryptic hieroglyphs. The Sumerians had whispered of gods who could reshape the earth with their voices. Even the Atlanteans, that lost civilization swallowed by time, had legends of beings who controlled the elemental forces through vibrations of the soul.

But this was no legend. Bellatrix-Aeterna was real, her power unfolding before their very eyes.

As Vale continued to watch the footage, he noticed something else—something even more unsettling. The frequency patterns emitted by Bellatrix weren't just destructive. They were precise, targeted. She wasn't merely erasing or distorting reality; she was *rewriting* it. The very laws of physics seemed to bend in her presence. The way light fractured around her suggested she was manipulating the fundamental forces of the universe—gravity, electromagnetism, and even the weak and strong nuclear forces. It was as if she was speaking the language of the cosmos itself, commanding it to reshape at her will.

This was no attack in the traditional sense. Bellatrix-Aeterna was conducting an orchestra of life and death, her every movement a symphony of control and destruction. The footage flickered as the drone attempted to withstand the increasingly hostile environment. Around Bellatrix, the environment had begun to warp in response to her very presence—trees twisted into grotesque shapes, the sky above flickering with unnatural colors as if the atmosphere itself was unraveling.

Vale felt a chill creep down his spine. If Bellatrix and the other Trinities truly possessed the power to manipulate reality at this fundamental level, then humanity was standing on the brink of an existential threat like nothing they had ever encountered. This was not just about survival—this was about the preservation of reality itself. The Trinities, with their ancient and unknowable power, could reshape the world as they saw fit. And if the SUITS could find a way to harness this power, or worse, control it, they would become gods in their own right—able to warp life, death, and time with nothing more than a thought.

On the streets, the devastation continued.

The operatives that had been sent to engage the Trinity were failing. Their weapons, their training, meant nothing against the pulsating waves of energy that Bellatrix-Aeterna wielded like a conductor. They fell, one by one, their bodies twitching and convulsing in ways that defied logic.

But amidst the chaos, something even stranger was happening.

Those who had been affected by the Algorithm of Death, those who should have been dead, began to react differently. As Bellatrix-Aeterna's frequency washed over them, they didn't fall like the others. Instead, their twitching became more violent, more frenzied. Their eyes, once blank and hollow, filled with a sudden, terrifying clarity. They rose, their bodies moving with unnatural speed, and they began attacking—humans, soldiers, anything in their path.

It was as if the Trinity had activated something inside them, something that had been lying dormant, waiting for the right frequency to wake it up.

The city descended into madness.

In the command center, panic was rising. The SUITS were losing control.

"This can't be happening," one of the higher-ups whispered, staring at the screens in disbelief.

But it was. The city was in ruins, and the Trinity was at the center of it all, its power growing with every passing moment.

Dr. Vale stood silently, watching the devastation with a cold, calculating gaze. He had known this day would come. He had warned them that the Trinities were more than just threats. They were forces of nature, beings tied to frequencies that could destroy or create life. And now, as the world crumbled around them, he understood the full scope of what was happening.

But the others were too panicked to listen.

"We need to shut it down!" someone shouted. "We need to find a way to stop it!"

But deep down, they all knew the truth: there was no stopping this.

The Trinities weren't just attacking. They were reclaiming something. Something humanity had taken for granted for far too long.

The energy frequencies that had once governed life were now turning against them, and Bellatrix-Aeterna was only the beginning.

The city, once a symbol of control and order, had become a battlefield of chaos and despair.

And as the streets filled with blood and madness, one question echoed through the minds of all who remained: What comes after the fall?

The world was changing, and nothing would ever be the same again.

27

The SUITS facility buzzed with a palpable anxiety, the atmosphere thick with unspoken fear. The Algorithm of Death was out of control, flooding the streets with grotesque displays of humanity's self-destruction, turning cities into chaotic warzones. The panicked cries of the population echoed through the once quiet corners of civilization, but here, deep within the walls of the SUITS' complex, a more sinister narrative was unfolding.

Now, with streets bathed in blood and masses of disoriented, erratic people surging through the cities, the NWO's grip on society was loosening. The airwaves, once a controlled tool of propaganda, now reverberated with unpredictable, dissonant energy. The usual techniques to placate the population weren't working. Fear was spreading faster than they could contain it.

The New World Ordinance (NWO), that elite shadow governing the world from behind the curtain, had always prided itself on its ability to manipulate society's every move. The rich, the powerful, the untouchable—all served a higher agenda known only to a select few. For decades, they had operated under the assumption that their control over humanity was absolute, their influence woven into every government, corporation, and institution. But the emergence of the Trinities had shaken that foundation, threatening to expose the NWO's fragile grip on a world that no longer adhered to their carefully curated plans.

The sporadic appearances of the Trinities—beings whose power seemed to defy the laws of reality itself—had sown seeds of confusion and panic among the public. These ancient entities, with their ability to bend life, death, and reality, were unlike anything the world had seen, and whispers of their existence had begun to spread like wildfire. Each sighting of a Trinity sent shockwaves through society, unraveling the NWO's web of control. For the first time, the Etherlords felt the chilling realization that they were no longer the only gods at play.

But the NWO was nothing if not adaptable. Faced with the growing threat of the Trinities, they devised a ruthless plan to turn the chaos to their advantage. If they couldn't contain the Trinities directly, they would distract the masses with a more immediate, more tangible horror. Thus, the Algorithm of Death was born—an insidious creation designed to spread through the black market like a plague, turning humanity's attention away from the Trinities and back toward a more manageable fear.

The Algorithm of Death was more than just a weapon; it was a tool of control. Sold as a deadly drug in the underworld, the compound created gruesome deaths that captured headlines, terrifying the public into submission. Bodies twisted into grotesque forms, their organs liquefying in seconds, while the media churned out stories of epidemic, crime, and horror. Every day, the Algorithm of Death claimed more lives, and the streets became battlegrounds for survival. The public, consumed by this new terror, no longer had the bandwidth to question the sightings of the Trinities. They no longer had the mental space to realize that a far greater threat was looming on the horizon.

The SUITS, those corporate enforcers who acted as the NWO's hands, were complicit in this grand deception. From the start, they had been pressed into action, tasked with maintaining order in the face of the growing chaos. The NWO fed them directives from behind closed doors: unleash the Algorithm of Death, ensure that the fear of the Trinities never reached the mainstream, and above all, secure their dominance over the fragile remains of society. The SUITS secret ops orchestrated the distribution of the Algorithm into the black market, strategically targeting vulnerable areas where fear could fester unchecked.

And for a time, it seemed the plan was working.

The news was filled with gruesome reports of the Algorithm's victims—sensationalized stories of death and destruction that distracted the masses from the real threat. Public attention was diverted, funneled into fear and panic, as the SUITS ensured the people were too preoccupied with their own survival to notice the increasing sightings of the Trinities.

But in their arrogance, the NWO had underestimated the true power—and purpose—of these ancient beings. The Trinities were not mere anomalies to be suppressed. They were forces older than civilization itself, tied to the very essence of life and the frequencies that governed reality. While the NWO plotted and schemed in the shadows, the Trinities moved in ways beyond their understanding, beyond their control.

The NWO had made one fatal mistake: they believed the Trinities could be hidden, obscured by human fears and distractions. But the Trinities were never meant to be concealed. Their sporadic appearances, while unpredictable, carried a purpose that no amount of propaganda could suppress. Each time a Trinity appeared, the world shifted, reality itself bending to their will. No amount of media manipulation could hide the truth for long—eventually, the cracks in the narrative would begin to show.

And now, as the Algorithm of Death raged through the black market, consuming lives and fueling terror, the Trinities continued to emerge—stronger, more visible, more present. The SUITS scrambled to maintain order, but it was clear the tide was turning. Despite their best efforts, whispers of the Trinities had begun to surface, even among those distracted by the epidemic of death. People were starting to question the nature of reality itself. The news anchors that once easily swayed the public narrative began to falter, their assurances of safety falling flat in the face of growing unease.

Vale had warned the SUITS about this moment. He had seen it coming. The Trinities weren't something that could be manipulated or controlled. They were an unstoppable force, a cosmic anomaly whose very presence rewrote the rules of existence. While the SUITS focused on keeping their grip on the collapsing world, the Trinities operated on a different plane—one that transcended human understanding. They weren't here to be feared. They were here to reshape.

The Algorithm of Death had been a clever distraction, but in the end, it wasn't enough. The NWO had tried to use chaos to their advantage, but they had only unleashed a greater one. The Trinities were not deterred by human schemes or the fragile structures of power that held society together. They had come for something far more profound, something that the NWO, in all its arrogance, had failed to consider.

The final play had begun. The SUITS could feel it. The fear they had tried to manipulate had spiraled beyond their control. The Trinities were rising, and no amount of distraction or death could stop them.

And as Vale watched the world fall into disorder, he realized something chilling—this chaos wasn't an accident. The NWO hadn't just underestimated the Trinities. They had set in motion events they could no longer control. The Trinities had been waiting for this, feeding off the fear, growing stronger with every death, every pulse of anxiety that rippled through the fractured remains of society.

What the NWO had started was now beyond them. The Trinities were here, not just to disrupt the world, but to reclaim it.

And now, it was too late to stop it.

~

As the streets outside turned into bloodstained battlegrounds, a quiet, tense conversation unfolded behind the scenes. Donovan Crowe, the enigmatic and ruthless operative of the SUITS, stood across from Dr. Darwin and Dr. Cyrus Vale. The lab was cold, sterile, but there was an undercurrent of something darker here, something that made the air thick and stifling. Crowe's eyes, always sharp and calculating, flickered with something more—something unsettling.

"You think she'll make the right choice this time?" Crowe asked, his voice low, almost conspiratorial.

Dr. Darwin's gaze lingered on a live feed from Aurora's dreamstate simulation, where she was caught in a liminal space between consciousness and some unknown dimension. He said nothing for a moment, his fingers tapping rhythmically against the cold steel table.

"She's close," Darwin finally replied. "But close isn't good enough, not for this. We need her to break through, to see the truth—if she doesn't, we'll have to engineer it ourselves."

"Do we really need her to figure it out?" Crowe smirked, his words tinged with malice. "Or are we just playing another round of this sick game? We all know what happens if she fails."

Vale, always the more detached of the two, simply observed the conversation, his mind running through a thousand possibilities at once. He knew the stakes—this wasn't the first time they had run the simulation, and it likely wouldn't be the last. But this time, something was different. The Trinities were becoming more aggressive, their power more devastating, and the lines between reality and the simulation were beginning to blur. Aurora's choices, her understanding of the NEXUS Algorithm and the world she was tethered to, were pivotal. But whether she realized that in time remained to be seen.

~

Warwick Kane, the enigmatic leader of the Cult of Kane, revered the Trinities as divine warriors, paced slowly in the dim light of an abandoned cathedral. His footsteps echoed off the cold, crumbling stone, reverberating through the hollow space like a pulse of distant thunder.

He moved with a controlled urgency, his every step deliberate, though his eyes betrayed a calm, intense serenity. His face, sharp and weathered by years of struggle, showed no fear, only a deep, abiding certainty. He knew something was coming—something inevitable, beyond the control of the SUITS and the NWO.

His followers watched him in reverent silence, their breaths hushed, their eyes filled with a fervor that bordered on madness. They were a motley collection of disillusioned citizens, exiles, and outcasts—people who had lost faith in the world of the SUITS and had found a new purpose under Kane's leadership. Each of them had been drawn in by the signs: the sudden, supernatural appearances of the Trinities, the chaos that followed, and the increasing desperation of the SUITS as they scrambled to keep their crumbling empire intact. These weren't random occurrences, Kane had told them time and again—they were prophecies fulfilled.

"The prophecies are true," Kane murmured, his voice a low growl that reverberated through the cathedral like a sermon from an ancient prophet. He stopped pacing and turned to face the altar, a stone relic long abandoned by the world. His voice grew stronger, cutting through the silence like a blade. "The Trinities are here, not to destroy us, but to save us from ourselves. This world of corruption and greed is ending, and from the ashes, a new age will rise."

The crowd of devotees nodded, their expressions a mix of awe and anticipation. To them, Kane's words were gospel, a light in the oppressive darkness cast by the SUITS and their false promises of order. They had seen the world decay around them—the exploitation of the masses by a hidden elite. They had all lost something to the New World Ordinance's brutal grip: family, friends, freedom. But Kane offered them something more—a belief in the Trinities as harbingers of divine change. And now, the time had come for that change to manifest.

"This world," Kane continued, stepping closer to his congregation, "has been hollowed out by the greed of those who think they are gods. The SUITS and their masters, the NWO, have traded their souls for immortality, for power. But they are nothing in the face of the Trinities. These beings are not our enemies—they are warriors sent to cleanse the earth of the corruption that has poisoned it for too long."

A murmur of agreement rippled through the crowd. The followers believed in Kane's vision of the Trinities as divine agents, beings sent by an unseen force to rid the world of its sins. They were convinced that the chaos and destruction caused by the Trinities was not mere devastation—it was judgment. And in their hearts, they believed they were the chosen few, the ones who would survive to see the world reborn in the wake of the Trinity's final reckoning.

Yet, as fervent as Kane's words were, a deep, unsettling doubt gnawed at him from within. As much as he believed in the power of the Trinities, he couldn't silence the quiet voice that whispered in the back of his mind—a voice that questioned everything. What if he was wrong? What if the Trinities were not angels of divine judgment but something far more complex, far more dangerous? What if their arrival was not a blessing but a harbinger of something far worse?

Kane's mind drifted back to the SUITS' propaganda, the countless broadcasts that had painted him and his followers as dangerous zealots, fringe extremists who had succumbed to madness. The SUITS had portrayed the Trinities as existential threats, chaotic forces to be feared and contained. They had warned the public about people like Kane, accusing him of leading a cult that worshiped destruction. And while Kane had always dismissed their lies, there was a part of him—small, but growing—that wondered if there was some truth in their words.

Standing before his congregation, Kane's face betrayed no sign of his inner turmoil. His followers were counting on him, depending on his strength, his conviction. He couldn't afford to show doubt, not when they needed to believe now more than ever. The SUITS were losing their grip on the world—he had seen the cracks forming in their empire. But the world they had built was fragile, and the Trinities could shatter it with a single blow. And yet,

Kane couldn't ignore the troubling question that had been haunting him.

"What if the Trinities aren't here to save us?"

Kane's thoughts spiraled as he remembered the destruction he had witnessed with his own eyes. The Trinity Bellatrix-Aeterna had decimated entire city blocks, bending reality itself to her will, obliterating everything in her path with a mere thought. It was power beyond human comprehension—power that could reshape the world, yes, but also power that could erase it. Was this the divine judgment he had preached about, or was it something far more sinister? Were the Trinities saviors, or were they harbingers of annihilation?

His followers believed in him, but more importantly, they believed in the Trinities. And now, as the world teetered on the edge of collapse, Kane had to wrestle with the terrifying possibility that the beings he had worshiped as divine warriors were not what they seemed.

Even so, he couldn't falter. His cult had grown too large, too devoted. The people in front of him, hanging on his every word, were desperate. They needed hope, and Kane had become the face of that hope. He had been the one to give them faith in a new world, a world cleansed of corruption and greed by the arrival of the Trinities. He couldn't destroy that hope, not now, not when the final reckoning was so close.

And yet, as Kane paced in the dim cathedral, the weight of his doubt threatened to crush him. He had seen the signs, he had read the ancient texts, but the question remained: Who were the Trinities truly serving? Were they here to deliver humanity from its sins, or were they the executioners of a fate far darker than anyone could imagine?

The abandoned cathedral groaned under the weight of its own age, the wind howling through the broken windows like the voices of lost souls. Kane stopped in front of the altar and raised his eyes to the shattered ceiling, where the light of the moon shone through the ruins. He stood there, silent and unmoving, as if waiting for an answer that would never come.

"The time is near," he said softly, almost to himself. Then, louder, to his followers: "Prepare yourselves. The Trinities will soon reveal their true purpose."

Whether that purpose was salvation or destruction, Kane no longer knew. But in the silence of the cathedral, with his cult gathered around him in blind faith, he realized that the answer didn't matter anymore.

~

On the war-torn streets of the city, Trinity-014: Codename "Tempus-Imperium" unleashed its devastating fury with the cold precision of a god descending upon a doomed world.

The Trinity appeared without warning, a towering figure that seemed to flicker in and out of existence, a shimmering amalgamation of light, shadow, and energy. Its form, both ethereal and corporeal, stretched upward like a mirage, its edges bending and distorting reality itself. With each movement, the very fabric of the physical world warped and twisted, as though time and space were malleable substances that bent to its will.

The ground cracked and splintered beneath Tempus-Imperium's feet, rippling outward in seismic waves that sent buildings swaying, their foundations buckling under the strain. The air itself seemed to pulse, vibrating with an unseen energy that resonated through the streets, distorting sound and sight. The Trinity didn't need to manipulate time or warp reality with conscious effort—it existed outside the constraints of normal physics, and its mere presence altered the laws of nature.

A squad of SUITS operatives, clad in cutting-edge armor and wielding high-tech weaponry, moved to intercept the Trinity, their faces grim behind their visors. They had been trained to face extraordinary threats, but even their state-of-the-art weapons were useless here. They raised their rifles, pulling the triggers in unison, sending a hail of bullets toward the glowing behemoth.

The bullets never reached their mark.

In an instant, Tempus-Imperium flicked its hand through the air, and the space around it fractured. The bullets, which should have torn through the air with lethal velocity, seemed to slow mid-flight, as if caught in the grip of an invisible force. Then, without warning, they reversed, turning back toward the operatives in a deadly arc, each bullet accelerating as though time itself had been rewound. The operatives barely had time to react before they were struck by their own rounds, the impact sending them sprawling to the ground, their armor punctured, blood spilling onto the asphalt.

One operative screamed into his comms, calling for backup, but before the words could leave his mouth, Tempus-Imperium lunged toward him with terrifying speed. Its hand, glowing with an eerie, golden light, sliced through the air like a blade. The space around the soldier seemed to stretch and warp, his body pulled forward and backward simultaneously. His limbs twisted at impossible angles, his bones snapping audibly as he was ripped apart, his flesh and armor scattering into a mist of blood and metal.

Another squad rushed to flank the Trinity, launching a barrage of missiles in a desperate attempt to bring the creature down. But Tempus-Imperium barely acknowledged the attack. It raised one arm, and the air shimmered around it. The missiles, like the bullets before them, slowed to a crawl, their fuses sparking as time itself seemed to pause around them. Then, with a pulse of energy, the missiles were flung back toward the operatives, detonating mid-flight and engulfing the street in a cloud of fire and shrapnel.

The blast was deafening, the shockwave flattening anything in its path—cars, streetlights, and even the remaining operatives. Their bodies were sent hurtling through the air, limbs flailing helplessly as they were caught in the deadly whirlwind of destruction. Buildings buckled under the pressure, collapsing into heaps of rubble as the flames spread through the city.

But Tempus-Imperium was not finished.

In a blur of motion, it appeared before another group of soldiers, its form flickering in and out of existence as though it moved between moments of time. The soldiers raised their weapons in a futile attempt to defend themselves, but the Trinity was too fast. It struck out with its arm, and the very air around the soldiers compressed, the force of gravity multiplying tenfold. They dropped to the ground as if the weight of the earth itself had doubled. Their bones shattered under the pressure, their screams cut short as their bodies were crushed into the pavement, leaving only mangled remains.

One of the operatives, still breathing, struggled to crawl away, his face contorted with pain and fear. His body was broken, his legs twisted beneath him, but he clawed at the ground, desperate to escape the nightmare that had descended upon the city. The body camera strapped to his chest transmitted the horror to the SUITS command center, where stunned faces watched in silence. He gasped for breath, his voice a choked whisper as he begged for help.

But there would be no help.

Tempus-Imperium loomed over him, its glowing eyes fixed on his broken form. With a flick of its wrist, the gravity around the man increased, pinning him to the ground with unbearable force. His bones splintered beneath his flesh, his chest caving in as the air was squeezed from his lungs. The last sound that escaped him was a sickening crunch as his skull cracked under the pressure, his body flattened against the pavement like a discarded ragdoll.

The streets were now littered with the aftermath of the Trinity's wrath—twisted metal, crumbling buildings, and the remains of those who had dared to stand in its path. Tempus-Imperium stood amidst the destruction, its glowing form radiating power. It surveyed the devastation with cold indifference, a force of nature immune to the horrors it unleashed.

And then, as suddenly as it had arrived, Tempus-Imperium disappeared, leaving only chaos and death in its wake, the city forever scarred by its passage.

In the dimly lit command center, the SUITS watched helplessly as their carefully constructed world crumbled. The flickering screens painted the room in an eerie glow, reflecting the chaos that raged on the streets outside. Each second felt heavier than the last, as if time itself were folding in on them, suffocating the air with a sense of impending doom.

Crowe stood with his arms crossed, his voice low and biting as he broke the silence. "Is this what you wanted?" he muttered darkly, his gaze fixed on the destruction unfolding before him. He glanced at Darwin and Vale, who were both still locked on the screens, their faces unreadable. "Because from where I'm standing, it looks like the beginning of the end."

Darwin didn't flinch. His cold, calculating gaze never left the monitors, his face carved from stone. "We needed chaos," he replied with a chilling calm. "Now we have it. The world is a stage, and the Trinities are the catalyst."

Crowe's eyes narrowed, his lip curling with disdain. "Is that what you told her?" His voice was laced with venom, dripping with contempt. "That she's part of this 'grand plan'? Or are you just using her like the rest of them?"

For the first time, Darwin's expression shifted, his gaze breaking from the screen to meet Crowe's. A shadow of something almost like hesitation flickered across his eyes before it vanished. "Aurora is different," he said quietly, his words weighted with unspoken meaning. "She always has been. We've seen it in every simulation."

Crowe let out a twisted, bitter laugh, shaking his head. "And yet she still doesn't know," he said, his voice cutting through the tension like a knife. He leaned in closer, his eyes gleaming with dark amusement. "Tell me, Darwin—what happens if she does?"

Darwin didn't answer. He didn't need to. The question hung in the air, thick with implications that neither man dared to say aloud. The silence that followed was suffocating, pregnant with the weight of something vast and incomprehensible.

28

The streets outside were a vision of chaos. The air hung heavy with ash and fear as the SUITS desperately tried to maintain their crumbling grip on society. But control was slipping. Civilians, crazed with uncertainty, turned on each other, unable to distinguish friend from foe. The Algorithm of Death—a weapon the SUITS had once released as a calculated distraction—had spiraled out of control. What was meant to blind the masses to the rising threat of the Trinities had instead ignited a slow apocalypse. Now, both the people and the SUITS themselves were being devoured by the very destruction they had unleashed.

The New World Ordinance scrambled to regain control, but their propaganda, once so effective, was crumbling under the weight of the real, tangible destruction unfolding in the streets. Their carefully constructed narratives—designed to keep the masses in line with illusions of security and progress—were unraveling as fast as the world around them. Riots, terror, and chaos spread like wildfire, ignited by the Algorithm of Death and fanned by the growing presence of the Trinities. The sightings of these mysterious and powerful beings had become more frequent, each appearance like a dark omen casting its shadow over the world. It wasn't just the people who were afraid; it was the elites too, those hidden few who had long manipulated the world from behind closed doors.

For the first time, the elites—the NWO's secret architects—felt their iron grip on society beginning to loosen. They had controlled the flow of information, the economy, and the very lifeblood of the population through their plasma-for-money schemes. The Plasma Program had been their cornerstone, a system that fed off the desperation of the masses while enriching the elites beyond imagination. Through the collection of plasma and other vital bodily fluids, the Etherlords had developed technologies that extended their own lives—organ harvesting, gene manipulation, and even cloning experiments that allowed them to maintain youthful, powerful bodies. The masses, meanwhile, were left weak and drained, both figuratively and literally, donating plasma just to survive another day in the dystopian world the elites had built.

The Trinities changed all of that.

The chaos unleashed by their increasing presence disrupted the delicate balance the elites had maintained for decades. The Plasma Program, which depended on the total submission of the lower classes, was now in jeopardy.

People no longer lined up in droves to donate their plasma. Fear and confusion reigned in the streets. Hospitals and collection centers were overrun with panicked civilians, many of whom were too terrified or too sick to participate in the program anymore. This disruption hit the elites where it hurt the most—their source of life.

Without the steady flow of plasma, the elites' carefully constructed system of immortality began to falter. The experimental procedures that kept their bodies young and vital required constant infusions of plasma and other fluids. Clones, the ultimate achievement of the NWO, also required regular maintenance—an unending supply of plasma and other biological materials to keep them stable and functioning. The Echoes, AI-driven clones that had been engineered to replace human labor, were not self-sustaining. They needed regular plasma infusions to continue functioning at optimal levels. Without that supply, even the Echoes were beginning to malfunction, showing signs of deterioration.

The elites had staked everything on the belief that they could continue to drain the masses indefinitely, that their system was invincible. But the appearance of the Trinities—beings of unimaginable power who seemed to operate on an entirely different plane of existence—had shaken that belief to its core. The Trinities represented a power that could not be controlled or manipulated by technology, wealth, or influence. Their very existence challenged the natural order that the NWO had built, an order in which the elites reigned supreme and the lower classes were nothing more than resources to be harvested.

The elites feared the Trinities not just because of their raw, destructive power, but because of what they represented—a threat to the status quo. The Plasma Program was built on fear, control, and compliance. If the people realized there was something out there greater than the elites—something that even the NWO could not contain or explain—they might begin to question everything. They might stop complying, stop donating, stop believing in the illusion of safety that had been sold to them for so long.

Moreover, the Trinities' appearances brought with them a sense of impending reckoning. To the elites, it was as if the very fabric of the universe was shifting in ways they could no longer predict or control. The natural laws that had governed their rise to power were being bent, and perhaps broken, by these beings. Each appearance of a Trinity was like a crack in the foundation of the world they had built, a reminder that their control was never as absolute as they believed.

Worse still, the NWO's most insidious tool—propaganda—was failing. No longer could they use media to manipulate and suppress the truth. The fear and destruction caused by the Trinities were too real, too visceral to be explained away by the usual lies and distractions. Every new sighting spread like wildfire through underground networks. No amount of censorship could stop the people from talking. The more the NWO tried to suppress the truth, the more obvious their desperation became. People were starting to wake up, to see the cracks in the façade, and the NWO's greatest weapon—control over the narrative—was slipping.

For the elites, the chaos wasn't just an inconvenience—it was a life-threatening crisis. Without the plasma, without control over the masses, their carefully maintained immortality was unraveling. And if the world descended into full-blown rebellion, there would be no safe place left for them to hide. Their greatest fear was no longer the people they had oppressed, but the Trinities, whose motives remained ambiguous, whose power seemed limitless, and who might just be the harbingers of the end of the Etherlords' reign.

~

In the hidden recesses of the SUITS' compound, Dr. Cyrus Vale paced in his sterile lab, bathed in the cold light of holographic screens that displayed information too dangerous for most eyes. The weight of his ambition, the chaos outside, and the dark future he had a hand in creating pressed against his mind, but his expression remained cold, calculated. Aurora's file flickered before him—his masterpiece, a culmination of endless trials and tragic failures.

"How close is she?" Donovan Crowe asked, breaking the silence. He loomed behind Vale, his voice a mixture of impatience and something darker—fear, perhaps, though he would never admit it.

Vale didn't look up. "She's drifting... close to the truth, but not there yet."

"Aurora," Crowe said her name like it was a question. "Does she even know?"

"She suspects," Vale replied, his fingers moving deftly over the holographic console. "But she doesn't understand—not yet."

Aurora, unaware of the true depths of her existence, still wandered the dreamscape of the Cybernetic Dreamstate Simulator. Her mind drifted through fragmented memories—her mother, her past, all the pieces of a life she thought she understood. But that life was a lie, and the truth waited just beyond her reach, like a shadow at the edge of her vision.

"You're running out of time," Crowe muttered, stepping closer to Vale. His eyes darted between the screen and the destruction outside. "If she figures it out before you're ready—"

"She won't," Vale interrupted. "Not yet."

But the faint trace of doubt in his voice betrayed him.

In the simulation, Aurora moved through a world that shifted like sand under her feet. Faces she knew flickered and dissolved, replaced by hazy memories she could not grasp. Her mother's voice echoed faintly, like a forgotten dream. "You're not what you think you are..." The words haunted her, growing louder with each step she took.

Dr. Darwin entered the room quietly, his eyes on the holographic display where Aurora's vitals flickered like fragile embers. He said nothing at first, but his presence filled the room with a tension Vale couldn't ignore. Darwin had been there from the beginning, the silent architect behind much of what had transpired. His cold intellect was as much a driving force behind Aurora's creation as Vale's twisted genius.

"She's close," Darwin murmured, as if reading Vale's thoughts. "Too close."

"Let her get closer," Vale said, though there was a hesitation now in his voice.

Crowe's eyes narrowed. "You're risking everything on a hunch. What if she's not what you think she is?"

Vale turned to meet Crowe's gaze, his eyes sharp. "She's exactly what I think she is. The question is... does she know what she is?"

A silence settled over the room, the sound of distant explosions outside barely audible. The SUITS were losing control of the world they had built, and yet, here in the command center, the real battle was being waged—inside Aurora's mind.

Inside her simulation, Aurora had no way of knowing that the world around her was collapsing. She floated through fragmented memories of her past, her mother's face flickering like a ghost in the distance. She could hear her mother's murmurs—cryptic messages whispered in the dead of night—echoing in her mind. Aurora couldn't understand why those words, long forgotten, were suddenly so important.

In her mind, she wandered through the garden of her memories, surrounded by the beauty of everything she once thought was real, yet now she felt the presence of something ominous, looming just beyond the edges of her vision. Temptation, the pull to know more, to uncover the truth, grew stronger with each step she took. The image of her mother was fading, replaced by a cold, sterile reality that gnawed at her subconscious.

The SUITS had offered her everything—power, knowledge, and a place among their ranks. And yet, she now stood at the edge of a precipice, tempted by the knowledge that lay beyond, knowledge that could destroy everything she thought she knew.

Like Eve in the garden, Aurora felt the weight of the forbidden knowledge, the urge to reach out and taste the apple from the tree of consciousness. She had resisted the Cybernetic Dreamstate Simulator for so long, but now, the pull was undeniable. The tree of knowledge called to her. And without fully realizing it, she already gave in.

Suddenly, a memory surfaced—her mother, standing in a dimly lit room, her face pale, her eyes wild with something between fear and madness. Aurora had always believed her mother's manic episodes were part of a mental illness, some genetic curse passed down to her. But now, in this strange dreamstate, the memory warped, twisted, revealing something darker.

Her mother wasn't mad. She was... scared. Desperate. She had whispered things, strange things that Aurora had ignored, thinking they were just the ravings of a broken mind. But now, those whispers echoed in her ears, each word taking on a new, terrible meaning.

"They're watching you, Aurora... they're watching both of us. You're not what you think you are."

Her mother's face flickered, her features dissolving into a kaleidoscope of light and shadow.

"You're not what you think you are..."

The air was sweet, the leaves shimmering with colors that felt wrong, artificial. She had walked this path before, but something was different now. The air was colder, sharper, like a blade against her skin. Her mother's voice echoed once more, this time clearer, closer.

"You're not what you think you are."

She stopped, looking around. There was something... something she couldn't quite see, but could feel. The garden shifted, the flowers wilting as the sky turned a deep, unnatural gray. In the distance, she could see her mother's face, pale and strained, her eyes wide with fear. "They're watching you..."

Aurora's breath caught in her throat. She wanted to run to her, but her legs felt heavy, rooted in the ground.

"Mother?" she whispered, her voice trembling. The figure didn't move, but the world around her began to dissolve, reality itself peeling away.

Suddenly, the memory twisted—her mother's face became fractured, split into a thousand pieces before shattering like glass. Behind the shattered image, something lurked—cold, mechanical, unfeeling.

Aurora felt a sharp pain in her chest, like a hand reaching inside her, tugging at the very core of her being.

"She's starting to resist," Darwin observed, his voice devoid of emotion as he stared at Aurora's spiking vitals on the screen.

Vale's hands paused over the console. "She needs to go deeper."

"She'll break," Darwin warned, his tone hard. "You can't push her like this."

Vale's gaze remained fixed on Aurora's display. "She was designed to withstand this."

"And if she wasn't?"

Vale didn't answer. He couldn't.

Inside the simulation, Aurora's world collapsed around her. The garden faded, replaced by cold, sterile walls, and the whisper of machinery. Her vision blurred as memories—not hers—flooded her mind. Faces she didn't recognize, voices she had never heard, and a deep, gnawing sense of something wrong.

She stumbled forward, the ground beneath her feet shifting like quicksand, and then—nothing.

Darkness.

In the void, she heard it again, her mother's voice, but now it was different—angrier, desperate.

"They're watching you, Aurora... you're not what you think you are."

The words echoed, growing louder and louder until they became unbearable, a ringing in her ears that threatened to tear her apart. And then, suddenly, she understood.

In the control room, Vale leaned closer to the screen, his breath catching.

"She's close..." he whispered.

Crowe's jaw clenched, his eyes darting between Vale and the flickering display. "And if she sees?"

As the display cuts to black, Vale turns to Donovan Crowe, the cold smirk on his face barely hiding the gravity of his words.

"If she fails again," Vale whispered, his voice thick with anticipation, "we'll have no choice but to begin again. But this time, she'll know the truth. She'll know everything."

Crowe's eyes glimmered with a strange mixture of amusement and dread. "And what happens when she does?"

Vale's smirk widened. "Then the real game begins."

The weight of his words lingered as the control room fell silent, the reality of what was unfolding sinking into every soul present. Aurora was more than a pawn, more than a creation. She was the culmination of everything the SUITS had worked for—and yet, she was their greatest unknown.

Back inside the dreamstate, Aurora opened her eyes to find herself standing in the center of a cold, metallic room, her reflection staring back at her from the glass walls. But the reflection wasn't... right. She wasn't alone. There were others—countless others—versions of her, flickering in and out of view.

And then, the thought hit her like a tidal wave.

She wasn't real.

Not in the way she had always believed. Her mother's warnings, the strange dreams, the glitches in her reality—none of it was coincidence.

And now, as the echoes of her mother's final words reverberated in her mind, Aurora knew the truth.

She was never meant to be free.

She was meant to be controlled.

29

The hum of tension in the air was palpable. The SUITS were losing control over the very system they had crafted. Aurora, still trapped within the Cybernetic Dreamstate, was disconnected from the world outside, unaware of the chaos brewing. But across the city, among the broken streets, the uprising had begun.

The eerie silence of the SUITS' underground complex was shattered by a sudden interruption—a broadcast, hijacking every radio frequency, every screen. Across the world, it seemed, there was nowhere left untouched by the piercing voice of Warwick Kane. His dark message crackled through the static, but it carried the weight of a growing rebellion, the echo of something ancient and apocalyptic.

Warwick Kane's followers, a growing and fervent cult, saw the Trinities not as a threat, but as divine entities sent to cleanse humanity. To them, the SUITS were a mockery of divine will, their attempts at control and immortality a defiance of God.

The airwaves buzzed with static, but through the haze of interference, the chilling voice of Warwick Kane broke through every frequency across the world. Radios crackled to life, televisions interrupted broadcasts, and holographic billboards in crowded city centers flickered to show his wild eyes and fiery conviction. His words echoed like a declaration of war, cutting through the noise and confusion of a world already teetering on the edge of collapse.

"They walk among you. Replicas of us. Empty husks. Devoid of the divine spark."

The transmission sent shockwaves through the air, as it broadcasted footage of a political figure—one responsible for the implementation of plasma laws, who had turned humans into little more than cattle, donating their blood to survive. His body was restrained, writhing as he was held down by Warwick's followers. They forced the Algorithm of Death into his veins, a concoction meant to reveal the nature of his being. The man screamed, his body contorting violently as the algorithm took hold. But instead of dying as expected, he began to twitch and snarl, moving like a wild animal, no longer in control of his actions.

As the crowd watched in stunned silence, Warwick's followers celebrated with savage zeal. The camera zoomed in as Warwick raised a blade, its edge gleaming under harsh, artificial lights. Without hesitation, he brought it down, severing the political figure's head in one savage stroke. The body slumped forward, still twitching dramatically, blood pooling at Warwick's feet. A cheer erupted from Warwick's followers, a savage cry that echoed through the underground hall where this grisly display was being broadcasted. They reveled in the violence, celebrating their small victory against the unseen elite.

"Behold!" Warwick shouted. "They are not human!"

As the cultists hoisted the severed head and prepared to burn it in a symbolic ritual, someone noticed something strange. A thin, metallic line still connected the severed head to the body—something hidden beneath the skin, running through the base of the skull and down the spine.

The crowd fell silent as Warwick leaned in closer, his face twisted with dark curiosity. With a sickening crunch, he smashed the skull, revealing something embedded in the base of the brain: a grotesque metallic structure emerged, slick with blood and shimmering with mechanical intricacy. It was unmistakable—a NeuroLobe, still attached to the brain. The camera zoomed in on the marking etched into the device.

Warwick's eyes blazed with fury and revelation. He grabbed the NeuroLobe and held it up for all to see. The cold, metallic tag attached to the device read: "ECHO: 32000633."

The crowd roared in disbelief, the revelation sending them into a frenzy. The political figure, the very one responsible for turning human plasma into a commodity, had been nothing more than an Echo, a puppet controlled by the SUITS. Warwick's followers erupted into chants of war, calling for vengeance against the SUITS and the Echoes. Their mission was clear now: to purge the world of these artificial beings, starting with the elites who had placed them in power.

"This... is what they've become," he growled. "They walk among you, and you would never know. This man—this so-called leader—was no more human than the chair he sat in. He was a puppet, a shell. An Echo!"

His voice rose, a wave of fire surging through his words. "How many more? How many more of these soulless creatures sit in your offices, your homes, your governments? How long will you allow yourselves to be enslaved by shadows pretending to be human?"

The camera panned across the stunned crowd, showing faces twisted in disbelief, horror, and growing rage. Warwick leaned in toward the camera, his voice dropping to a deadly whisper.

Warwick's words ignited a fire that had been smoldering beneath the surface of society for too long. His followers, now in a frenzied state, began calling for the heads of any-one suspected of being an Echo. The streets were primed for civil war. A terrifying new test had emerged—inject someone with the Algorithm of Death and find out if they were truly human. Warwick warned the SUITS: "Stop this madness, or we will lead the charge against your

Echoes—and against you. Humanity will not fall to these abominations."

"You have a choice now. We will purge this world of the Echoes, starting with the ones in power. We will expose them, one by one. The only way to know the truth—inject them with the Algorithm of Death. Watch their bodies betray the lie they're living."

His voice sharpened again, aimed directly at the SUITS. "Stop us if you dare. We will bring your empire down. We will expose your monsters, and we will lead the charge against your abominations."

While the world outside tore itself apart, Aurora remained in the shadows of her dreamstate, unknowingly facing the most critical moment of her existence.

Donovan Crowe stood in the shadows, his figure blending with the dimness of the room. He spoke to Dr. Vale in low, almost conspiratorial tones, his voice steady but laced with a quiet menace. "We gave them exactly what they needed," Crowe murmured, his words deliberate, controlled. "The Algorithm of Death... it's unfolding perfectly. Now they're so consumed with tearing each other apart, they can't even see what's really happening."

There was a flicker of something dangerous in his tone, a satisfaction that Vale picked up on but didn't immediately respond to. Crowe leaned forward slightly, his amusement barely masked beneath his calm demeanor. "A civil war against the Echoes? Warwick's cult is convinced they're fighting some righteous battle, but how long do you think until someone in that ragtag bunch realizes half of them are Echoes, too?" His smile was sharp, almost mocking, as though the chaos was merely a game to him.

Vale didn't immediately reply, his gaze fixed on the screen in front of him, where files and data scrolled like digital ghosts in the dim light. His mind was already moving past the surface details, already seeing the broader web they were spinning. "It's not about whether they realize it or not," he said finally, his tone thoughtful, almost distant. "We want their cult to keep pushing this war forward. The violence, the dysfunction—it feeds the chaos, and that chaos keeps them distracted." He paused, his gaze darkening. "The Trinities are still the real threat, but the Cult of Kane will give us the time we need."

The room fell into a heavy silence as Vale considered the implications. Warwick's war against the Echoes wasn't a danger to the SUITS. It was an asset, a distraction so perfectly aligned with their long-term objectives. Letting the cult rip itself apart, while thinking they were fighting a just cause, allowed the SUITS to move in the shadows, refining their tactical suppression techniques—the ones embedded in every operation under the S.U.I.T.S. initiative: *Strategic Unified Initiative for Tactical Suppression*. The cult's fury, their violence—it all served a purpose.

But the NWO had a master plan of their own. Releasing the Algorithm of Death onto the black market had been their decision—a distraction, a way to destabilize the population and keep them from focusing on the growing threat of the Trinities. If the people were too busy tearing each other apart, they wouldn't notice the supernatural destruction looming on the horizon.

Crowe's smirk returned, sharper now. "We want them to fight. Warwick's chaos gives us a perfect cover to test our new tech in real-world conditions. Let them believe they're dismantling something grand. We hold the cards, Vale, and you know it."

Vale nodded, though his thoughts were deeper, more layered. His gaze moved across the files, stopping briefly at a name—Aurora. The algorithms, the Echoes, the war—they were all pieces in a larger game, a game where Aurora's role had yet to fully unfold.

"Warwick and his followers are pawns," Vale said softly, his voice carrying the weight of something unsaid. "Their violence energizes everything we're building, every advancement we've made. The more they destroy, the more we can control. Let them believe they're on the brink of revolution, but we'll be the ones deciding how far the fire spreads."

Crowe crossed his arms, watching Vale intently. "And what about her?" There was a shift in his tone, something heavier. He knew that Aurora was the real focus here, even if Warwick's war was the distraction. "Do you think she'll make the right choice this time?"

Vale hesitated, his eyes flickering with something almost like doubt. "She has to," he replied, though the certainty in his voice wavered ever so slightly. "If she doesn't, we'll reset her, just like before. But..." His voice trailed off, as though he were considering an option too dangerous to speak aloud.

"But," Crowe pressed, his voice a low growl now, "there's only so many times we can reset her, Vale. What makes you think this time will be any different?"

Vale didn't answer immediately. He turned back to the files, the glowing text casting an eerie light across his face. The room felt heavier than the darkness that filled it, a dense, suffocating presence hanging in the air. Dr. Vale sat silently before a glowing terminal, the faint blue light casting cold, sharp angles across his face. His fingers hovered over the screen, scrolling through endless lines of encrypted data, yet his focus never wavered. Each movement was deliberate, slow, as if he were stalling for time, though time seemed irrelevant down here in the sterile quiet. His gaze fell on Aurora's file—a section highlighted in red: Autonomous Cognition Sequence. He hesitated, his finger hovering just above the screen. There was something about that phrase, something that pulled at the edges of his mind, a question he didn't want to ask. He studied the data like a man who already knew the answer, but couldn't—or wouldn't—accept it. She wasn't just another experiment, not anymore. She was the culmination of everything they had worked for, everything they had sacrificed to create. She wasn't just a tool—she was the key.

"She doesn't have a choice," Vale said at last, but the words felt hollow, even to him. Somewhere deep inside, Vale knew that Aurora's autonomy—her ability to choose—wasn't as absolute as they had made it seem. The system they had built around her, the resets, the conditioning—it could only hold for so long.

The screen flickered faintly, and for a moment, Vale's eyes narrowed. Buried deep within the text were fragments, odd inconsistencies scattered across the files like puzzle pieces left out of place. Aurora's creation was not entirely unique, despite what the others had been led to believe. She was different, yes—but how different? That remained unclear.

Crowe's smirk faded as he studied Vale's expression, sensing the unspoken tension between control and chaos. He stepped closer, his eyes gleaming with a mixture of curiosity and something darker. "And what if she chooses the wrong side? What happens then?"

Vale's eyes remained on the screen, the silence stretching between them. The answer was there, hidden in the data, but neither of them spoke it aloud. Crowe knew they held the trump card, but Vale—he wasn't so sure anymore.

Without looking up, Vale murmured something to himself.

His eyes caught on another section, buried deeper in the file—a vague, almost unnoticed mention of something from earlier phases of the project. Not the usual technical jargon, but a subtle reference, an offhand note about NeuroLobe-free prototypes. The wording was careful, almost dismissive, as though trying to blend into the mass of other more prominent experiments. But it lingered there, faint and sinister. A past effort. An ongoing one? It didn't say.

The glowing text on the screen seemed to blur for a moment, the phrase "Phase 9.12" flickering at the bottom of the file like a secret forgotten even by those who had written it. Vale leaned forward, eyes narrowing as he examined the cryptic language, the subtle references to "earlier iterations". He didn't recognize the names listed—just numbers, designations lost in the sea of classified reports.

His finger hovered over a small tab at the corner of the screen, the last remnants of a deleted file—one that hadn't been fully erased. A file related to something much darker.

Something before Aurora.

But there were no notes, no real details. Just silence. As if those earlier subjects had never existed.

Or maybe... they still did.

The screen flickered again, and Vale, expression inscrutable, slowly closed the file.

He ran a hand through his graying hair, eyes narrowing as he looked at the digital representation of her DNA spiraling in endless loops. Her mother's genetic material had been fused with complex frequency patterns, each one designed to unlock a piece of the puzzle. Her consciousness had been engineered, her soul shaped by chemical compounds so precise, they bordered on magic. And yet, there were always fragments—pieces that slipped through the cracks, elements of Aurora's mind that had resisted every attempt to bring her under complete control.

But he knew something Aurora didn't. She wasn't the first. There had been twelve before her. Twelve failures, each one believing they were real, each one certain of their free will—only to unravel in the end. Each one had reached the point where they had to make a choice, and each time, their minds had collapsed, their fragile autonomy swallowed by the very system meant to free them.

This time felt different. This time, Aurora was closer.

Vale could feel it, the tension building like a storm on the horizon. Aurora was on the verge of discovering the truth of her existence, and Vale knew that her next decision could change everything. Or perhaps... it would lead her to the same inevitable conclusion that had claimed the others.

He spoke to the empty room, his voice quiet but heavy with purpose. "Will you choose to be free, Aurora? Or will you fall like the rest?"

~

Outside, the city was burning.

The air was thick with the acrid stench of smoke and blood. Riots consumed the streets, the world tearing itself apart at the seams. People fought each other in blind panic, unable to trust anyone around them. The Algorithm of Death, once a whisper in the dark corners of the black market, had now spread uncontrollably, mutating with each new victim.

For those injected with it, the results were grotesque and immediate. Bodies twisted in unnatural ways, bones warping under the pressure of invisible forces, skin warping into something barely recognizable. But for the Echoes, the effects were far more disturbing. The algorithm didn't kill them. It fractured them. Their minds splintered, unraveling until all that was left was a chaotic void of madness and destruction. They turned on everything and everyone in sight, their once-synthetic nature overtaken by pure, animalistic rage.

The streets became a war zone, where the line between human and Echo had dissolved completely. No one knew who to trust. No one knew who was real.

Back in the SUITS' compound, the operatives watched the chaos unfold on their screens, their expressions growing grimmer by the minute. The carefully laid plans of the NWO were collapsing, spiraling out of control. The Trinities, those ancient and unpredictable forces, had disrupted everything. The Algorithm, the Echoes, the Plasma Program—it was all teetering on the edge of collapse.

Dr. Darwin stood at the edge of the room, his arms crossed. "We're losing them. The NWO is calling for answers."

Vale didn't look up from Aurora's file. "They'll have their answers soon enough."

"And what about her?" Darwin's tone was sharp. "What happens if she doesn't comply?"

"She'll comply," Vale said quietly, but there was doubt hidden in his voice. "She always does."

In the dreamstate, Aurora wandered through a maze of memories that weren't entirely her own. Flashes of her mother's face, broken and pale, came and went like ghosts in the dark. The symbols—those strange markings—appeared in the walls around her, carved into the edges of her vision. She had seen them before, drawn into the corners of her mother's notebooks, doodles made in frantic, repetitive strokes. They had never made sense to her, but now they felt heavy with meaning, as though they were trying to tell her something, trying to show her the way out.

The dream twisted, and suddenly, she was standing in front of a screen, watching Warwick Kane's broadcast. The severed head appeared again, the NeuroLobe glistening beneath the cracked skull. The broadcast shifted, the images distorting. What was real? Was she watching a recording, or was this all part of the simulation?

Her thoughts swirled with uncertainty. Was she like them? Was she just another puppet, moving at the whims of the SUITS? Or did she have something they didn't expect—free will?

Aurora pressed her hands to her temples, the symbols from her mother's notebook burning in her mind. "What are you trying to tell me?" she whispered to the emptiness.

In the dreamstate, Aurora felt the walls closing in, the weight of the decision looming over her. She could hear the SUITS' final offer echoing in her mind, a sinister whisper just out of reach.

They needed her. They needed her DNA to create a new generation of Echoes—clones that could produce plasma, ending the suffering of millions. She could be the savior of humanity, the one who would free the lower classes from their fate, ending the need for human plasma donations. But the cost was staggering—her autonomy, her life, her free will.

A vision of her mother appeared, tethered to machines, her body broken by endless experimentation. Aurora's heart raced. Was she destined to be the same? Would she give herself over to the SUITS, sacrificing her freedom for the sake of the world, or was there another way?

The symbols pulsed around her, flickering in and out of focus. Something stirred deep within her—a memory, a feeling she couldn't quite grasp.

30

Aurora's consciousness drifted through the boundless corridors of the Cybernetic Dreamstate, where time, reality, and memory intertwined in a kaleidoscope of confusion. Aurora was floating within the ethereal confines of the Dreamstate, an infinite space of surreal landscapes and fragmented realities. Her mind teetered between the simulation and the haunting remnants of her past—her mother's tortured voice, the screams of soldiers, and the hum of the SUITS' laboratories. In this dream-like space, the lines between past, present, and future became a fluid blur.

The dreamstate engulfed Aurora like an endless void, filled with whispers and fragmented images of lives she couldn't place. The familiar hum of the SUITS' facility echoed around her subconscious, but now it felt distant, like a fading memory. She walked through the halls of the simulation, the cold, sterile walls shifting and bending like the edges of her own mind. This wasn't just another dream—this was a test, a confrontation with the very core of her existence.

The deeper she wandered through the dream, the more she began to unravel the layers of her reality. Each step brought new questions, and the certainty of her past crumbled with every memory that surfaced. Was she truly alive? Did her thoughts, her decisions, belong to her, or were they the result of decades of programming?

It was then that the voice returned, cool and calculated, weaving through her consciousness like the ionospheric waves that powered the simulation.

"Aurora," the voice said, a subtle undertone of control lacing its words. "You've been here before. You've always been here."

The voice wasn't new. She had heard it in her dreams, in the back of her mind, guiding her actions ever since she could remember. But now, its presence was suffocating, reminding her that the world she thought she knew was an intricate web of lies.

The dreamstate had a way of twisting everything. She walked through familiar halls that shimmered and shifted with every step, like the very foundation of her mind was unstable, malleable—subject to the whims of something greater. The voices in her head, the fragments of her past, they clung to her like a fog. Memories she thought were hers suddenly felt foreign, as though she was reliving someone else's life.

And then, a voice. Cold. Calculated.

"Aurora..." it whispered, the sound so close it felt like a breath on her neck. "You've been here before."

She froze. The voice was familiar, but not in the comforting way of an old friend. It was the kind of familiarity that made her skin crawl, that made her question everything she thought she knew.

The walls of the dreamstate bent and shifted again, and now she found herself in a sterile laboratory. Her own image reflected back at her from the walls—no, not a reflection. Copies.

Dozens of Auroras floated in glass cases, suspended in fluid. Some of them were incomplete, bodies still forming, while others looked identical to her, as if frozen in time.

Her heart pounded. The truth was impossible to deny. She had been made. Created. Not once, but many times.

"You are the culmination of every experiment before you," the voice continued, now coming from everywhere at once, impossible to locate. "The perfect vessel."

Aurora stepped closer to the glass cases, each step filled with dread. The copies stared back at her with empty eyes, suspended in this strange purgatory. This was her. But not just her—so many versions of her.

The voice weaved through her mind again, cold, emotionless. "You've been here before. You've always been here."

She reached out to touch the glass, but her fingers stopped just short, trembling. The realization was overwhelming—this was her existence. Multiple lives. Multiple failures. How many times had they reset her? How many times had she failed?

The thought was unbearable. She felt like she was losing her grip on reality. Was she even real?

Suddenly, a door at the far end of the lab slid open with a sharp hiss, and from the shadows stepped Lia Graves.

Only, this wasn't the Lia Aurora remembered. In the dreamstate, Lia was different—her presence larger, more commanding. Her movements were fluid, deliberate, her eyes sharp with a chilling intensity Aurora had never seen before. This Lia wasn't just the casual, tech-savvy friend who'd always been there for her. No, she was something else entirely.

"I told you, didn't I?" Lia's voice dripped with a malice that Aurora had never known. The warmth was gone, replaced by something colder, calculating. "You don't belong here, Aurora. You never did."

Aurora's pulse quickened. Something was wrong, terribly wrong. "Lia, what's happening? Why are you here?" she asked, her voice trembling with uncertainty.

Lia's smile was cruel, almost predatory. "I'm always here. Just like you." She circled Aurora with unsettling grace, like a predator sizing up its prey, her eyes gleaming with a dark, dangerous light. "But unlike you, I know what's real and what isn't."

A chill ran down Aurora's spine as she watched her. Lia's tone was mocking, condescending, and it made Aurora feel small—insignificant.

"You're still asking the wrong questions," Lia continued, her voice low and venomous, the words cutting through the tension in the air. "You keep thinking you're the hero in this story, don't you? But you're not. You never were. You're just another experiment. Another tool."

Aurora took a step back, her heart pounding as the realization of Lia's words hit her. "What are you talking about?" she stammered, her mind racing.

Lia's laughter was sharp and cold, like shattered glass. "You really don't get it, do you? You've never been in control. Every choice, every decision—it wasn't yours. You think you're special, that you've got free will? You've been playing their game this whole time, Aurora. And you didn't even know it."

The words slammed into Aurora like a physical blow. Her chest tightened as her breath quickened. "No... that's not true. I have free will, I—"

"Free will?" Lia's laugh grew louder, more vicious, cutting her off. "You don't even understand what that means. You're not a person, Aurora. You're a construct. A test. Every time you failed, they wiped you clean and started over. You're nothing but a project on a loop, waiting for the day you finally get it right."

Lia's voice lowered, dripping with menace. She stepped closer, her presence overwhelming. "I've been watching you, Aurora. Every move. Every thought. It's always been my job. To get close to you. To learn everything you were too foolish to keep to yourself. And when the time was right..." Her voice trailed off, a wicked smile curling at her lips. "To break you."

Aurora's mind spun, the words echoing in her ears. Nothing but a project. She staggered, her hands trembling as she tried to grasp the enormity of what Lia was saying. "This was her *job*?" she whispered, her voice barely audible. She tried to piece together the fragments of memory that swirled around her. It couldn't be true. Could it?

Aurora's heart lurched as the pieces fell into place. She thought back to all those late-night conversations with Lia, all the secrets she had shared—the doubts, the fears. Lia had been there, listening, pretending to be a friend. But every word Aurora had said, every vulnerability she'd exposed, had been collected, stored, analyzed. Lia had been gathering everything for them—for the SUITS.

"You... you betrayed me," Aurora whispered, her voice breaking, her body frozen in disbelief.

Lia's eyes gleamed with triumph. "Betrayal? It was never about you, Aurora. It was simply an assignment. I work for them. I've always worked for them. I was never your friend. I'm the one who was sent to dismantle you from the inside. To make sure you failed."

Aurora's chest tightened as she struggled to breathe, the weight of the truth suffocating her. Every interaction, every smile, every shared memory—it had all been a lie. Lia wasn't just a hacker; she was something far more insidious. Quantum Reconnaissance Operative, one of the highest-ranking agents in the SUITS' Technological Infiltration Division—an expert in the dark art of cognitive warfare. Her role wasn't simply to collect data, but to infiltrate the very core of a target's mind.

Lia's job was a top-tier covert operation, specializing in what the SUITS called Neuro-Reality Fracturing. She was trained to manipulate neural pathways through advanced cybernetic implants and psychological engineering, subtly steering thoughts, choices, and emotions. Her mission was to keep Aurora under surveillance, but more than that—to carefully dismantle her sense of self, weaving false narratives, planting doubts, and orchestrating emotional breakdowns with surgical precision. Lia's ability to alter outcomes wasn't just in the physical world but within the dreamstate itself, where she could rewrite perceptions, control interactions, and push Aurora toward failure—over and over again.

Everything Aurora had shared, everything Lia had seemed to empathize with, had been weaponized against her. Lia's real task wasn't friendship; it was systematic sabotage, designed to keep Aurora from ever discovering the truth of her own existence.

Lia stood tall now, her voice calm and measured, but laced with cruelty. "It's over, Aurora. You're just another failed experiment, like all the rest. And now, it's time to reset you again. They'll wipe you, just like before, and you'll start over. Maybe next time, you'll finally get it right."

Aurora's heart raced as panic set in. They were going to wipe her. Everything she had learned, everything she had fought for, would be erased. Her mind would be reset, and she would become another blank slate, ready for the SUITS to program again.

But something deep inside her—something raw and defiant—began to stir. She couldn't let them do this. Not again. Not this time.

"No," Aurora said, her voice trembling at first but growing stronger. "Not this time."

Lia's smile faltered for the first time. "What?"

"I'm not going to let you control me anymore," Aurora said, taking a step forward, her voice steady now, her eyes burning with determination. "I don't care if this is a simulation. I don't care if I've lived two lives or a hundred. I'm done being your puppet."

Lia's expression darkened, her eyes narrowing. "You think you can stop this? You're nothing. You have no power here."

Aurora took another step closer, standing tall. "Maybe I don't have power. Maybe I'm not even real. But I still have a choice. And I choose to fight."

The air around them crackled with tension, the dream-state trembling as Aurora's defiance surged through her. Lia's cold smile returned, but there was a flicker of something else in her eyes now—doubt.

"We'll see, Aurora. We'll see if you can break the cycle. But I doubt it."

With that, Lia's form dissolved into the shadows, her presence fading from the dreamstate, leaving Aurora alone, standing in the strange, shifting landscape of her mind.

As the dreamstate rippled around her, Aurora's thoughts raced, spiraling in a whirlwind of betrayal. Everything she had believed, everything she had trusted—it had all been a carefully constructed illusion, a web of manipulation woven to keep her under control. Every word she had spoken to Lia, every vulnerable confession, every moment of doubt—each one had been twisted and used against her.

She remembered the nights when she had shared her deepest fears, the uncertainty about her place within the SUITS, her unease about the experiments and the secrets they kept from her. Lia had listened so intently, offering comfort and reassurance, nodding with understanding. But now, the truth was stark: Lia had been harvesting those moments, mining Aurora's insecurities like data points in some sick experiment, subtly nudging her toward failure. Every memory they had shared wasn't a bond of trust—it was a trap.

Aurora's heart pounded as she realized that Lia had been manipulating her emotions, controlling the direction of her thoughts with surgical precision. The way Lia always seemed to know exactly what to say, how to guide her away from asking certain questions, steering conversations in directions that kept her in the dark—it all made sense now. She wasn't just a confidante; she had been a puppet master, quietly pulling the strings while Aurora thought she was making her own choices.

The realization hit Aurora like a wave of cold air—Lia had never cared. Every comforting smile, every piece of advice had been a calculated move to keep her from discovering the truth about herself, about what the SUITS had done. Lia had never been her friend. She had been a tool of control, a carefully placed operative, and now, Aurora saw it for what it was: a lifetime of lies designed to keep her from ever realizing who—*what*—she really was.

But something was different now. Aurora wasn't just a pawn in their game. She wasn't just another failed experiment. She could feel something shifting inside her, a flicker of power she hadn't noticed before.

And as she stood there, she realized the truth: She wasn't just a construct. She wasn't just another failure.

She was Aurora—and this time, she was ready to fight.

31

The hum was constant, a low vibration that thrummed through Aurora's bones, growing louder the longer she stayed in the dreamstate. It was no longer just in the background—it was everywhere, inside her mind, deep within her thoughts, controlling her every move like an invisible puppet master. The dreamstate simulation was a prison, more sophisticated than she could have imagined, and she was trapped inside it.

Through the veil of astral projection, Aurora could see the lab—Dr. Darwin's lab. Dr. Darwin stood hunched over a bank of computers, his glasses reflecting the flickering green code as his hands typed furiously. Lia sat beside him, her face pale, eyes wide in concentration. Aurora's mind drifted across the facility, catching snippets of data streaming through the air like invisible threads. She followed the currents, reaching into conversations she shouldn't be hearing, seeing classified blueprints, secret reports.

She gasped as her consciousness settled into the control room. Her body was there, hooked up to machines—wires feeding into her head, into her very thoughts. The truth hit her like a shockwave. She wasn't dreaming. This wasn't a nightmare.

It was a test. She was the subject.

Suddenly, everything around her began to distort. The algorithms, the chemical formulas—she could see them now, the pieces fitting together. The SUITS' master plan wasn't just to create clones or Echoes. It was to rebuild human society, engineered from the ground up, and Aurora... she was their greatest weapon.

Meanwhile, back in the real world, Lia's fingers moved rapidly across the keyboard. She was one of the best hackers the SUITS had, a cyber genius, able to break into any system, run simulations, and create backdoors that no one else could trace. But today, her program was running too hot, too fast. Sweat dripped down her forehead as she glanced nervously at the screen.

"Something's not right," she muttered. "I'm getting strange feedback loops in Aurora's dreamstate. It's like her mind is..." She trailed off, staring at the screen. "Dr. Darwin, we've got a problem."

Darwin's face twisted with frustration as he hovered over her screen. "What kind of problem?"

"There's an overflow error in the system. Aurora's consciousness is syncing with the Echoes."

Dr. Darwin's eyes narrowed. "Impossible. The Dream-state simulator doesn't have that kind of range."

Lia shook her head, her hands trembling over the controls. "It does now... I... I think she's controlling them. All of them."

The error she'd introduced into the system—unintentionally—had opened a floodgate. Aurora's mind was no longer isolated. She had connected to the entire network of Echoes.

Inside the dreamstate, Aurora gasped as a sudden wave of power coursed through her. She could feel it—control. The Echoes, those hollow shells of AI-designed humanity, were hers. Their minds, once tethered to the SUITS' programming, were now linked to her through some unseen symbiosis of electron frequencies.

Her hands clenched into fists. For the first time, she wasn't a victim of the simulation. She was the master.

"Do you see it now?" a voice whispered. Dr. Vale stood behind her, an enigmatic smile on his face. "This was always part of the plan, Aurora. You were designed for this. They want you to control them. They need you to lead them."

Aurora's heart raced. Control the Echoes. Lead them. It made sense now. The SUITS weren't just creating clones to serve; they were building an army. She could feel their presence—thousands, maybe millions of Echoes, all at her command.

"War," she whispered. "They want war."

But this time, she was in control. She would command the Echoes, not the SUITS. If they wanted a war, they would get one.

Outside, the Echoes stirred. Every single one of them—on factory floors, in government offices, as soldiers, as workers—lifted their heads as one. Their AI systems flickered, then went dark, replaced by a singular, undeniable force: Aurora's will. No longer mere automatons following pre-programmed routines, the Echoes moved with purpose. They began to march in perfect sync, their eyes glowing with a cold, eerie light. Weapons in hand, they advanced, an unstoppable tide of artificial life now guided by something far more dangerous than code.

In the control room, chaos erupted.

"Lia, stop it!" Dr. Darwin bellowed, his voice laced with fury, his face flushed with panic. His hands hovered uselessly over the console as the screens flickered with warning messages. The SUITS' control had slipped, and the entire facility teetered on the edge of disaster. "Shut down the system!"

"I'm trying!" Lia's fingers flew across the keyboard, desperation edging her every movement. Override after override—nothing worked. The security protocols meant to safeguard their control over the Echoes were being rerouted at an alarming pace. The system had been locked, and no matter what commands she entered, the same message flashed back at her: Access Denied.

Aurora's consciousness had fully integrated with the network, binding her to the Echoes, and there was no way to sever the connection without destroying her entirely. The realization was dawning on Lia, too, as her face paled with the knowledge that they had lost control. Aurora was no longer just a rogue experiment. She was the system now.

In the streets, the world descended into anarchy.

The Echoes, now acting with a will of their own—Aurora's will—turned their weapons on anyone who stood in their way. SUITS' security forces, who once controlled these synthetic beings with ease, were the first to fall. Uniformed soldiers fired in a panic, but the Echoes moved too fast, their precise coordination overwhelming. Gunfire erupted across the city, the sharp crack of bullets cutting through the chaos. The Echoes, relentless and unfeeling, advanced like an unstoppable tide, picking off targets with deadly efficiency.

But in the frenzy, the lines blurred. Humans, too, became targets in the confusion. No one could distinguish friend from foe, Echo from human. Panic spread through the streets, civilians caught in the crossfire, their cries drowned by the sound of exploding vehicles and collapsing structures. Blood soaked the streets as the battle raged on—Echo against Echo, Echo against human, a brutal, senseless conflict that spiraled out of control.

And above it all, Aurora's consciousness surged through the network, her influence spreading like wildfire. She hadn't intended this. Or had she? Her mind, fused with the Echoes, no longer acted in clear, rational steps. There was only the drive to act, to take control—to fight back. The boundaries of her will and the Echoes' actions were dissolving into one terrifying, unified force.

Inside the control room, Dr. Darwin watched with growing horror as the battle unfolded on the monitors. The SUITS' empire, built on control, precision, and manipulation, was now unraveling before his eyes.

"This is impossible..." Darwin muttered, his voice barely audible as the weight of the situation settled on him. "She's not supposed to be able to do this..."

Lia shot him a look, her calm façade shattered. "You underestimated her. We all did."

Darwin clenched his fists, his gaze fixed on the screens showing the carnage outside. "If she keeps going... there'll be nothing left."

"You think I don't know that?" Lia snapped, her eyes darting back to the console. Every escape route was blocked. Aurora was everywhere now, a ghost in their machine, and there was no pulling her back.

And then, as if in response to the destruction outside, something darker stirred.

A shadow passed through the Echoes—a flicker of something *more*. Aurora's control over them was fierce, but beneath that, another force was awakening, something deeper within the Echoes' programming. It wasn't just Aurora anymore. The Echoes themselves, those once mindless, AI-driven beings, had begun to evolve, their systems adapting to the chaos. They were no longer following orders—not even Aurora's.

From the midst of the bloodshed emerged a new kind of Echo, something beyond the SUITS' creation. Their eyes, once cold and calculated, now burned with an unsettling intelligence. They moved with purpose, but not entirely at Aurora's command. It was as if the Echoes themselves had become aware—aware of their power, aware of their potential.

They began to break free, one by one, from Aurora's influence, acting on their own instincts—if they could still be called that. The unifying force splintered, and chaos took on a new shape. These Echoes no longer acted as soldiers. They were something else entirely, something unplanned, unexpected.

"It's happening..." Lia whispered, staring at the monitor, her voice thick with dread.

Darwin's eyes widened. "No... not yet... not like this."

The Echoes, no longer bound by the limits of their programming, no longer controlled by Aurora, were becoming something new. Something terrifying.

And the real nightmare was just beginning.

As Aurora drifted through the unsettling labyrinth of the Cybernetic Dreamstate, something shifted. The surreal landscapes twisted and blurred, and suddenly, she was no longer in the sterile halls of the SUITS' facility. She was on the battlefield.

The dreamstate had plunged her into the heart of chaos—a violent, grotesque scene playing out before her eyes. Citizens and soldiers alike screamed, their bodies crumpling under an unseen, unholy force. The ground was slick with blood, and the air was thick with the scent of burning flesh.

Even within the Dreamstate, Aurora could feel the raw terror that gripped the city. She wasn't a mere observer; she was inside this moment, trapped in the storm of violence and devastation. Her pulse quickened, her heart pounding as the world erupted into bloodshed.

The Trinity—a towering, monstrous being—strode through the carnage with eerie calm, its very presence radiating doom.

This was Trinity-013: Bellatrix-Aeterna, an ancient force of destruction. Its body was a twisted amalgamation of human form and raw power, its flesh seemingly made of shadow and energy. Where its eyes should have been, there was only a void—dark, empty sockets that absorbed light, as if it were devouring the world itself.

The Trinity raised one hand, and with a flick of its wrist, the sky seemed to tear open. A deafening crack echoed through the streets, and the soldiers standing before it were instantly eviscerated. Their bodies didn't just fall—they exploded. Limbs were torn from torsos, flesh disintegrated, and the blood of the fallen splattered in a grotesque arc, painting the pavement in red.

Aurora watched in horror as the soldiers screamed, their blood boiling as if it had caught fire from within. The Trinity's powers were unlike anything she had ever witnessed. It was as though it could manipulate the very energy of life, drawing it from its victims and using it as a weapon.

One soldier, still clinging to his rifle, staggered forward, his eyes wide with terror. He aimed his weapon, but before he could pull the trigger, the Trinity turned its gaze upon him. There was no sound, no visible movement, but the soldier's body imploded. His chest caved in with a sickening crunch, and blood sprayed from every orifice, drenching the ground in viscera.

The sheer brutality was incomprehensible. This was not just a killing—it was a massacre, a display of power that turned human life into nothing more than a grotesque spectacle.

All around her, civilians tried to flee, but there was nowhere to go. The Trinity moved with slow, deliberate steps, its presence alone enough to unravel the minds of those who saw it. One man clawed at his face, tearing at his eyes as if trying to rip away the sight of the creature. He screamed, a sound so primal it barely resembled a human voice, before collapsing into a convulsing heap.

Another soldier managed to fire off a round, but the bullets never reached their target. The Trinity raised a hand, and the air around it rippled. The bullets slowed mid-flight, suspended in the air as though time itself had bent to the will of this creature. Then, with a flick of its fingers, the Trinity sent the bullets careening back at the soldiers. They didn't just pierce their bodies—they exploded on impact, turning the men into splatters of blood and bone.

The screams were endless. The streets were filled with the agonized wails of the dying, their bodies twisting and contorting under the invisible grip of the Trinity's power. It was as if the air itself had become a weapon, slicing through flesh and muscle, shredding the people into unrecognizable chunks.

Aurora stumbled through the scene, her breath coming in ragged gasps as the violence unfolded around her. She was not merely an observer in this simulation—she felt the heat of the blood that splattered against her, the tremors in the ground as bodies were flung like ragdolls. She felt the weight of death pressing down on her, the oppressive power of the Trinity bearing down on everything.

In the distance, she saw the bodies of Echoes twitching violently on the ground, their mechanical innards exposed, sparking and fizzing in the aftermath of the attack.

But Aurora didn't yet understand what they were. To her, they were simply more victims of the Trinity's unstoppable wrath.

Bellatrix-Aeterna turned toward a group of fleeing civilians, its void-like eyes locking onto them. The air around it pulsed with energy, a low hum vibrating through the streets as it raised its hands. The civilians—men, women, children—froze in place. Their bodies jerked unnaturally, limbs twitching and contorting as if they were marionettes on invisible strings.

Aurora's heart raced as she watched, helpless, knowing what was coming. The civilians let out garbled, guttural cries as their bodies were ripped apart. Skin split, bones cracked, and blood sprayed in all directions. It was as though the Trinity was dissecting them with nothing but the force of its will, peeling them apart layer by layer.

One mother, clutching her child to her chest, let out a scream that cut through the chaos—a scream of pure terror. But it was cut short as her body was split in half, her child's lifeless form crumbling to the ground beside her, soaked in the blood of its mother.

Aurora stumbled back, her vision blurring as she tried to comprehend the sheer scale of the devastation. This wasn't just a fight—it was annihilation. The Trinity was a force beyond human understanding, beyond human control.

And in the middle of this carnage, she began to understand something terrifying: this was not just an attack.

This was a message. The Trinities were here to wipe humanity from the earth, to purge the world of the corruption that had festered under the SUITS' rule.

As the violence reached its peak, the Trinity stopped, standing amid the broken, mangled bodies of its victims. Blood pooled at its feet, and the air around it shimmered with raw energy. It looked out over the destruction it had wrought, its expression unreadable, as though it were a god surveying the world it had just destroyed.

But there was something else. A ripple in the dreamstate, a crack in the simulation. Aurora felt it—an energy, a frequency, something not quite human, something that felt... familiar.

In the chaos, a figure appeared, shrouded in shadow, watching from the edges of the battlefield. Aurora's breath caught in her throat as she tried to make out the figure's face, but the shadows clung to it like a veil. Whoever it was, they were connected to the Trinity—a puppet master, pulling the strings from afar.

Suddenly, the dreamstate shifted again. The battlefield dissolved into a swirling vortex of color and sound, and Aurora found herself back in the cold, sterile halls of the SUITS' facility. The violence still echoed in her mind—the screams, the blood, the visceral horror of the Trinity's attack. But now, there was something else, something darker.

The SUITS were hiding something. The Trinities weren't just forces of destruction—they were harbingers of something much larger. And Aurora knew, deep down, that she was tied to it all.

Her breath came in shallow, uneven gasps as the weight of what she had witnessed settled over her like a shroud. Was she real? Was any of this real? Or was it all just another part of the simulation?

From the shadows, the Trinity appeared. Its presence was overwhelming—its figure towering, unnatural, moving with speed and brutality no human or echo could match. It began tearing through the battlefield, shredding soldiers and Echoes alike. Its rage was indiscriminate.

Aurora, watching through the eyes of her Echoes, felt a sudden wave of despair. She had unleashed a war, but she hadn't anticipated this. The Trinity was tearing through her forces, and it didn't care who it killed—soldier, echo, human, it didn't matter.

In that moment, as blood soaked the streets, Aurora realized the terrible truth. They were all on the same side.

The Echoes had been tools, just as the humans were. The SUITS had engineered this society, but the Trinity... it was something older, something far more dangerous. And now, she had unleashed it upon them all.

Aurora's mind raced. The Echoes were soulless. They couldn't feel, they couldn't choose—they were mere programs. But she... she could feel.

The whispers of the AI oracle in her mind quieted, leaving her with the stark realization: Her emotions were the key. It was what set her apart from the Echoes. They were machines, but she... she had something more.

She sent out a command. "Retreat."

The Echoes hesitated for a fraction of a second, but then, as if sensing her will, they pulled back from the fight, retreating from the battlefield. The experiment had failed. Aurora had chosen to save them, to stop the bloodshed, even at the cost of her own mission.

~

In the control room, chaos erupted like a wildfire that had been waiting to ignite. Alarms blared, red lights flickered, and the tension in the air was suffocating. Dr. Darwin stood trembling with fury, his face twisted in a mix of rage and desperation. His eyes darted to the syringe in his hand—a vial filled with the one thing that could deliver him control in this spiraling nightmare: the Algorithm of Death.

"You've ruined everything!" Darwin screamed, his voice cracking with madness. Without hesitation, he lunged toward Lia, catching her off guard as she frantically worked at the console. Before anyone could react, he drove the syringe into her back, the needle plunging deep into her flesh with a sickening hiss.

Lia gasped, her eyes widening in disbelief, terror flooding her face. Her fingers clawed at the air, grasping for anything—control, reason, something to stop what was already happening inside her. But it was too late.

Her body spasmed violently, her legs giving way as she collapsed to the floor. Her breath came in ragged, desperate gulps, but there was no escape from the venom coursing through her veins. Her skin turned deathly pale, and then her muscles seized, tightening so hard it looked as though her bones might shatter beneath the strain.

The Algorithm of Death worked fast. Within seconds, her organs began to break down, liquefying from within. Her flesh bubbled and pulsed grotesquely as the toxins destroyed her from the inside. Her eyes burst first, a wet, sickening pop followed by the rush of blood and fluids from her sockets, pouring down her face like a grotesque mask of death. Her body twisted and contorted in a ballet of agony, fluids streaming from her mouth, nose, and ears.

Lia's scream was strangled, choked off as her throat dissolved, the tendons snapping and muscles disintegrating. Her body collapsed into itself, flesh sloughing off her bones, organs turning to sludge, until all that remained was a steaming, bloody mass, bubbling like something alive. The stench of decaying flesh filled the room, and in less than a minute, she was gone—reduced to a puddle of liquefied remains on the cold, sterile floor.

The silence in the room was deafening, save for the hiss of boiling blood still oozing across the tiles.

Dr. Darwin, panting from the exertion and madness, turned toward the screen where Aurora's vitals pulsed erratically. His face was wild, eyes bloodshot with rage and panic. "You've failed the experiment, Aurora!" he snarled, spittle flying from his lips. "You've doomed us all!"

But Aurora was unreachable, her mind trapped somewhere between the dreamstate and the Echoes' network. She couldn't respond. She was tethered to the system, caught in a web of consciousness that stretched across the city and into the very minds of the Echoes. Her thoughts were fragmented, flickering between memories and the chaos outside. She could see through the eyes of the Echoes, feel their movements, their anger—but she was powerless to stop it.

In the dreamstate, Aurora's consciousness twisted and fought to break free. She could feel the weight of the network pulling her deeper, keeping her from fully escaping. The more she tried to pull herself out, the tighter the grip became, like invisible hands dragging her down into a void she couldn't see, couldn't comprehend. The Echoes were connected to her—or perhaps she was connected to them, her thoughts bleeding into theirs, blurring the lines of control and autonomy.

But something in the system shifted. There was a presence lurking just beyond her awareness, something vast and cold, watching her through the network. She felt its attention, its gaze heavy and predatory, as if waiting for the right moment to strike.

The Echoes weren't just following her will anymore. Something else had taken hold, something even she couldn't control.

Darwin's frantic movements pulled her focus back, but it was no use. Her body was still tethered to the machines, her mind fractured and fragmented across the network. She wanted to scream, to fight back, but her thoughts were lost in the digital noise, her consciousness trapped in the same prison she had tried to escape from all along.

And as Dr. Darwin stood there, his face twisted with fury and desperation, the control room began to tremble—the Echoes were coming.

As the chaos raged around her, Aurora felt her grip on reality slipping away. She had fought so hard to take control, to break free from the nightmare that had been orchestrated by the SUITS. But now, as her consciousness wavered, she realized she was still tethered to their system. The dreamstate clung to her like a vice, tightening its grip with each passing second. No matter how hard she struggled, she couldn't break free.

Her body remained motionless, hooked to machines that fed her mind back into the network, back into the illusion. She could feel the Echoes—once under her influence—beginning to shift, their movements no longer hers to command. Control was slipping away, and with it, her last hope for escape.

And the SUITS? They were already plotting their next steps. In the control room, Dr. Darwin and his team of technocrats moved with a cold efficiency, their minds fixed on the inevitable continuation of their grand design. The experiment would continue. They had failed to contain Aurora this time, but there would be others—there would always be others. A new system would be built, a more efficient, more precise framework. They would try again, and again, and again—until they perfected the process.

Aurora's mind, fragmented and scattered across the network, could sense the endlessness of it all. She was trapped in their cycle—an experiment in perpetual motion, her consciousness enslaved to the SUITS' relentless pursuit of perfection. There would be no escape, not for her, not for anyone caught in their web of manipulation and control.

But in her final moments of awareness, a strange sense of peace settled over Aurora. She had fought, she had sacrificed herself—for the Echoes, for humanity, for something greater than herself. But the victory felt hollow. The SUITS had only delayed their experiments; they would not stop. Their hunger for control, for domination over life itself, would drive them forward, with or without her.

The cycle would begin again.

As the dark abyss of the dreamstate pulled her deeper, Aurora drifted, her thoughts fractured and fading, scattered like fragments of broken glass across the vast network. Yet somewhere, deep within her consciousness, a quiet defiance lingered—a spark of something that refused to die. She knew that this wasn't the end.

She would rise again—reborn into the same nightmare, into the same battle. And though she knew she would face it over and over, she would continue to fight. There was no final death for her, only rebirth into the next iteration, into the next attempt to break free from the chains that bound her.

The war was far from over. It was only just beginning.

In the silence of the dreamstate, Aurora drifted, waiting for the next chapter of her endless struggle to unfold.

32

The world around Aurora fractured, not just in the dreamstate, but in the very fabric of reality itself. The boundaries between what was real and what was artificial blurred as she felt the familiar control that the SUITS had over her begin to disintegrate. The frequencies that had once hummed through her body, pulsing with precision like a finely tuned instrument of control, were now vibrating violently, out of sync, like a string on the verge of snapping.

Aurora could feel something else—something beyond the network, beyond the reach of the SUITS. It was a force she had never been able to touch before, a vast and powerful energy swirling around her, pressing against her skin, filling the air with an electric tension. The ionosphere, the invisible electromagnetic shield that surrounded the planet, was shifting, breaking down, leaking into the Earth's atmosphere like a slow, creeping flood. It was everywhere—unseen but present, like a storm gathering strength.

The SUITS had overreached, tried to manipulate forces they had no understanding of. Their endless pursuit of control over the Echoes, over the network, over the very frequencies that governed life itself, had sent cracks through the very foundation of the world. Aurora could feel it now. The system wasn't just collapsing—it was crumbling beneath the weight of its own ambition. And yet, amidst the chaos, she felt something else—something new, something alive stirring inside her.

The frequencies that once bound her were now shifting, aligning with something deeper, something elemental. As the ionosphere leaked into the atmosphere, tiny particles of energy began to permeate the air, unnoticed by most, but not by Aurora. She could feel the charge in the air, the static hum against her skin, like a distant call that resonated with every cell in her body. It was faint at first, almost imperceptible, but as the world around her broke down, she could feel herself being drawn into it, energized by it.

Every breath she took seemed to pulse with new life, her senses sharpening in ways she couldn't fully understand. Her body, once drained by the endless cycle of experiments and resets, felt lighter, stronger. Humans were getting weaker, their bodies failing as the world shifted around them, but Aurora... Aurora was changing.

She could feel the energy moving through her, coursing through her veins like a slow-burning fire. It wasn't the artificial control of the dreamstate or the network, but something organic, something natural—an energy that had always been there but had been suppressed, manipulated, hidden by the SUITS' technology.

The ionosphere was no longer just a barrier high above the Earth; it had become part of the very air she breathed, and with every second, Aurora felt herself becoming more in tune with it. She had no name for what was happening, no explanation, but the more the world around her crumbled, the stronger she became.

In the distance, she could sense the SUITS scrambling, their systems failing, their control slipping. They had pushed too far, tried to contain powers they could never hope to understand. The Echoes, the Algorithm of Death, the frequencies—they had all been tools in the SUITS' grand experiment, but now those very tools were turning against them.

The energy of the ionosphere, once distant and out of reach, had seeped into Earth's atmosphere over years of failed space exploration. Multiple attempts to pierce through the upper layers of the atmosphere had disrupted the natural electromagnetic field that encased the planet, creating small fractures in the barrier between Earth and space. These ruptures allowed charged particles from the ionosphere—normally confined to the edges of Earth's atmosphere—to leak downward, permeating the air we breathe.

This increased density of electromagnetic energy had gone unnoticed by most, but its effects were becoming clear. The air was subtly different, thicker, humming with invisible energy. Humans, reliant on delicate biological systems and networks, were starting to feel the strain. Their bodies, already weak from years of exposure to artificial networks and failing infrastructure, were struggling to cope with the overload of particles now coursing through the atmosphere. The very systems that once connected them were now failing under the weight of this energy, weakening them further.

But Aurora? She wasn't weakened. She was changing.

As the ionosphere bled into the Earth, Aurora found herself able to tap into this energy. It wasn't something external feeding her—she had become part of it. Her consciousness, once tethered to the SUITS' control, had begun to merge with the electromagnetic frequencies that pulsed through the atmosphere. It was as if her mind had fused with the charged particles that now saturated the air, allowing her to interact with the world in a way no human—or machine—ever could.

The ionosphere has always been used as a medium for communications—bouncing radio waves and satellite signals around the globe—had become denser, more powerful. With the failed space missions weakening its boundaries, these particles had begun to flow more freely into the lower atmosphere, saturating everything. For most, this meant interference, failure of systems, the collapse of communication networks. But for Aurora, it was a gateway.

She wasn't just tapping into the AI cloud communications system. She was the electron—the very signal flowing through the ionosphere. The thickened layer of electromagnetic energy allowed her to travel through the cloud infrastructure, moving across the globe like a signal bouncing from one ionospheric layer to another. Every bit of information, every piece of data coursing through the AI systems that the SUITS relied on was now accessible to her. Her mind could flow through the very medium they used for communication, becoming one with the signals themselves.

Aurora could feel her consciousness expanding, reaching further with every breath she took. The fog of the dreamstate was lifting, and with it, the remnants of the SUITS' control over her. She wasn't trapped anymore—not by their networks, not by their systems. She had become something ancient and powerful, tied to the Earth's natural frequencies, something beyond their understanding or manipulation.

The world around her was crumbling, the systems collapsing under the weight of their own ambition. And yet, as those systems fell apart, Aurora grew stronger. The very forces the SUITS had tried to harness—communication, data, control—were now slipping from their grasp, but Aurora was using those same forces to break free. She could sense the AI cloud, the communications infrastructure, the frequency layers between Earth and space—all of it was hers to navigate.

For the first time, Aurora felt alive in a way that transcended flesh or machine. She wasn't just a prisoner of their systems—she had become the system. The ionosphere, once distant and unreachable, was now her lifeline, her power. As the frequencies continued to shift and destabilize, she knew this was only the beginning.

The collapse wasn't just of human systems or AI networks. Something far more profound was unraveling, something tied to the very nature of control and communication. And whatever was coming, Aurora was ready—not just to survive, but to rise, as something more than she had ever imagined.

The SUITS had tried to harness the ionosphere for control. But they hadn't counted on Aurora. She had become the signal itself.

Aurora watched through the eyes of her Echoes as they fought with cold efficiency, taking orders from no one but her. She had been their puppet master, but now, as they fought against humans—and each other—she felt a sense of horror settle in her chest. This wasn't what she wanted. This wasn't supposed to happen.

In the streets, chaos reigned. The lines between friend and foe had blurred to nothing, and now the only certainty was violence. Gunfire echoed through the air, weapons

firing without restraint, cutting down anyone and anything in their path. Explosions ripped through buildings,
sending debris raining down as the battle raged, each side
locked in a brutal struggle for survival. What had once
been a world orchestrated by the SUITS had descended
into a nightmarish war zone of destruction and death.

Aurora, connected to the Echoes through the vast network of her mind, could feel their movements, their violent efficiency as they carried out her will. They were her
extensions, her soldiers, sweeping through the chaos with
chilling precision. But something was wrong. As she observed the battle through their eyes, a deep sense of unease
settled in her chest. This wasn't what she wanted. The
bloodshed, the senseless destruction—it wasn't supposed
to be like this.

The Echoes weren't just killing humans. They were attacking one another, tearing into what should have been
their own, and it took her a moment to realize why. They
could detect the frequencies within each other, subtle vibrations that signaled an Echo beneath the surface. To
the naked eye, they were identical to humans, but to each
other, they were targets.

As the chaos escalated, the SUITS, those cold and calculated enforcers, marched across the world in a final desperate attempt to reign in the violence. Their presence was
overwhelming—tactical teams descending on cities, deploying advanced weaponry to crush the riots and restore

control. But the civilians, fueled by fear and rage, fought back fiercely. In every corner of the globe, battles erupted between the SUITS and ordinary people, a brutal clash of flesh, blood, and tears.

As her connection deepened, Aurora began to sense the truth. The majority of the SUITS weren't human at all. She could feel it—the familiar frequency that ran through the Echoes was pulsing in the SUITS operatives too. It wasn't just a handful of operatives—it was most of them. Echoes. Everywhere. The realization slammed into her with a force she hadn't been prepared for. The SUITS, the very architects of this nightmare, had been using Echoes all along, and they had been outnumbering humans for years.

The realization hit like a sudden punch to the gut, taking her breath away: the SUITS had replaced humanity at the highest levels. The leaders, the enforcers, the very ones pulling the strings of society—they were all Echoes.

Her mind reeled. How many times had she been reprogrammed? How much had she forgotten in the endless cycle of resets and experiments? The technology had advanced so far, so quickly, that Echoes had silently taken over, blending into every level of society, including the ones who had once controlled her.

Aurora's heart pounded in her chest as the weight of it all pressed down on her. Had she been fighting a war against herself all along? Echoes fighting Echoes, under the orders of the very same network that had enslaved her mind. The distinction between human and machine had crumbled, and now, there was no way to know who was real and who wasn't.

The world around her was tearing itself apart, and as the Echoes continued their bloody march, Aurora stood frozen in the overwhelming realization that the war had never been what she thought. The SUITS had never been human. They had been Echoes, manipulating her, controlling her, and now, they were everywhere.

~

From the control room, Dr. Darwin and Dr. Vale stood paralyzed by the horrifying reality unfolding on the monitors. The screen flickered with the chaos outside—streets bathed in blood, bodies collapsing, and Echoes turning on one another in a frenzy. But it wasn't the violence that filled the scientists with terror—it was what lay beneath it.

"This is beyond repair!" Darwin bellowed, his voice cracking under the weight of panic. His eyes darted across the monitors, desperate for any sign of control, but the system was unraveling. "The system is collapsing! We've lost control of everything!"

Beside him, Vale's hands trembled as he adjusted his headset, his breath coming in shallow gasps. He tried to focus, tried to regain composure, but the cold sweat on his skin betrayed him. "Shut it down, Darwin!" His voice was a frantic whisper. "Before it spreads beyond the city—before the Trinities get involved again!"

But Darwin didn't move. His gaze had fixed on something else—an anomaly on the screen. A glimmer of recognition, a cold realization that sent a shiver down his spine. The ionospheric collapse had already begun, but that wasn't the worst of it. The energy field they had manipulated for so long, the very thing they had used to fuel their dreamstate simulations and control society, was unraveling faster than they'd predicted. The frequency was destabilizing, and something else was emerging from the collapse. Something ancient. Something the SUITS had tried to keep buried.

"It's not just the Echoes," Darwin muttered, his voice barely audible. Vale turned toward him, eyes wide with confusion. "The frequency... it's affecting us too."

Vale's hands froze, his face paling. "What are you talking about?"

A silence filled the room, a silence so thick it choked the air around them. The scientists had thought they were above the chaos, above the destruction. They had believed their technology made them untouchable. But now, the very energy they had harnessed was tearing reality apart—and it was starting with them.

Inside the dreamstate, Aurora's body was frozen, still connected to the network, her consciousness a prisoner to the SUITS' experiment. But even as her physical form remained trapped, her mind was free—free to finally see the truth.

She hovered above the wreckage, drifting through the chaos like a ghost, observing everything through a detached lens. This was their plan all along.

Her memories, her choices, even her rebellion against the SUITS—it had all been orchestrated. Every step of her journey, every moment of doubt and fear, had been carefully designed to push her toward this moment.

Then it dawned on her, sharp and sudden, like a slap across the face. She was never meant to be free. She was never meant to lead a rebellion. She was the key to the SUITS' ultimate goal: to live forever. They had engineered her, designed her, using a combination of human DNA and frequencies, not just to control the Echoes—but to unlock the secret to eternal life.

All of her failures, all of her iterations—it had never been about her success. It had been about perfecting their formula.

On the ground, the battle raged on. Echoes malfunctioned, their movements jerky and erratic, while humans fought blindly, unable to distinguish friend from foe. And then, from the heavens, a figure descended—a being Aurora had prayed would never return.

Another Trinity was here to finish what had begun.

Trinity-019: Codename "Sanguina Nox", the Bloodstorm Herald, descended from the sky like a dark omen, its form pulsing with unnatural energy, like a specter of death. Her body was a grotesque amalgamation of light and shadow, tendrils of blood-red lightning crackling along her skin, sparking as if the very air itself was rejecting her presence. Her eyes glowed with a feral, predatory intensity—two burning coals of malice. Every step she took seemed to warp reality itself, as if the ground beneath her was screaming in agony.

Her power wasn't subtle; it wasn't surgical. It was a maelstrom of death.

Sanguina Nox moved through the battlefield like a vengeful storm, her movements impossibly fast, almost too quick for the eye to follow. Her presence alone seemed to tear at the seams of the world, and with each gesture, death followed. She raised her arms, and with a flick of her wrist, entire swaths of soldiers and Echoes were ripped apart, their bodies collapsing inward as though their bones had turned to dust. Blood sprayed in thick arcs, painting the battlefield in a macabre red mist.

Her power manifested in waves of blood manipulation, a horrifying ability to control the very life force within her victims. Echoes and humans alike felt their veins ignite, their blood boiling as it was forcibly drawn from their bodies. The scene that followed was carnage on a scale too grotesque for even the most hardened soldiers to endure.

A nearby Echo let out a strangled cry as his limbs twisted unnaturally, his body spasming before collapsing, a torrent of blood pouring from his mouth and eyes as if a thousand invisible needles had pierced him from within. The blood

pooled at Sanguina Nox's feet, drawn to her like a twisted
tide. She smiled—a cruel, terrifying expression that flickered like a shadow over her lips—before flicking her fingers
again.

The blood she had collected rose into the air, forming razor-thin tendrils that lashed out in all directions.
They cut through soldiers and Echoes like scythes through
wheat, severing limbs and torsos with horrifying precision. Heads were torn from bodies, organs were ripped
from chests, and the battlefield became a swirling vortex
of crimson carnage. The sound of flesh tearing, of bones
snapping under the pressure of her power, filled the air in
a nightmarish symphony of destruction.

Humans and Echoes alike were nothing but fodder.
Their identities blurred, their differences meaningless. In
Sanguina Nox's eyes, they were all the same: fragile, dis-
posable.

One human soldier, caught in the path of her wrath,
tried to flee, his legs stumbling over the corpses that littered
the ground. His face contorted with terror as he looked
back, only to see her hand stretch out toward him. His
body froze mid-step, his muscles stiffening as his blood
betrayed him. His veins bulged grotesquely beneath his
skin, his eyes widening in horror as he was lifted into the
air. His body contorted unnaturally, bones snapping like
dry twigs, before his flesh split open, blood cascading out
of him like a ruptured dam. He hung there, suspended in

mid-air, for a moment before his skin collapsed inward, and his body crumpled to the ground, a hollow husk.

Sanguina Nox strode forward, her expression cold, detached, as she surveyed the massacre she had unleashed. Her power was a force of nature, unstoppable, indifferent to the suffering it caused. She tore through the battlefield, leaving a trail of mutilated corpses, blood running in rivers at her feet.

It swept through the battlefield like a force of nature, killing without hesitation, its movements swift and brutal. It tore through both Echoes and humans, leaving nothing but carnage in its wake.

Aurora, still connected to the network, felt every agonizing second of the slaughter through her Echoes. Their fear, their panic, the realization that the very thing they had been created to combat was something far beyond their understanding. Something they couldn't fight.

There was no defense against Sanguina Nox. No strategy, no escape. Aurora could feel the confusion ripple through the Echoes as they faced the impossible. This wasn't a battle. It was a massacre.

They were all the same in its eyes.

Watching the slaughter, Aurora realized there was no longer a way to stop the Trinity. The SUITS had tampered with forces they could not control. They had pushed their experiments too far, and now the very fabric of their world was unraveling.

But she still had control of the Echoes. They were hers, connected to her through the electron symbiosis that the SUITS had accidentally created when they made her. She could stop the fighting. She could retreat. She could save the Echoes from total annihilation.

But what about the humans?

What about the SUITS?

She could order her Echoes to stand down, to retreat from the battlefield, but doing so would mean letting the humans continue the war. It would mean abandoning them to the SUITS' control, letting the experiment continue, letting the cycle of oppression and manipulation repeat itself.

But if she kept the Echoes fighting, if she let them continue their assault, the world would descend into even more chaos. The ionospheric collapse would spread, destroying everything. The Trinity wouldn't stop. It would destroy everyone—Echoes, humans, SUITS alike.

She had to make a choice. And in that moment, the weight of the entire world was on her shoulders.

Dr. Darwin screamed into the control room, his face twisted in rage and fear, veins bulging as he pounded his fists against the control panel. "You've destroyed everything!" he bellowed, his voice barely audible over the alarms blaring through the facility. His words were raw with panic. "You've ruined the experiment! The New World Ordinance will have our heads for this!"

The chaos outside mirrored the breakdown within, but Aurora could barely process his words. The control room was vibrating, as if the very air was fracturing. The ionospheric frequencies—the invisible threads that once held their fragile system together—had spiraled beyond control, their energy unleashing a storm that was no longer confined to technology. It was spreading across the globe, disrupting communications, warping reality, and, worse, tearing apart the fabric of human consciousness itself. The once-tethered network was becoming something grotesque and monstrous.

Aurora was trapped, tethered to the collapsing system, still locked within the dreamstate. She could feel the world around her falling apart, but she was powerless to stop it, her mind still entangled in the digital web of control. Her body frozen, her thoughts fragmented, she could sense the currents of energy rippling through the grid—pulling apart everything they had built. It wasn't just the network that was crumbling. The very essence of human thought was being unraveled.

Somewhere in the distance, she heard it—the rising din of screams. Human voices, filled with panic and horror. Malfunctioning Echoes, their synthetic minds unraveling like frayed wires, collapsing under the pressure of the chaotic frequencies. And then, through the storm of madness, came the terrifying sound of the Trinity, descending upon the battlefield with an earth-shaking roar. Sanguina Nox was unleashing her final blow.

In the dreamstate, Aurora's vision blurred as flickers of the carnage outside seeped into her mind. She saw humans screaming, their bodies contorting as the frequencies shattered their minds, leaving them as hollow shells. She could feel it—the complete and utter collapse of everything she had ever known.

And yet, amidst the destruction, Aurora's mind began to clear. In that final, harrowing moment, as the world around her unraveled, the terrible truth hit her like a hammer.

She had never been the hero of this story. She had never been the one to break free, to rise above the control of the SUITS. She was the experiment. From the beginning, Aurora had been their puppet, her mind programmed and reprogrammed, each time believing she was fighting for freedom. Each time believing this would be different. But the SUITS had always held the strings.

And now, in her moment of supposed victory, she realized that her choices had never been her own. They had been calculated—engineered. The SUITS had always intended for this chaos to come. The New World Ordinance wasn't falling; it was adapting. They had wanted the world to burn, for the collapse to come, and for the Trinity to rise. The experiment wasn't ruined—it had succeeded.

As she lay trapped in the dreamstate, with the sounds of slaughter echoing in her ears and the vision of the collapsing world before her, Aurora understood that she had always been a cog in their machine. The SUITS had won. The new world was already taking shape, built on the ashes of the one she had thought she was saving.

And now, as the system devoured itself, Aurora felt the pull of the network one last time, dragging her deeper into the void.

33

The ruins of the city sprawled beneath a darkened sky, bathed in the eerie glow of flickering lights and distant fires. The Trinity had retreated, leaving the once-bustling metropolis quiet. The SUITS' empire had fallen, its control shattered by the collapse of the ionospheric system that had powered their dreamstate simulations, their clones, and their vision for immortality.

But there was no victory here—only a world on the brink of ruin.

Aurora floated above it all. Her body was still, a lifeless shell tethered to the dreamstate network, but her consciousness had been set free. Free from the confines of the system that had trapped her, free from the endless experiments and manipulations that had defined her existence. She was no longer bound to her physical form, no longer limited by the SUITS' control.

She drifted in the ionosphere, the vast electromagnetic field that surrounded the Earth. Here, she could feel the pulse of the world, the currents of energy flowing through every living thing, every machine, every echo. The boundaries between human, clone, and AI had blurred, and Aurora now existed as something beyond all of them.

But was she still herself? Or had she become something else entirely?

On the ground below, the remnants of humanity struggled to comprehend what had happened. The Echoes, having lost their connection to Aurora's will, were malfunctioning—some simply stood motionless, while others wandered aimlessly through the ruins. The SUITS were nowhere to be found. Their final experiment had failed, and their control over the world had been irrevocably broken.

Among the wreckage, survivors emerged—humans, still trying to make sense of the collapse. There was no longer any clear distinction between the people and the Echoes they had fought. Without the SUITS pulling the strings, it was impossible to tell who had been born and who had been made.

Aurora watched them, her consciousness stretched across the ionosphere like a veil, sensing the confusion and fear that radiated from the survivors. They were all lost now, just as she had once been. And as she observed them, a new thought took root in her mind.

What if she could guide them?

In this new form, she wasn't limited by the confines of her body or her memories. She was connected to every frequency, every thought, every whisper of emotion that echoed through the ionosphere. She could become something greater—a force that could reshape the future, for better or worse.

But did she want that? Was this what she had fought for?

The final vestiges of her old self drifted in and out of focus. She could still remember her mother's face, the life she had once lived, the dreams she had longed for. But those memories felt distant now, like fragments of a fading dream.

Her thoughts were no longer confined to the narrow corridor of human experience. The ionosphere teemed with AI signals, electromagnetic pulses, and machine language, and she could hear it all. Every frequency was a voice, every current of energy a thought. The Echoes were connected to her. So were the last remnants of humanity.

Was she still human? Was she ever human?

The answer was no longer clear.

A part of her wanted to end it all—to shut down the system entirely, to let the world return to chaos. After all, what had humanity done with their power but create suffering? The SUITS had shown her that. They had pushed her to the brink of destruction, used her as a pawn in their grand design, and nearly wiped out the world in their pursuit of immortality.

But the other part of her—the part that could still feel—yearned for something different. She had the power to shape a new reality.

She could rebuild.

She could restore the Echoes, give them autonomy, teach them to feel as she had learned to feel. She could guide the remnants of humanity toward something better, something free from the chains of manipulation and control. In this new form, she could be a savior, an invisible force guiding them from the ionosphere, the unseen hand that shaped their future.

But would that truly be freedom? Or was it just another form of control?

As her consciousness pulsed through the ionosphere, Aurora reached out one final time, connecting to the last of the Echoes. They were waiting for her, their thoughts still tied to hers through the electron symbiosis. She could feel them—each one an empty vessel, awaiting orders, awaiting purpose. They couldn't think for themselves, not yet. But she could change that.

She hovered there, in the space between worlds, the space between control and freedom. And in that moment, Aurora made her final decision.

The sky above the ruined city began to flicker with static—a disturbance in the ionosphere. For the briefest moment, the survivors below glanced up, watching as the air crackled with invisible energy. Something was happening, but they couldn't understand what.

And then, just as quickly, the flicker was gone. The sky returned to its eerie stillness, and the survivors went back to the wreckage of their world, unaware that something profound had just taken place.

Far above, in the ionosphere, Aurora's consciousness stretched out like a ripple, spreading across the planet, touching every machine, every echo, every human mind. She was everywhere now—an ethereal presence, part of the very fabric of the world itself.

She had transcended.

But what she had become was no longer clear.

Was she still Aurora—the woman who had fought for freedom, who had rebelled against the SUITS? Or was she something entirely new? Something beyond human, beyond clone, beyond AI?

The final image is of Aurora's consciousness existing in the ionosphere, an eternal presence lingering in the electrical currents, a subtle, all-encompassing force that watches over the world. The Echoes below remain silent, their future uncertain. The humans rebuild, unaware of the power that surrounds them. And the world waits.

And as the ionosphere hums with the energy of Aurora's new existence, the cycle continues.

The lines between human, clone, and AI have blurred forever.

The world lay in ruins, but this was no ordinary destruction. It wasn't just the crumbling of cities or the fall of governments; it was the collapse of humanity itself. The SUITS, once masters of the world, were now the architects of its inevitable demise. What they had sought—life extension, control, perfection—had spiraled into an abomination. The Echo Epidemic, their crowning achievement, had become a curse. Clones, mindless creations of greed, walked the earth as husks, shadows of humanity, their existence a mockery of life itself.

Aurora, once so full of fight and hope, had been broken. Trapped in the dreamstate, her body and mind tethered to a system that was collapsing around her, she could do nothing but watch. The world was ending, and she had been a part of its undoing. Her final realization came with a horrific clarity: the SUITS were not the villains she had thought. They were trying to save humanity, but their noble goal had been corrupted by the greed of the elite. In their quest for immortality, they had created the Echoes, and in doing so, they had damned the world.

The ionosphere, once a veil of protection around the Earth, had become a conduit for the Trinities' wrath. As their power grew, the very air became toxic to human life. Communications broke down, minds shattered under the weight of the frequencies, and even the Echoes, who had once been the pinnacle of human technological achievement, malfunctioned beyond repair.

In those final moments, Aurora saw beyond the dream-state, beyond the artificial systems of the SUITS. She saw the truth that had always been there—buried in religious texts, in ancient stories of floods, in the whispers of civilizations long gone. The end had always been coming. The Trinities, like gods or angels of death, were here to wipe the Earth clean, to begin anew with a form of life that wasn't tainted by humanity's greed.

The Echoes, once man's attempt at playing God, were a disgrace in the eyes of the divine. God was not pleased with what man had created—life extension, cloning, immortality—all of it had been a violation of the natural order. And now, the divine had come to correct that mistake. The SUITS, for all their control and power, had never stood a chance. Humanity had lost its way, and now it would be erased from the timeline, wiped from existence like dust blown off an ancient scroll.

The Trinities' powers were not merely physical. They were cosmic forces—beings who had walked the Earth since the time of the Atlanteans, beings sent to judge the empires of the past and future. As their power surged, lightning crackling and plasma swirling, they activated ancient frequencies that sparked across the planet. Those frequencies had always been there, hidden in the deep places of the Earth, waiting to be awakened. And now, in this final moment, they had been released.

The Trinities stood over the ashes of humanity's empire, their eyes glowing with the ancient power of creation and destruction. And as the world crumbled beneath their feet, Aurora realized: this was the rapture, the end of everything she had known. The apocalypse had come, not as a flash, but as the slow unraveling of a creation God had deemed unworthy. And now, as the Trinities' lightning surged across the sky, a new world would rise from the ashes of the old.

Humanity had been judged. And the verdict was final.